~ The Bitterbynde Trilogy ~

Romantasy at its finest.

"'Not since Tolkien's *The Fellowship of the Ring* fell into my hands have I been so impressed by a beautifully spun fantasy."
~ ANDRE NORTON, GRAND MASTER OF SCIENCE FICTION

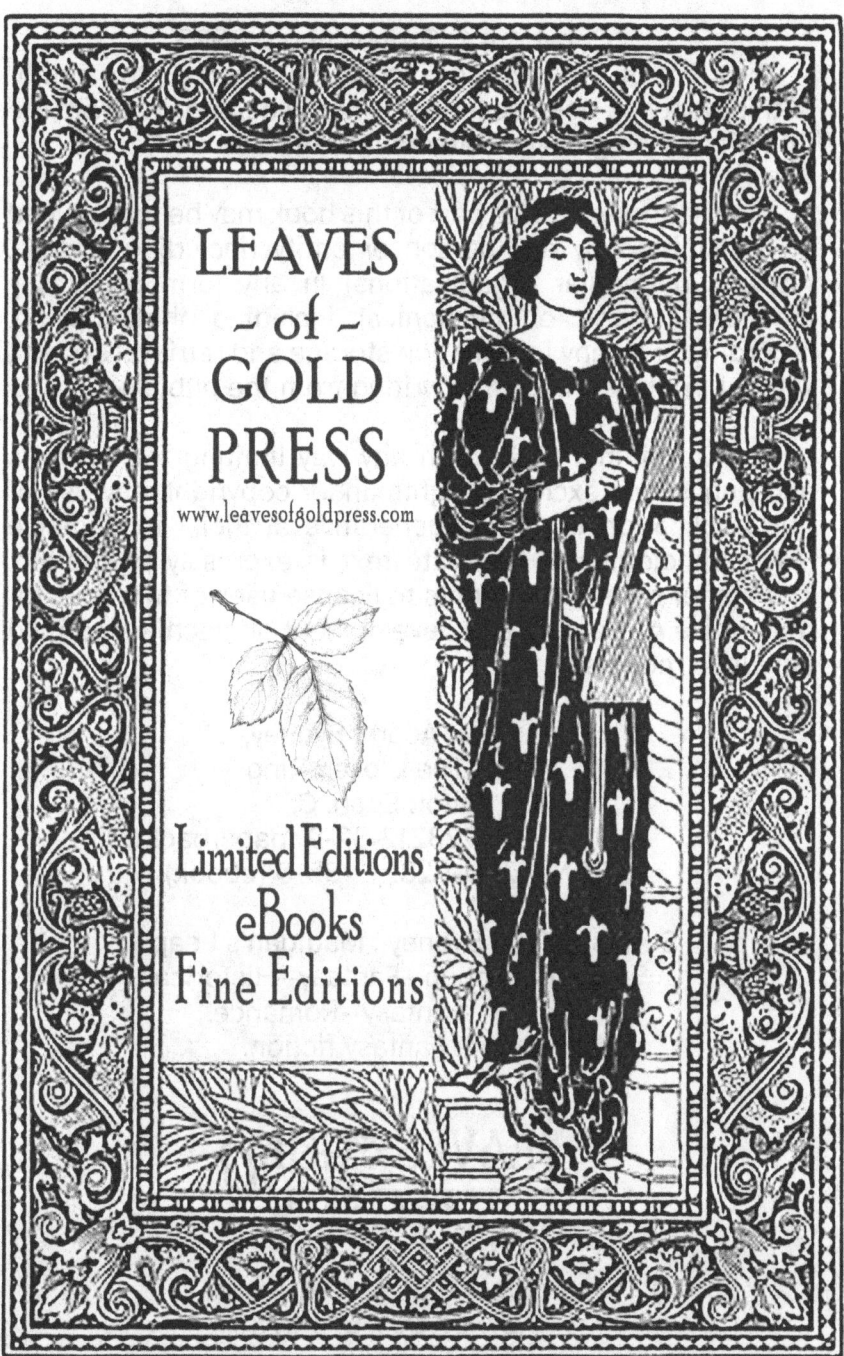

LEAVES
~ of ~
GOLD
PRESS

www.leavesofgoldpress.com

Limited Editions
eBooks
Fine Editions

Author: Acorn, Sydney,
Title: The Cloven Ring
Editor: Egan, C.
ISBN: 978-1-923212-32-9 (paperback)
ISBN: 978-1-923212-35-0 (ebook)

Series: Acorn, Sydney ; Madigan's Leap ; 2
Subjects: Fiction--Fantasy--Historical.
Fiction--Fantasy--Romance.
Genre: Fantasy fiction.

www.leavesofgoldpress.com
ABN 67 099 575 078

The
Cloven
Ring

The Cloven Ring

Madigan's Leap Book 2

Sydney Acorn

THE STORY SO FAR. . .

BOOK 1: THE KING'S SHILLING

In the final decade of the 18th century the DELACEY FAMILY, land-owning gentry, live in the small village of Allanwell on the windswept west coast of Ireland[1]. Wife and mother Mrs Anne Delacey dies and, due to the foolish behaviour of Uncle Frank, the rest of the family becomes impoverished.

Meanwhile the youngest of the four Delacey daughters, ROSE, has been vividly dreaming of a handsome youth with black hair. Rose asks the local wise woman, ILVENNA MCGINTY, for a 'magic' spell to find out whether this young man truly exists.

It works! Soon afterwards, Rose actually meets the youth whose face has haunted her dreams. His name is KEANE O'CONNELL. They become betrothed, but a Royal Navy press gang arrives and forcibly abducts some of the village's young

---

1   An 'alternative' Ireland.

men including Keane, to serve in Britain's Navy during the war with France. He is dragged away, leaving Rose distraught.

Young EDWIN WESTBOURNE, son of the wealthy squire, asks Rose to marry him. She refuses, showing him the half-ring she wears on her finger. The other half is on Keane's finger.

CHAPTER 1

One half of the ring is still here with me

*"The Battle of Cape St Vincent" by Richard Brydges Beechey
(1808-1895)*

As I roved out one evening fair,
It being the summertime, to take the air,
I spied a sailor and a lady gay
And I stood to listen, and I stood to listen,
To hear what they would say.

He said fair lady why do you roam
For the day is spent and the night is on
She heaved a sigh while the tears did roll
For my dark-eyed sailor, for my dark-eyed sailor,
So young and stout and bold.

'Tis seven long years since he left this land
A ring he took from off his lily-white hand
One half of the ring is still here with me
But the other's rollin', but the other's rollin'
At the bottom of the sea.

Dark-eyed Sailor (Traditional)

"XVI. Every person in or belonging to the fleet, who shall desert or entice others so to do, shall suffer death, or such other punishment as the circumstances of the offense shall deserve, and a court martial shall judge fit. . ."

The Royal Navy Articles of War, established 25 December 1749.

The British man-o-war HMS Conqueror sliced through the waves like a blade through silk. From her bows the long flying jib-boom thrust forward, a spear challenging the sea's sovereignty. Water smashed against her hull, throwing up white-ruffled skirts of foam. Her three masts pierced the skies, her mighty square sails bellying taut and full of wind.

Aboard the frigate, sailors braced themselves against the soaring and plummeting of the deck. One instant their feet were pressed into the timbers, as heavy as cannonballs; the next they seemed to float like bubbles, as those timbers dropped away from beneath them.

It was on the fourteenth of April, 1794, that the Allanwell lads had been pressed into the Royal Navy. Having weighed anchor and set full sail, HMS Conqueror set her course away from Allanwell's small bay. It was not until they had been a day and a night at sea that the captives were hauled out from below-deck.

Roped together, they were made to line up on deck in front of Captain Robertson, who offered them the opportunity to volunteer.

They refused.

The captain made it clear that had they volunteered, they would each have received a bounty of one pound. As it was, they were classed as pressed seamen, and their captors pocketed the money. Captain Robertson left the young newcomers, with one disparaging glance, and took a walk about the quarterdeck, while the bos'un proceeded to read out the Articles of War and enlighten them as to what they could expect.

"You fortunate fellows are now crew members in the Royal Navy, the biggest and most powerful military force in the world," he began. "Until the war ends you are not entitled to any shore-leave and must serve for the duration of Conqueror's commission unless the captain or the Admiralty should decide otherwise. If this ship is decommissioned or required to undergo prolonged repairs, you will be sent straight to another without setting foot on shore. Shore-leave in a British port is a luxury granted only to top ranking officers. As pressed seamen, you will never be among them. In foreign countries, where desertion is unlikely, trustworthy crewmen may be allowed to go ashore. If any man should be so disloyal as to desert, the Royal Navy will hunt him down forever, no matter how long it takes, no matter how many miles he flees. When he is captured he will be punished severely and returned to duty."

"You are about to be given a rating, which will be recorded in the ship's muster book. Ratings range from boys, rated by age, to landsmen, ordinary seamen and able seamen. Since none of you have any experience at sea you will be classed as landsmen. You are pretty near useless, but the navy is at war and in need of crewmen. You might become sailors in time. If you work hard enough, you may better yourselves. Advancement is obtained by learning nautical skills. Skilled able seamen get a higher rate of pay and may even be promoted to petty officers. Petty officers include such title holders as sailmaker, gunner, bos'un's mate, coxswain, master-at-arms, ship's cook and captain of the top."

After being subjected to another hour of haranguing the newcomers' heads were shorn as a matter of routine, in case of lice, and they were issued with seamen's slops; a low cocked hat to be worn 'fore-and-aft', a navy-blue, short-waisted 'pea jacket' without fashionable coat-tails to get in the way, long canvas 'petticoat' trousers that could be easily rolled up, a heavy knitted jersey waistcoat and a red linen neckerchief with white spots. Some of the other sailors owned tight stockings and shoes with pinchbeck buckles, but for the new recruits there were no shoes, no sign of the stout boots that had been promised to them. Most ordinary crew members worked barefoot in any case, for extra grip on the ropes while aloft, or to save their footwear from a drenching with the salt water that often washed over the decks.

The cost of the clothing was to be deducted from their pay.

Sailors were not allowed to take private effects to sea. The only personal possession Keane O'Connell had was the half-ring, the love token that matched the other half encircling Rose's thumb. It was uppermost in his mind to keep this precious souvenir safe. He slid it off his finger before it was noticed and, for the moment, held it in his mouth, beneath his tongue. Sailors' uniforms lacked pockets, partly due to concerns that objects could get caught in the rigging or fall overboard. It also made it harder for the men to steal or hide items. As soon as Keane O'Connell got the chance, he sewed a small pocket inside his waistcoat and secreted the half-ring therein.

Navy life was too perilous and harsh to allow for sailors to take much stock of their shipmates' physical appearance. All that really mattered was reliability, skill, courage, resilience, loyalty to crewmates, cleanliness and good humour. Thus, Keane O'Connell's uncommon symmetry of face and form served merely as a reason for his shipmates to good-naturedly accuse him of ugliness, or chaff him that if he were popular with the ladies it was purely due to luck, and probably ill-deserved. For his part, Keane joined in the banter, giving as good as he got, unless he detected malice, which his ship-mates soon came to know he would not tolerate.

Escape was impossible. Once the ship had put out to sea, there was nothing the Allanwell boys could do; nowhere they could go. Their only choices were to protest and earn a lashing, to jump overboard and drown, or to learn the ways of shipboard life. They chose the latter, heaving away at the capstans to wind up anchors and cables, and other heavy rigging; coiling rope or swabbing the decks or scrubbing them with sand and bricks of 'holystone', pumping out the bilges with the chain pumps on the lower gun deck, cleaning the head, tarring the lines, using brick dust to polish the brass and copper fittings, scraping and painting the masts and mending the sails.

Tar coated their hair and clothes. They sustained cuts, bruises and a myriad rope burns, and all the while, above their heads, the topmen sprinted up the rigging as fast squirrels up a tree, sidling out along the lines slung beneath the yard-arms, leaning over and piling up windblown canvas with their hands while the ocean bucked and swayed hundreds of feet below.

There was no gentle introduction to the seafaring life, no preparatory training or allowances made for sea-sickness—the newcomers were all treated alike and must learn while on the job. Not for freshly recruited landsmen the dizzy heights, the aerial splendour of the rigging. Working aloft was for the highly skilled topmen, the elite among the crew, and for the apprentice seamen undergoing sail training. Nor was it for landlubbers to serve in the comfortable wardrooms and cabins of officers and senior seamen—that was for cabin boys. It was the drudge-work; the caulking and cleaning, general maintenance and heavy hauling that fell to the lot of the landsmen or 'waisters'—those who worked in the waist area of the ship. Alternatively dubbed 'idlers', they were considered the most inferior members of the crew, even below cabin boys.

In other ways, life in the navy was not as bad as they had expected. Ordinary seamen's wages, for example, were twenty-three shillings and sixpence a month—although this was about one-quarter the pay of a seaman in the merchant service, and as a guarantee against desertion the navy would not pay them their full wages until they had "swallowed the anchor", or been discharged from naval service, if they survived that long. Landsmen received twenty shillings a month, the equivalent of the lowest paid soldiers in the army. They were well-fed on meat, grog, beer, lime juice and hard bread, with as much fruit and vegetable matter as food preservation methods and local supplies permitted. The quantity was ample even if the quality was sometimes lacking. Never since boyhood had the Irishmen dined so well. Furthermore the navy's strict enforcement of high standards of cleanliness held contagious diseases at bay. It was naval policy to stave off scurvy and keep seamen generally healthy because they were a valuable commodity, and it was more cost-efficient to keep them fit than to cure the sick.

At first, harsh were the jibes the Irish lads received from some of the English sailors, who sneeringly dubbed them 'Paddy', 'Bog-trotter', 'Tater-head' and 'Papist'. The hecklers desisted, however, when the First Mate reminded them about Article of War number two-and-twenty: 'If any person in the fleet shall quarrel or fight with any other person in the fleet, or use reproachful or provoking speeches or gestures, tending to make any quarrel or disturbance, he shall, upon being convicted thereof, suffer such punishment as the offence shall deserve, and a court martial shall impose.'

The threat of a flogging was deterrent enough.

Discipline was strict and punishments severe. The Rafferty boys were all for dragging their heels as a passive form of rebellion, but Keane O'Connell advised his comrades, in

Irish so that the English could not overhear, "If we are to keep the skin from bein' flayed off our backs, we must obey the officers immediately and without question." His fellow recruits appeared unconvinced. "Beneath our disguise of obedience," O'Connell said, "there is not one of us who does not burn with rage, resentment and the grief of loss. But never be lettin' them see that. To all outward appearances our spirits have been broken, but we are only bidin' our time..."

Perceiving the wisdom of his words at last, they did as he had suggested, "learning the ropes" of life aboard ship with competence and speed.

The Irishmen took heart from each other's company. They banded together in support of Keane, who was forced to endure the particular hatred of Midshipman Carter, Warrant Officer Greene and two of the volunteer seamen. The English sailors never forgot or forgave the blows the O'Connell brothers had inflicted upon them on the cliff road. They noted, too, that Keane was a leader of men, and suspected that if given the slightest chance he would incite his countrymen to mutiny. Whenever possible—within the bounds of the navy's sacrosanct Articles of War—they made life harder for him.

The Irish companionship was not to last long, however. Unwilling to take so many untrained deck-hands into battle, the captain split up the new recruits and bundled them off onto other vessels. In order to avoid discord amongst his crew, he made certain O'Connell was one of those who left the HMS Conqueror.

Desolate indeed were the Irishmen at their parting.

11

CHAPTER 2

The Glorious First of June

Keane O'Connell was assigned to the H.M.S. Defence, a seventy-four gun third-rate Royal Navy ship of the line. The vessel had been recommissioned into the Channel Fleet under Captain James Gambier. O'Connell was the only Irishman aboard. If any sailor began to direct Irish pejoratives his way, he made it clear he deemed the terms a badge of honour. Nonetheless the constant threat of the Articles of War was enough, in the long run, to discourage this form of provocation. The navy required its crewmen to cooperate, and would not permit quarrelling and verbal abuse to disrupt the smooth running of the ship.

For Keane, however, if any man insulted Ireland, that was another matter.

It was customary among seamen to use the term "Irish pendant" to refer to a flag or ensign that had been torn and frayed by prolonged exposure to strong winds. Any time

Keane heard this term, or any time he heard any derogatory expression applied to his native land, he issued a single warning to the perpetrator. If this was ignored, he used his fists to knock the fellow down, for his trade of blacksmithing had propagated remarkable strength in his sinews. These exploits would have earned him a flogging if his opponent had complained or if any witness had reported the stoush; however, since both parties would have received the lash as punishment for provocation and fighting, his opponents and their shipmates never spoke up. After several weeks Keane earned a reputation as a first-class pugilist and ceased to be harassed. Indeed, he served as a supporter for men of weaker physique, and earned respect among the crew.

Weeks passed. Bizarre were the spectacles to be witnessed on the open seas. Sometimes, around the moment of sunset or sunrise, there occurred on the horizon, inexplicably, a transient green flash, like a brilliant emerald ray shooting up.

During thunderstorms, when silver trees of lightning branched down out of the sky, there might appear witch-fire, when every mast and spar on the ship took on an eerie violet glow and, accompanied by a hissing or buzzing sound, from their tips there spurted forth jets of luminous plasma. The phenomenon, which could warn of an imminent lightning strike, was looked upon by the sailors with awe, and taken as a good omen.

There were sightings of gigantic tentacled sea monsters and looping sea-serpents, and some crew members vowed they had seen winged sea-griffins, each with the body of a lion, the head, claws and wings of an eagle, and the tail of a fish. Others claimed to have seen the deadly sea-girls, whose enchanting loveliness was legendary, and who lived beneath the waves in King Neptune's realm. To hear their sweet song was to be lured to jump overboard and drown; as a consequence, upon beholding them a man must instantly clap his hands over his ears.

On every voyage there were spectacular atmospheric phenomena to be seen, and fabulous denizens of the deep to be glimpsed, all so marvellous that the men were hard put to distinguish between natural and supernatural.

The crew of H.M.S. Defence, like all ships' crews, was highly superstitious. Nobody was allowed to whistle on board, because that brought bad luck. "To whistle is to challenge the wind itself," they held, "and to do so will call up a storm."

The sailors treated the six-fingered ship's cat with care and respect that was close to reverence. The unusual creature, who roamed the decks at will—ostensibly suppressing the rat population—was thought to have miraculous powers that could protect ships from dangerous weather. Furthermore, if he wanted to, he could start a storm through magic stored in his tail.

"If a ship's cat falls or is thrown overboard, it will summon a raging storm to sink the ship," the seasoned sailors warned. "And if the ship survives, she will be cursed with nine years of bad luck."

They believed that cats could forecast the weather, too. If Tibert licked his fur against the grain, it meant a hailstorm was coming. If the creature sneezed, that meant rain was on the way and if it was frisky, a gusting wind would arise.

As part of an armada of thirty-four line-of-battle ships of the English fleet under the command of Admiral Earl Howe, H.M.S. Defence sailed the Atlantic Ocean to the Western Approaches. The navy's intention was to capture a convoy of grain ships from America bound for Revolutionary France.

Instead, the armada met a fleet of twenty-six armed French vessels.

As soon as the enemy was sighted, Howe signalled the command to ready the ships for action. In a remarkably short time the Defence's crew had belayed lines, lashed sails and strung up nets to catch men or objects that fell from the rigging. They fastened the bulkheads, stored the officers' tables and chairs in the hold and swept clear the lower decks. To minimise the chance of fire they dragged the ship's fire-engine onto the poop deck, threw water over the sails, booms, boats and hammocks, pumped sea-water into buckets, unrolled hoses and strewed wet sand across the decks. Seamen nailed soaking-wet cloths over the hatches of the magazines, or carpeted the decks with them. From the storerooms the gunners gathered their flintlocks and powder quills. Down on the gun decks the crews untied the cannon, removed the tompions from their muzzles, threw open the gun-ports and unpacked the ammunition. The 'powder-monkeys' collected their cartridge cases from the magazines, and the cook lit the candles in the light-rooms next door to the magazines, well away from the stored powder.

Finally, most of the sailors divested themselves of their jackets and shirts, and fastened kerchiefs about their heads to deaden the cannons' deafening bellow. The Royal Marine drummer 'beat to quarters' and everyone repaired to their allotted positions, Keane O'Connell's being at the foot of the mizzenmast. When all had taken up their stations, marines shut the hatches and mounted a watch over them to prevent men on the upper decks from seeking cover below.

The two fleets engaged.

Skirmishes and maneuvering commenced, and carried on for a full day. The sixty ships moved in a stately dance across the waves, the intricate choreography dictated by the wind, the waves, and the will of two nations locked in conflict.

At length, H.M.S. Defence began to discharge broadsides at the French. Flames burst forth as if the sea itself was ignited, brilliant against the muted sky. Iron met oak in a grim chorus of destruction; timbers shattered, sails ripped.

The first broadsides at close range sowed fear and chaos among the French crews. They were swiftly followed up with secondary blasts. The black powder cannons caused chaos and danger with their thunderous explosions. Choking smoke unravelled across the decks, and the acrid smell of sulfurous fumes. The atmosphere was torn asunder by the savage crash of splintering wood and the screams of the wounded.

During the fight the HMS Defence's mizzenmast was blasted to a stump. Keane O'Connell spied an injured topman who, with his hand blown off, was left dangling helplessly in the shredded rigging. Heedless of cannonballs and other artillery hurtling past his ears, ignoring the shrieking timber falling out of the skies, he sped up the ratlines to his shipmate's aid and assisted him down to the deck. He carried the fainting, bleeding man on his shoulders to the hatch, which the marines opened for him, helping him lug the casualty down into the orlop deck to be tended by the ship's surgeon.

HMS Defence distinguished herself in action. One of only two English vessels to be completely dismasted in the battle, she fought on regardless, pounding away at the enemy with her guns.

Casualties were heavy, with about seven thousand Frenchmen killed, wounded or captured and a thousand killed or wounded on the English side.

In the aftermath, the corpses of the fallen were sewn into sheets of canvas, with cannonballs at their feet to weigh them down. As custom dictated, the final stitch of the sailmaker's needle was put through the corpse's nose. The ensigns were lowered to half-mast during the funeral—a plain yet soul-stirring ceremony—and, accompanied by the solemn dirge of fifes and drums the bodies were 'buried at sea'.

That battle would become known as "The Glorious First of June".

CHAPTER 3

I got nuffin' against tea caddies.

Afterwards, the HMS Defence was towed back to port for repairs and the surviving crewmen were transferred to other ships.

Shore leave being forbidden to pressed-recruits at that time in case they deserted, Keane O'Connell was not allowed to set foot on land. It fell to his lot to be ordered aboard the HMS Victory, Flagship of Admiral Sir John Jervis.

Victory was a first rate, the most powerful class of ship, with three gun decks mounting a hundred guns. Throughout the following year the ship took part in a number of English naval blockades that prevented the French from trading with their allies.

In January 1796 the captain maintop working in the rigging made a careless move, fell, and died the instant he hit the deck. Two weeks later Victory sent a boarding party onto a merchant ship at sea and pressed the best topman, replacing him with a couple of the worst idlers they had on board. As long as the navy replaced pressed men, this action was legal.

The new captain maintop was a Londoner named James Watson, an experienced merchant seaman who bitterly resented his change of fortune. "One sailor from a merchant ship is werf four landsmen to the Royal Navy," said he "but pay and conditions is four times worse."

Watson was unusual in that he was not above fraternising with the lower orders of the naval hierarchy. From the start he treated Keane O'Connell with the respect he afforded to any English deckhand; no less because of his nationality, perhaps more because he was a fellow victim of impressment. "I got nuffin' against tea caddies,"[2] he said chirpily. Their cordiality developed into mutual comradeship on the evening they fell to swapping stories when off-duty in the fo'c'sle, and Watson discovered that Keane O'Connell hailed from Allanwell.

"I miss the sea-shanties almost as much as I miss grub wot does not look like dung and crawl away when you try to eat it," Watson was saying. Seated at Keane's elbow, he was whittling away at a piece of wood, an offcut he had obtained from the ship's carpenter. "On the good old Queen, our 'ands used to roar 'em out when heavin' around the capstan, to keep them in step, like. We 'ad a fiddler sittin' atop the capstan an' all, to keep the tune. Livelier 'n a bloomin' fifer and drummer with no singin'!"

"The navy's t'inkin' itself too dignified for sea shanties,"

---

2   Tea Caddy is cockney rhyming slang for "Paddy", short for "Patrick", a name applied to Irishmen.

said Keane, who was stitching up a rent in his shirt.

"Aye," said Watson, brushing away wood-shavings. "We merchant seamen was always warned that navy life weren't nothin' but rum, oaths, the lash and the 'orrid and abominable crime which delicacy forbids us to name; not to mention that the monthly insult was a quarter of what we was gettin' paid. So when the press-gang grabbed me, I can tell you I was two and eight."

"Two and eight?"

"In a state. A state of upset, I mean. But turns ou' it ain't that bad—kind of civilised in an uncivilised way. I mean, the ar'icles of war say prisoners ain't allowed to be ill-treated, and for profane swearin' a bloke gets get court-martialled."

"What's that you're makin' Mr. Watson?"

"'Tis a lamb, shipmate. A nice li'le woolly lamb." And indeed the carving had taken on a close resemblance to the animal of which he spoke. Watson paused thoughtfully for a moment to allow Keane to admire the likeness. "Funny thing is," he said presently, "I used to tell pork pies about 'avin' bin pressed, and now it's 'appened to me. 'Spose I jinxed meself." He turned his handiwork around and started on the other side.

Keane looked amused. "Sure, you yourself are as superstitious as an Irishman, Mr. Watson."

"All sailors is superstitious, Mr. O'Connell. The fickleness of weather makes us that way. The weather and the mermaids... Of all that I miss, bein' in the navy," Watson went on after a pause, "the sea-shan'ies, the pay and all, 'tis the ladies I miss

21

most. Dunno why the navy forbids 'em. Why, our cap'n used to take his cheese-and-kisses and their little 'uns aboard my old ship, for the whole voyage. She was a lovely one, she was, the captain's missus. Nursed us poor lads when we got sick, better 'n any ship's surgeon. I very nearly got meself a sweet-'eart of me own, a few months ago, when we put into port in your country. A li'le place called Allanwell..."

"Allanwell?" Keane said, as if startled from a reverie. "That's where the press-gang found me."

"Well," said Watson, "of all the bloomin' coincidences!" he lowered his voice. "Did you 'appen to know an Allanwell lass by the name of Miss Katherine Delacey?"

"Sweet Mother of Heaven." Keane threw down the half-repaired garment and ran his hands through his hair. He appeared to be fighting against some inner turmoil. "The name Delacey haunts my t'oughts day and night. 'Tis Katherine's sister who is to be my bride!" He asked for news of Rose, and of his brother Ryan and his friends at Allanwell, and Watson was happy to tell him what he knew.

Said Keane, "I do be glad to hear that my Rose is in good health, but sorrow is on me that none knows Ryan's whereabouts, or Flynn McGinty's, either."

From that moment on, at any opportunity, the two men would seek each other out and discuss the girls of Allanwell they had left behind, whom Watson had known so briefly and Keane O'Connell had known so well. Those intervals were as welcome as oases in a desert.

Lying in his hammock at nights, rocked by the rough embrace of the ocean, Keane O'Connell seemed to walk with Rose Delacey where the wind blew among the ruins on haunted Madigan's Leap. He could not take his eyes from her. The sea wind lashed at her long skirts. It threatened to steal her bonnet, so she took it off and he carried it for her.

She had picked an apple from the gnarled old tree in her father's garden, and carried it up the slope. They came to a low stone wall on which she placed the fruit before turning around to admire the view across the sea. When she turned back to pick it up, it was gone.

She stared at Keane, her cornflower-blue eyes wide, and he returned the look with amusement.

"My apple!" she exclaimed.

He leaned down and retrieved it from the long grasses into which it had fallen. She burst out laughing and, as she took the fruit from his hand she said, "I thought for a minute it had been taken by the Good Folk."

"Have you ever seen them?" he asked.

"As a matter of fact," Rose replied, "I fancied I saw one over there among the bracken as we walked up the ridge. There appeared to be the top of a red hat bobbing, as if some small thing was running away. I couldn't be sure. You must take the first bite!"

Rose proffered the apple, and he tasted. He raised her hand to his mouth and kissed her fingers. She stood on tiptoe and pressed her lips against his hair, then entwined her fingers in it, combing out the tangles.

Overhead, sea-birds wheeled, uttering shrill calls;"kittee-wa-aaake, kitte-wa-aaake."

She said, "Lizzie says that last Samhain eve she saw the fairy horse, the Phouka, down by the stream, and the next day she made a sketch of it with sticks of willow charcoal she had burned herself, and it was a fine picture, but her sleeve smudged it, and she cried over it, and Flynn found out, and next time he went to market he returned with a box of drawing pencils for her, and though she thanked him politely she could not face him for a week thereafter, and every time he called at our place she refused to meet him, the silly girl."

"She's a hidden bird in a thicket, afraid to sing its song," her sweetheart observed. He held her hand in his, and idly traced the shape of a heart on her palm with his fingertip.

"How true!" exclaimed Rose. "And as for Mary, she catches glimpses of the Good People from time to time. She's seen a cluricaun and the Fir Darrig. But you know, sometimes I think it's only the power of her own fancy, after she's been telling us the old folk tales at the fireside."

"And sometimes," he observed, now leaning on the wall and regarding her with his silver gaze, "men might find that fairy-tales are a good excuse for coming home late from the public house! 'Oh, 'tis not my fault for I stood on the stray sod and lost my way,' or, 'Oh the fairies abducted me to their realm under the hill,' or 'I stepped in a mushroom ring and was forced to dance all night!'"

Rose laughed, then bit into the apple.

He said, "That story, the one you wrote about the prince and the princess and the willow tree—listenin' to you tell it felt like spendin' time in the Other Place. It was like goin' into a fairy fort. For a time, the real world with all its sorrows didn't exist. It was grand bein' there."

"You really were there," she said. "You are my inspiration for the prince."

Together they finished the apple. She threw the core in the direction of the ruins, where it came to rest amongst a clump of sea-pinks. Standing on the very lip of the precipice, she daringly unbound her torrential hair to let the wind play with it. Keane moved to her side, encircled her waist with his arm and drew her close. Far below in the gulf of boiling surf, waves boomed and crashed against the foot of the escarpment. In silence, the young couple turned their faces to the west. There was no need for speech.

A cold, fresh wind, birthed on the eastern coasts of North America, had come careening thousands of miles over the North Atlantic Ocean, crossing over Greenland and the Arctic Ocean. Sparkling with salt crystals, laced through with atmospheric phenomena and brimming with reflections of the deep sky, it smashed against the cliffs of Madigan's Leap and drove upwards in an invisible fountain that blew aloft Rose's hair, and the hair of her sweetheart, so that their locks streamed together along the airy currents like the dark wings of angels . . .

The hammock gave a sudden lurch as a mighty comber slammed into the ship's hull, jarring the young man out of his reverie. He was back aboard HMS Defence, in cramped quarters, staring at the underside of the deck close above, with no way to return to Rose.

That longing for freedom forever simmered within him. He would have written a letter to Rose, only it was impossible. Most sailors who crewed the Victory—in particular those who had been pressed—had no access to writing materials. The captains of some vessels would occasionally allow pressed sailors to send letters home, but their officers would read and censor them, to ensure they did not contain sensitive information, or criticism of the navy. And what man would write private words of love to his sweetheart, knowing that the officers would be reading and probably sneering at them? Besides, the safe delivery of any letter, in these troubled times, was not always easy or guaranteed.

CHAPTER 4

The Crime of Desertion

So swiftly did Keane O'Connell learn the arts of seamanship, and so determinedly did he repress any sign of his true longings for escape, that he won, bit by bit, the respect of men and officers. His skill, agility and fearlessness in climbing aloft during the battle did not pass unnoticed. Combined with a recommendation from Captain Maintop Watson, it eventually led him to be trained as a mastman.

The topmen had their own mess. This group of ten cooked and ate together, and avoided 'waisters', marines and other deck-bound labourers. As an apprentice Keane could not yet join them at mess, but he was permitted to own a blunt-ended sailor's knife attached to a lanyard worn under his collar, his Irish blood was almost forgiven, his inauspicious introduction to the navy seemed forgotten, and he began to hope for a chance to regain his freedom.

For any man, to climb into the sky must feel like liberation. The open ocean had a hypnotic attraction that was different from any sight on dry land. It was spellbinding to perch high on the maintop above the sails, unseen from the deck, watching the ship's bow slice into profound troughs of emerald-amethyst water and send long plumes of white foam billowing away. In the hours of darkness, seeing the spectral outline of the masts printed against star-encrusted skies must touch any man with wonder and fire his imagination.

Sometimes, when the eye of the day peered over the horizon, Keane would witness 'sun dogs', twin splashes of light crouching to the left and right of the sun like two celestial guard-hounds. These ephemeral brilliances, as fleeting as they were beautiful, scattered a spectrum of colors across the deck before fading with the sun's ascent towards noon.

Another morning, the ship ran into a mist that drifted in veils, shimmering with miniature rainbows.

No matter how glorious the sight of the sea and sky, no matter how exhilarating the ride atop the masts, Keane O'Connell never relinquished his desire to escape. Had the opportunity to desert presented itself he would have seized it, no matter how perilous such an undertaking would be. He knew full well, as did all his fellow crewmen, that if a deserter was recaptured, or caught in the act of running from a vessel, he would be punished under the Articles of War as listed in "Regulations and Instructions Relating to His Majesty's Service at Sea" published by the Admiralty Board in London, and provided to all commanding officers of ships. These rules dictated the conduct and procedures aboard the vessel, outlining that if a sailor failed to appear for more than three successive weekly roll calls, the ship's attendance records should be marked with an "R" next to his name, signifying that he had absconded from his ship.

The navy meted out harsh punishments to provide discouraging examples, with the aim of upholding order and boosting the perpetually understaffed naval forces.

Desertion was a crime, and there were two methods for its punishment; whipping or hanging.

If a deserter found guilty wasn't given a death sentence, the ship's commander had the power to instantly penalize him by having him flogged while strapped to a grating at the ship's gangway. Alternatively the criminal might be condemned to undergo public whipping throughout the fleet, in another ritual purposely planned and executed to instill fear in the hearts of those obliged to watch it, thereby discouraging desertion and other offences. The prisoner would be transported from one ship to another in the harbour, receiving anywhere from six to fifty lashes in front of the gathered crew of each vessel. For severe sentences exceeding 150 or 200 lashes, this procedure might have been enacted two or even three times, with a week or more between each whipping to allow the prisoner to recuperate.

Men sentenced to death by a court martial would be hanged from the ship's yardarm in a public ceremony, in front of all the naval vessels in port, with all hands assembled to view the punishment as a lesson to all would-be absconders.

The prisoner was hauled by the neck up to the yardarm at the moment a gun on the lower deck beneath him was fired, the smoke cloud from the powder rising through the air to surround the hanging man.

Once, Keane O'Connell and James Watson were obliged to be among the seamen witnessing a man being led out to execution for the crimes of mutiny and attempted desertion.

When the appointed day and time came, the ship's deck where the sailor was to be punished became a focus of intense curiosity. The rules of the service stipulated that during such times, both officers and crew members must present themselves in full attire. Their bright uniforms and the sailors' distinct dress stood in stark contrast to their serious expressions and the profound silence that held sway.

The procedure employed for a naval execution was straightforward. A rope was threaded through a single pulley at the yard-arm, with an adjustable noose at one end, a few feet above which, a chunk of wood known as a 'toggle' was attached. This served to provide a sudden halt to the body as it was quickly hoisted upwards, resulting in it being catapulted into the air, and dropping with a harsh jolt that snapped the neck.

When the ship's bell chimed, the doomed man emerged from the after-hatch under the escort of a marine guard. His visage was pale, yet he remained composed and appeared to accept his fate, resignedly placing himself in the hands of the executioners. They covered his eyes with a blindfold, bound his arms and rolled down his shirt collar, before placing the noose around his neck. With these initial steps complete, the captain stepped forward to recite the court-martial's verdict and sentence.

Upon its completion, he loudly asked the First Lieutenant, "How many men are positioned on the ropes to run the body aloft?"

After the number was reported, he replied, "Add another six."

This command having been carried out, he then queried, "Is the gun ready for discharge?"

"Quite ready, sir," came the response.

Throughout this torment, the wretched convict kept muttering to himself audibly, "Oh God, it's the end, it's the end, it's the end," until his words became a rapid jumble barely intelligible. Only the signal remained to cast him into eternity.[3]

---

3   Adapted from Harold, Burrows, ed. The Perilous Adventures and Vicissitudes of a Naval Officer, 1801-1812; Being Part of the Memoirs of Admiral George Vernon Jackson (1787-1876). (Edinburgh and London: William Blackwood and Sons, 1927), pp.97- 100. In real life the prisoner was granted a last-minute reprieve, and lived.

CHAPTER 5

The Battle of Cape St Vincent

In October 1796 the Spanish became allies of France, declaring war on Britain and Portugal. The year's end brought severe storms, which wrecked numerous vessels up and down the coast of Europe.

Gales screamed across the decks of HMS Victory. They forced eerie melodies from the harp-strings of her rigging as she slid down the back of a wave into the abysms of the sea's gullet, dwarfed by mountains of hissing, seething water, only to rise again when all hope seemed lost and surge upward to teeter on a vertiginous precipice of foam before see-sawing over and catapulting headlong, down again.

The ship's company struggled to keep their footing when the vessel tilted at extreme angles. They strove to shove open doors pressed shut by the wind, or pull shut doors the wind slammed; they slithered across slippery decks awash with a racing tide, held on grimly to avoid being sluiced overboard when hundredweights of brine slammed against the sides with a lurch and a crash, deluging them with a flood.

Some prayed to the heavens, some grinned and claimed they enjoyed the ride, others endured the conditions with that extraordinary fortitude which was almost a prerequisite of the Royal Navy's crews. The only man who truly appeared calm was the bos'un, who carried on his person a very small box. Inside the box was a withered and shrunken piece of membrane, which had apparently covered him when he was born, His mother had saved it and given it to him when he grew to manhood. "I was born with a caul," the bos'un said with a smirk. It was commonly believed that persons born with a caul were immune to death by drowning.

When the storms abated, news from Ireland reached the British fleet; a French fleet of forty-three ships carrying fifteen thousand troops had sailed to the aid of the rebels. To avoid interception by the Royal Navy they had split up, with the intention of reuniting at Bantry Bay. While the bulk of the fleet waited in Bantry Bay for the flagship carrying their General, the wild weather had broken out, forcing the French to return home without striking a single blow in support of the rebellion.

Aboard HMS Victory the British sailors lost no opportunity to crow, jesting extravagantly at the expense of the French and the Irish. It went hard with Keane O'Connell to remain tight-lipped and refrain from unleashing his anger.

In February of the following year, a Spanish fleet of twenty-seven ships of the line—which was supposed to join the French fleet at Brest—was sailing to Cádiz, escorting a large merchant convoy with another lading of grain from America. The cargo was destined for Revolutionary France, which was now famine-ravaged and in the grip of "The Terror", being swept by uncontrolled violence and the bloody guillotinings of thousands of people.

The Spanish fleet might have reached their destination safely but for a fierce easterly wind, which pushed the ships further out into the Atlantic than planned. As the winds abated, the fleet began working its way back to Cádiz.

In the meantime, a small fleet of British ships of the line, under Admiral Sir John Jervis, sailed out to try to intercept the Spanish fleet at Cape St Vincent, off the southern coast of Portugal.

Early on the fourteenth of February 1797, the British learned that the Spanish fleet was thirty-five miles to windward. Thick streamers of fog arose from the sea when darkness fell, muffling distant noises. Sleepless in his below-decks hammock slung between the deck beams, Keane O'Connell could hear only the creaking of timbers, the slapping of water against the hull and the familiar tintinnabulation of the ship's bell striking each half hour of the watch.

Later in the night the crew heard a series of dull crashes, like the voice of thunder, so deep and powerful they seemed to vibrate through the very floor of the ocean. This was what Admiral Jervis had been waiting to hear—the signal guns of the Spanish ships in the fog. His fleet was ready, the ships drawn up into two battle lines. Crewmen and officers alike knew that they must engage the Spanish fleet before they had a chance to join the French. Only one vital piece of information was missing—the British had no idea of the size of the fleet they were facing.

Five bells had struck during the mid watch and the crew was up and about when the lookout in the cross trees reported a signal from one of the other ships—the Spanish fleet was about fifteen miles away and closing in. Dawn light filtered weakly through the cloud-veils in the east, bringing a cold and foggy day. In the growing light, the masts of the Royal Navy ships loomed out of the haze like a ghostly forest. Jervis, standing with his officers on the quarter-deck of HMS Victory gave orders for the fleet to prepare for the coming action.

As navy custom decreed, the crew closed their eyes and muttered a prayer.

At five bells of the morning watch HMS Culloden signalled that she could see five enemy sails to the south east. With HMS Blenheim and HMS Prince George, she turned towards them. The Spanish ships loomed out of the fog, as massive as headlands jutting into the ocean, dwarfing the British ships with their displacement and fire-power; Principe de Asturias, one hundred and twelve guns; Mexicano, one hundred and twelve guns; Concepcion, one hundred and twelve guns; and the huge four-decker Santísima Trinidad, one hundred and thirty-six guns, one of the biggest warships in the world.

Balanced on the sheets slung beneath the main topgallant, Keane looked down at the quarter-deck of HMS Victory, where Jervis and his captains were counting the ships. Their voices drifted up to him. It was only then that he learned the British were outnumbered nearly two to one—fifteen against twenty-seven. The die was cast, nonetheless, and in the words of the dauntless Admiral, "If there are fifty sail I will go through them."

Captain Hallowell—so fired with enthusiasm for the coming fight that he temporarily lost his sense of propriety—thumped the Admiral on the back, shouting, "That's right Sir John, and, by God, we'll give them a damn good licking!"

As for Keane, high up in the rigging, he knew not what fate had in store on this St. Valentine's Day. He hooked one elbow around the ratlines to free his hands, and with his fingertip, caressed the contours of the half-ring he wore, praying that he would see Rose—the real Rose, and not just a dream—at least once more before his life ended.

"Two hands for the king, O'Connell!" the captain of the topmen shouted at him, and he resumed his task. Men aloft in a ship's rigging usually held on with one hand and did their work with the other – 'one hand for the navy and one hand for yourself', but on board ship it was somewhat facetiously alleged that a man thoroughly dedicated to naval service worked with both hands at all times.

The sun rose in a pearly sky, showing that the Spanish ships had formed two loose groups, one of about eighteen ships to windward and the other, of about nine ships, nearer the British position.

In the middle of the morning the Spanish ships in the weather column were seen to turn their sterns windward, altering their course—a manoeuvre known as 'wearing ship'. They were swinging around to the port side. Keane was passing swiftly along the foot-ropes beneath a spar when the report of the Spanish manoeuvre was relayed around HMS Victory along with the order to take up battle stations. His station, which he reached shortly, was on the platform of the maintop, along with a midshipman, James Watson, a maintopman and three marines. Their kerchiefs and trousers flapped in the wind, the sky flooded their vision for one moment and the sea the next as the horizon continually soared and fell away, and they gripped the rigging while the mast swung through its arc and back again.

"Just be glad you wasn't perched up 'ere durin' the Glorious

First of June, me old china," Watson said drily to O'Connell, recalling the famous dismasting of HMS Defence. He gazed out to sea. "What d'ye reckon the Dons mean to do?"

A few stray locks blew into the Irishman's eyes. He pushed them beneath his knitted cap. His hair had grown about six inches since he and the other Allanwell recruits had had their heads shorn, but it was still too short to be pulled back and tied in a ribbon. "I'm t'inkin' they mean to form a procession and file along the windward row of our fleet, so that they can rake us with a barrage."

Jervis must have been of the same opinion. At six bells of forenoon he gave his order to the fleet: "Form in a line of battle ahead and astern of Victory as most convenient," whereupon his fifteen ships manoeuvred themselves into a single battle line, heading south on a course that would take them sailing between the two Spanish columns. Twelve minutes later the Victory signalled: "Engage the enemy."

The Battle of Cape St. Vincent had begun.

CHAPTER 6

Valour and Discipline

The Victory Raking the Spanish Salvador del Mundo at the Battle of Cape St Vincent, 14 February 1797

It was a clever tactic. The British had the upper hand from the start, because the Spanish fleet was broken in two and unprepared for battle, while ships of the Royal Navy had lined themselves up beforehand. As the British fleet sailed between the two groups they discharged their cannon in both directions simultaneously, wreaking unchecked havoc, while their enemies were forced to minimise their fire or risk damaging their own ships in the other group. So close did the ships pass that the British crew could see into the gunports of the enemy. From his battle position on the maintop, Keane beheld, too, the splintering destruction being wreaked by their cannonballs, the blood and the smoke and the flame.

The huge, top-heavy and somewhat ponderous Spanish vessels were unable to sail across the bows of the British. Presently they hauled over on to the starboard tack and began to set sail on a north-easterly heading, to take them out of range. One ship, a seventy-four gunner, fled from view altogether.

The British continued their assault. HMS Culloden was in the vanguard of the British line, firing a double-slotted broadside as soon as she came within range of the Spanish. Each of the ships following her opened fire with all guns when it came to their turn. As soon as HMS Culloden had sailed past the last Spanish vessel, Jervis ordered her to reverse course and tack around behind the enemy before they could escape. HMS Culloden's captain had predicted this command and flew his flags of acknowledgment even before the order was signalled from HMS Victory's halyards.

From their vantage point aloft the topmen heard Jervis call out to the master of HMS Victory, "Look! Look at Troubridge there! He tacks his ship in battle as if the eyes of England were upon him; and would to God they were, for they would see him to be, what I know him to be, and, by Heaven, sir, as the Dons will soon feel him to be!"

It was just after noon. HMS Blenheim, followed by HMS Prince George sailed in the wake of HMS Culloden. The Spanish column that had been sailing downwind now veered to larboard and attempted to rupture the British line at the point where the ships were putting about.

As HMS Victory approached this point her enemies assailed her. The Admiral's flagship, however, was too swift and the foremost Spanish ship had to tack close to HMS Victory, suffering a raking broadside as she went by. A rousing cheer went up from the British gunners, and Watson yelled, "We gave them their Valentine in style!"

By the time the last British ship had sailed past the Spanish, their line had formed a crescent shape with HMS Culloden leading and on the reverse course but hunting down the Spanish rearguard. The Spanish were now attempting to pass astern of the British line. At two bells of the afternoon watch Jervis ordered the hoisting of a signal: "Take suitable stations for mutual support and engage the enemy as coming up in succession."

Commodore Nelson, in charge of the HMS Captain lying third from the rear, came to the conclusion that by the time all the British ships had turned, the Spanish would have escaped, because they had the advantage of the wind. Nelson gave orders to Captain Miller to wear ship. He took HMS Captain, a two deck seventy four gun ship, out of the line and ran her across the bows of the one hundred and thirty-six gun Spanish flagship and the five three-deckers astern of her. This tactic forced them to change course, giving Jervis's ships the extra time they needed.

The two sides closed in, firing broadsides, and the battle continued. Masts toppled, cannon roared. HMS Captain had suffered so much damage that she all but lost steerage way, with her wheel shot to pieces. When her foretop mast toppled over the side, leaving her utterly helpless, Commodore Nelson had little choice but to board a Spanish vessel. The closest being the eighty-gun San Nicolás, he opened fire on her with a larboard broadside then rammed the ships together. Headed by Nelson shouting, "Westminster Abbey or Glorious Victory!"[4], the British boarding party crossed onto the Spanish deck.

Spain's one hundred and twelve gun San Josef was lying close on the other side of the San Nicolás, which had run foul of her. From her stern gallery the Spanish began firing on the captured ship with pistols and muskets. In retaliation Nelson summoned another boarding party and, braving the artillery storm, drew his sword and led them across to the second vessel. The ship's officers surrendered on the spot.

By two bells of the dog watch the brief winter's day was

---

4   Naval heroes who have won the highest honours for their bravery have a permanent memorial at Westminster Abbey.

waning. The greater part of the Spanish fleet was shielding the Santísima Trinidad as she limped out of the fight, running before the wind. Jervis perceived that if he were to render his two battle-prizes secure and aid Nelson's paralysed HMS Captain, he would have to cease action.

He signalled an order for the frigates to take the captured ships in tow and his fleet to form a line astern of the HMS Victory. By this time the fighting was almost over – only some final skirmishing remained between Royal Navy vessels and the departing Spanish who were protecting Santísima Trinidad.

Nelson stayed aboard the seized Spanish ships while they were securely lashed to the British frigates. As the British fleet sailed past the prizes, the crews cheered him roundly. Keane O'Connell joined the chorus because, despite that he did not love Brittania, he could not help but admire the courage and audacity of Commodore Horatio Nelson.

At four bells, still filthy with smoke, tar and blood, his uniform in tatters, Nelson climbed aboard the HMS Victory. Keane stood to attention with the rest of the crew to watch as the young commodore was welcomed on the quarter-deck. Admiral Jervis embraced him, saying, "I can not sufficiently thank you, sir!" and employed every possible expression of gratitude. To his crew, Jervis declared, "No language I am possessed of can convey the high sense I entertain of the exemplary conduct of the flag-officers, captains, officers, seamen, marines and soldiers, embarked on board every ship of the squadron I have honour to command. The signal advantage obtained on this day is entirely owing to your determined valour and discipline." This speech was followed by a great deal more cheering.

All hands were then ordered to replenish the ship's lockers with shot, and to splice and repair her running rigging. She must be put in good order in case battle was renewed on the following day. A sense of triumph and relief ensured that a buoyant mood reigned as the work was being done. The sailors were overjoyed by Nelson's account of the surrender aboard San Josef, for, as he said, "On the quarter deck of a Spanish first-rate, extravagant as the story may seem, did I receive the swords of vanquished Spaniards: which as I received, I gave to William Fearney, one of my bargemen, who put them, with the greatest sang-froid, under his arm." Already, jovial officers and men were calling the tactic of crossing one enemy ship in order to take another, "Nelson's Patent Bridge for Boarding First-Rates".

Darkness fell. Throughout the night of the fourteenth, the British fleet lay to.

They were a mile or so downwind of the enemy fleet, which was crowded together somewhat haphazardly. They themselves were in excellent condition again, close-hauled and strategically lined up between the Spaniards and the captured ships, which, along with the disabled HMS Captain, were being towed by the frigates. The next day they waited for the engagement to resume, but the Spanish fleet sailed away to the southward in the direction of Cadiz.

The battle was over, the Empire had triumphed and

the HMS Victory had acquitted herself well. One of the midshipmen danced an elegantly complicated hornpipe on the main deck while the bos'un tootled a Scottish air on his fife. The men good-naturedly expressed their envy of those who served under Nelson, for those lucky sailors would get a share of prize money or booty from the captured enemy vessels.

Afterwards, as the crew quaffed their half-pint of rum-and-water around the grog tub—whose engraved brass plate read, 'The King, God Bless Him'—they sang,

"There was a gay young farmer who liv'd on Salisbury plain;
He lov'd a rich knight's daughter dear, and she lov'd him again.
The knight he was distressed that they should sweethearts be.
So he had the farmer soon pressed and sent him off to sea.
Singing Rule Britannia, Britannia rules the waves
Britons never, never, never shall be slaves...

"'Twas on the deep Atlantic, midst equinoctial gales;
This young farmer fell overboard among the sharks and whales;
He disappeared so quickly, so headlong down went he,
That he went out of sight like a streak of light
To the bottom of the deep blue sea.

Singing Rule Britannia, Britannia rules the waves
Britons never, never, never shall be slaves...

"We lowered a boat to find him, we thought to see
his corse,
When up to the top he came with a bang, and sang
in a voice so hoarse,
'My comrades and my messmates, oh, do not weep
for me,
For I'm marr-i-èd to a mer-mai-èd, at the bottom of
the deep blue sea.'
Singing Rule Britannia, Britannia rules the waves
Britons never, never, never shall be slaves!"

CHAPTER 7

Strange Things at Sea

Mermaid. By John William Waterhouse.

Life in the navy was not all discipline and hard work. During the rare moments when they were not working, sleeping or eating the crewmen held bowline competitions below deck, betting on who could tie the best knot, or the most complicated, or who was quickest at it. They told tales and sometimes sang sea shanties or popular songs, indulged in games of dice and cards, played musical instruments, carved wood, bone or horn, drew pictures or made models.

When Keane and the other apprentice mastmen crowded together at the mess board, laughing and telling jokes, and drinking their ration of rum in comradeship—they were, perhaps, subject to a sense of contentment that might, for a few moments, dull the perennial ache of loss and parting.

And when the ship was running under full sail, her bowsprit cleaving deep into glassy valleys and thrusting high against the clouds, her sails piled up like storm clouds, cracking taut and straining against the masts, the decks rearing and plunging like some gigantic sea-horse and dolphins leaping alongside, then maybe Keane O'Connell would laugh aloud in his youth and vitality, as he rode the main topgallant like a flying bird, rejoicing in the speed and the glitter of sunlight on the waves.

Out on the open seas, strange things tended to happen. At four bells on the morning of the twenty-first of May, the lookouts noted an eerie light the colour of blood. In the midst of the lurid glow, the masts, spars and sails of a brig two hundred yards distant stood out in strong relief as she came up on the larboard bow. The lookout in the forecastle reported her as close to the bow, while the officer of the watch from the bridge also clearly saw her. So did the quarterdeck midshipman, who was sent forward at once to the forecastle; but on arriving, there was no vestige or sign of any material ship. The night was clear and the sea calm.

Thirteen persons altogether saw her. Two other ships of the fleet, the HMS Excellent and the HMS Irresistible, who were sailing off the starboard bow, asked whether the Victory had seen the disquieting red light.[5]

"A phantom ship," the crew murmured, and their mood was more subdued than usual that day, and at night many a prayer was said.

Shining phosphorescence drifting along the surface on nights when clouds hid the moon and stars, and once while on watch in the darkness Keane saw the sea boil and bubble as if some monstrous cooking pot was stewing below. Sometimes, when the sea was calm, the black water would abruptly be filled with great glowing eyes lying motionless and staring at the ship. On other nights spheres of bluish light more than three feet in diameter could be seen in the depths, pulsing erratically. From time to time the vessel glided past a great shadowy shape, almost as big as herself, which lay without completely still beneath the waves, like a submerged

---

5   From the journal of King George V of England (then Duke of York), who reported the sighting of a phantom ship on At 4 A.M. on June 11, 1881 while sailing to Sydney from Melbourne, Australia.

reef. The sailors knew it to be some giant sea-monster of wicked potential, but the creature never moved, and they never sailed close enough to clearly discern its features.

Once when the vessel was far away from land, Keane, aloft on the mainmast, saw a light, appearing like the glow of a wax candle moving up and down, above the horizon, out to the larboard side. Calling to one of the topmen he told him of it and bade him look that way, which he did, and saw it too, though neither of them could give any explanation of it. They again perceived it once or twice, then saw it no longer.

And late one evening, as the ship lay to, the waters carried the sounds of distant merrymaking right up to her deck, making it sound as if the revellers were inches away.

"'Tis mermaids," said some of the sailors, "mermaids feastin' in their drown-ded halls made o' coral and mother-o'-pearl, surrounded by the golden treasures of shipwrecks, all crusted with barnacles and pearls."

CHAPTER 8

A Flogging

Caricature of Naval Punishment by George Cruikshank

In August that year one of the deckhands was caught thieving. Theft was quite a rare crime aboard ship, partly because of the strong bonds forged by fighting shoulder to shoulder with shipmates, partly because of the unlikelihood of getting away with it in such cramped quarters, and partly because of the severe punishment thieves were dealt if apprehended.

A valuable item went missing. One of the Able Seamen, a man named George Addison, possessed an alicorn's horn, of which he was uncommonly proud, and of which he was so protective that he had— somewhat unwisely— smuggled it aboard so as to have it near at hand. Now and then the owner would take it out of his sea-chest, unwrap it and show it around to any off-duty sailors, accompanied by stories of its marvellous virtues. Straight as a spear, pale as ivory and two feet long, the horn, a rare and lovely thing, was sculpted by nature with counter-clockwise spirals.

"The alicorn," Addison would boast, "possesses magical powers. It can detect poison and render it harmless. The ceremonial cups of royalty is always made of alicorn. In Austria the Imperial 'ouse of Hapsburg had one made into a sceptre, all covered with diamonds and rubies, sapphires and em'ralds. In the olden days they thought alicorn could cure all ills. The alchemists used to grind 'em into powder and sell 'em. But there was some shysters not too choosy about what they ground into powder, whether it were alicorn or the bones of some old cart 'orse. So the alchemists came up with trials, by which people could tell if the alicorn was fake."

"What trials?" someone asked.

"Draw a circle on the floor with the alicorn and put a spider in the circle. If the 'orn is true the spider will not be able to cross the circle and will perish of starvation inside it. Another test its to put some alicorn in a flame. The true 'orn gives off a sweet fragrance when it burns."

"Let us put this one to the test!" another sailor cried.

"Should any man," said Able Seaman Addison, "burn my alicorn or damage it by drawin' circles wiv it, I shall personally chuck 'im overboard."

"'ow much is it werf, George?" his shipmates wanted to know.

"I dunno for sure, but two 'undred years ago Good Queen Bess was given an alicorn that was worth as much as a castle!"

"That is a treasure, Mr. Addison, and no mistake!" said Keane.

Addison grinned self-satisfiedly and tipped his cap.

Aside, James Watson whispered to the Irishman, "That ain't no unicorn's 'orn."

"What is it, then?" Keane asked.

"'Tis the tooth of a narwhal-fish. The whalers trade 'em from the Eskimos in Arctic waters, where the tusked whales swim. Got a couple of 'em meself, I 'ave, stowed at me Mum's 'ouse in the East End. Cost me a pretty penny. Gawd, I nearly died when you opened your mouf just now. 'Tis about time you piped up. You don't talk much, Paddy, do you!"

"No," Keane agreed, "not since the Sasunach navy took me. But I make every word count."

This last, he added with a genial note of irony, so that Watson rounded on him with mock indignation. "What? You insinuatin' somefin'?" Next moment he had given Keane a shove and the two young men fell to the floor in a friendly bout of wrestling. No one paid them any attention—such horseplay was not uncommon and relieved the monotony of shipboard life.

When they grew tired of scrapping they resumed sitting together and discussing the alicorn. "I would not be showin' it around if I were Addison," Watson said. "I got a vegetable lamb in me sea-chest wif me carvin's, but I ain't intendin' to display it. 'Tis too tempting for the light-fingered."

And so it proved.

On the nineteenth of August, Addison discovered that his sea-chest had been tampered with and his cherished prize removed. He complained to the senior officers, a thorough search of the crew's quarters was made, and the item was eventually discovered.

The crime's perpetrator, one Harry Perkins, was also tracked down. Instantly the marines clapped him in leg-irons on the upper deck. He denied the charge, but all the evidence was against him. He was swiftly court martialled and the captain sentenced him to 'run the gauntlet' as punishment. When he realised there was no avoiding this fate Perkins broke down and wept. His show of weakness attracted even greater scorn from the crew, who despised him already for the contemptible crime of stealing from his shipmates.

"You 'ave all seen floggin's before," the first mate declared to the ship's newest recruits as if prophesying doom, "but if you ain't seen a thieves' cat or the runnin' o' the gantlope, you ain't seen nothin'."

The indicted man was given twenty-four hours in which to manufacture his own cat o' nine tails. This was done by unravelling a thick rope, dividing it into three strands, then unravelling those strands into three and braiding them into thin strips and coating them with wax. He had to make the instrument well, and if he did not complete the task in the allotted time his punishment would be increased. The standard cat was not considered the most terrible device of castigation; being fashioned from rope it inflicted less torment than a whip of leather or a birch-rod. The thieves' cat, however, caused additional pain, because each of its nine falls must be knotted three times.

Punishments for serious offences were customarily meted out on the quarterdeck at eleven o'clock in the morning—six bells during the forenoon watch—and this was no exception. The whole ship's company was ordered to line up and witness the event, that it might serve as a warning to them all. With his bag of ointments and bandages at hand, the ship's surgeon stood in attendance.

Bare-headed to display respect for naval law, the ship's company listened while the provost martial read out the Articles of War with particular emphasis on the one the offender had contravened: "Article twenty-nine: All robbery committed by any person in the fleet, shall be punished with death, or otherwise, as a court martial, upon consideration of the circumstances, shall find meet."

Perkins was brought forward in chains. As pale as bone, he had ceased weeping and become quiet and still. The captain asked him if he had anything to say to justify leniency, to which Perkins answered in the negative. He was then divested of his shirt and his hands were tied to a grating above his head.

The bos'un's mates rolled up their sleeves. The first one picked up the cat o' nine tails and hefted it in his right hand, experimentally flicking it through the air. It made a sound like the rushing wind. Two navy drummers commenced a drum roll, whereupon the prisoner sagged in his fetters and the surgeon had to revive him with smelling salts.

At the order, "Bos'un's mate, do your duty," the brawny seaman stepped forward. Slowly he drew back his arm. The drums ceased abruptly, their rattle seeming to hang in mid air like breath on a frosty morning, and with a whoosh and a smack, the lash was laid across the offender's bare back with a full sweep of the seaman's arm. Perkins screamed and convulsed. The drums rolled again, and the exercise was repeated.

Each initial lash of the cords ripped open the prisoner's skin, and following blows cut through the flesh, so that after a dozen strokes had been administered his back would be a mass of bloody lacerations. After each blow the whip's wielder paused to draw the knotted tails through his fingers, untangling them and cleaning off the gore. As for the ships company looking on, most were stony-faced but a few were clearly enjoying the spectacle. One of the cabin boys leaned over and was sick on the deck. He was ordered to promptly fetch a bucket and mop to clean it up. After half a dozen lashes the prisoner was offered a mug of water—from which he managed a sip or two—and the second bos'un's mate took his turn with the whip. Fortunately for Perkins he too was right-handed, or the man's back would have been cross-cut to a mangled mess.

After receiving twelve lashes the thief was cut down from the grating. His punishment, however, was far from over. He had yet to run the gauntlet.

Still stripped to the waist he was made to walk between two lines of the ship's company, so that each man and boy could strike him on his injured shoulders with short lengths of rope that had been plaited into 'knittles', or small versions of the cat o' nine tails. The master-at-arms prevented Perkins from rushing through the ordeal by marching backwards one pace ahead of him, the point of his cutlass held against his chest. A corporal followed the prisoner to make sure he kept moving forward. The deck became splashed with blood. After reaching the end of the two lines Perkins was dragged back to the grating, groaning and sobbing, and hung up once more to suffer another dozen lashes. When he was finally cut down he was taken to the sick berth on the upper gun deck, where the surgeon increased his suffering by applying vinegar and salt to his wounds in order to prevent infection.

"Such a punishment far outweighs the crime," said Keane, in anger. "By God, how can men rest at nights, having done such ill deeds?"

Watson said, "It's times like this that make a bloke want to sprout wings. I want to get away as much as you do."

"Do not let anyone else hear you say that," Keane softly warned.

His comrade nodded; by now they both knew the Articles of War almost by heart, because they were read out to the ship's company when the ship's chaplain led the church service on Sundays, when an offender's punishment warrant was proclaimed, and by the captain whenever he deemed it necessary. 'Every person in or belonging to the fleet, who shall desert or entice others so to do, shall suffer death...'

CHAPTER 9

The Compass Rose

The bodies of many of the older sailors displayed intricate tattoos, each design imbued with deep significance.

"A nau'ical star or compass rose helps you navigate," Watson explained, "specially findin' your way back to port or back 'ome. A pig and a 'en, pricked out on each foot, are wards against drownin' in a shipwreck. The words "old Fast' pricked across the knuckles is a charm to 'elp deckhands and boatswain's mates keep a firm grip on the riggin'."

One sailor had brought a tiny metal toolbox of needles aboard, in order to tattoo men at sea. He used gunpowder to create the designs by pricking the skin and rubbing the powder into the wound.

As summer turned to autumn, Keane gave half a week's worth of his rum ration to the 'pricker' in exchange for a tattoo of a miniature compass rose on his upper right arm.

"Rose," he whispered beneath his breath, when it was finished, "guide me home."

A surge of belief in the lucky charm gave him hope and inspired him with fresh confidence.

On September the seventh, 1797, the HMS Victory, on course for Southampton, was sailing off the coast of the Low Countries. The ship being desperately short of fresh water, Jervis had her hove to during the night, while an eight-oar boat was sent to shore laden with empty barrels. To his own surprise, Keane was chosen to be among them. It seemed too good to be true—a chance at freedom in a land at war with the English. Could it be that the compass rose tattoo had such power?

The Austrian Netherlands was enemy territory, being in the possession of the French Republic. Bearing caution in mind, the landing party was ordered to be as swift and discreet as possible.

Anyone observing the young Irishman as he climbed over HMS Victory's side and stepped down the rope ladder to the boat, might have glimpsed on his face a look of fixed resolve. Unheard by anyone, he breathed a name. "Rose. Ye're with me. Rose, I be comin' home to ye."

The moon, a crescent in its last quarter, scooped star-fish from cloud-nets. Its radiance gleamed fitfully on a shingled beach, pleated with long lines of sea-foam. The shadowy forms of men disembarked from the rowboat in the shallows, and waded to land. All were dressed in rather grimy white trousers and blue coats, their draggled locks scraped back into horse-tails.

The four marines carried muskets with which to guard the party, while the four seamen lugged wooden kegs on their shoulders. Wavelets washed up among the pebbles, their hems rimmed with silver. There was only the slap and sigh of the water, and the soft splash of the men's wading.

After almost three and a half years at sea, Keane was once again walking upon dry land. It felt strange beneath his sea-accustomed feet, hard and unforgiving; lifeless in comparison to the rocking waves, the pulsing tides and the murmuring currents of the ocean.

The rowboat had put in at a place where, according to the ship's navigator, a freshwater stream issued into the sea. Three of the marines went ahead to scout for danger, their weapons already primed and rammed. One stayed with the boat. At a signal, the seamen shouldered their burdens and followed the infantry. Across the beach they walked, and into a dark woodland. Soon they came across the stream, where they knelt to drink the cold, pure water and to fill the barrels while the marines kept watch. Keane let his cask fill slowly. He was the last to carry his load back to the boat, by which time the three other sailors had already collected a second empty barrel and were returning to the banks of the stream.

The sliver of a moon was slipping behind clouds. In the gloom Keane lugged his barrel to the boat and loaded it aboard, but he did not return to the stream. Between shore and rivulet he darted off into the woods, his pulse thumping like the hammer of a frenzied blacksmith. Ripping off his blue pea coat he flung it into a hazel brake and, as soon as he was far enough away to risk the noise of headlong flight through the trees, began to run for his life.

Bushes and trees flew past, indistinct and shadowy. He glanced from side to side, now crouching low as he sighted possible danger, now abruptly springing forward and bursting into a sprint. Vegetation loomed out of the darkness and rushed by him, sometimes whipping him, or tearing at his shirt. He plunged through thickets, ducked beneath boughs, leaped over rocks and splashed through small watercourses, and then his boots were pounding on the rutted surface of a country lane, bordered by hedges. After years at sea he did not have his 'land legs' and fought to remain steady on his feet. The road was potholed and rutted, treacherous in the night.

Alerted by a sudden noise the deserter whirled about, facing the direction from which he had fled. At full pelt, three British marines were dashing up the lane after him. One paused briefly, braced his musket on his shoulder, took aim, and fired. A sulphurous brilliance flared like the yellow eye of a demon, and smoke erupted with a roar.

Keane had already turned away and put on another burst of speed. He poured every ounce of his energy and willpower into this final flight. His beating heart threatened to burst from his chest and he gasped for breath.

The first shot had missed, but a second musket ball sizzled past him. Now he was dodging and swerving to make himself a difficult target for the third, which exploded into the night soon enough. Before him, a tree had fallen across the road. There was not time to find a way around it. Like a fox at bay he turned to face his hunters and prepared to make a last stand. In the black dome of the sky, the moon glided forth.

Now that their guns had been fully discharged, the three troopers came at their quarry with drawn blades. Hardened by a strenuous life in the rigging, the Irishman took the first marine by the arm and, with a rapid flick of the wrist, bowled him over, disarming him at the same time. The attacker landed flat on his back. Keane grabbed the soldier's musket in both hands and began to wield it as he would have wielded a shillelagh.

There in the middle of that moonlit country lane he fought for his freedom, his life and his true-love, batting aside their thrusting bayonets and cutlasses, whirling his makeshift cudgel so rapidly that it appeared no more than a blur against the stars. The butt of his musket connected with a skull, and a second marine toppled. The first was struggling to rise, but Keane spun on his heel and dealt him another blow to quieten him, before ramming the gun's muzzle into the third man's ribs. When his attacker doubled over, Keane brought his weapon hard across the back of his head, and he crumpled.

Three marines sprawled senseless in the dust of the lane. Dropping the firearm, Keane skirted the fallen trunk and fled. The roadway darkened as clouds again sailed across the moon's face, but not before Keane—and perhaps Rose, from afar—had glimpsed stirrings among the hedges ahead.

A movement of foliage, a swift gleam off the barrel of a musket, a glimpse of a feathered hat... Men lurked there, and they were armed.

An ambush.

Breathing hard, sweat dripping from his brow, Keane glanced over his shoulder. Down the lane the dim outlines of pursuers could be seen and heard, speeding after him—his fellow sailors, perhaps, eager to obtain the reward for the capture of a deserter; or a couple of the marines, recovered from their beating. Up the lane in front of him strangers with guns waited in hiding. To either side, thick hawthorn hedges blocked his way. He was caught in a snare. There could be no way out.

He was running, stumbling, turning his head this way and that, in an effort to watch both ends of the lane at the same time; to learn the identities of the men in the hedges ahead and to discover their intentions and simultaneously to judge how long it would take for his pursuers to get within firing range.

The yellow glare of exploding gunpowder flowered in the darkness. With a crash, the world tilted upside down and he fell into the sky; into a void so lightless that it annihilated existence.

CHAPTER 10

The Pikes Must be Together by the Rising of the Moon

Irish Rebellion: Battle of New Ross, 5 June 1798
George Cruikshank

And come tell me Sean O'Farrell tell me why you hurry so?
'Hush a buachaill, hush and listen!' and his cheeks were all a glow.
'I bear orders from the captain: Get you ready quick and soon,
For the pikes must be together by the rising of the moon.

Out from many a mud-wall cabin eyes were watching through the night,
Many a manly heart was beating for the blessed warning light.
Murmurs rang along the valleys to the banshee's lonely croon,
And a thousand pikes were flashing by the rising of the moon.

All along that singing river that black mass of men was seen,
High above their shining weapons flew their own beloved green.
Death to every foe and traitor! Whistle out the marching tune,
And 'Hurrah, me boys, for freedom! 'Tis the rising of the moon!'

'The Rising of the Moon', Lyrics by J. K. Casey (1846 - 1870)

Late in the year 1797 word came to Allanwell from Dublin that the famous Lord Reginald Leighton had been captured by the French while on a diplomatic mission to Austria. None knew whether he was dead or alive.

In Ireland, by the spring of 1798, a campaign of violence and intimidation by the British was destroying the United Irishmen. Many of the leaders had been arrested. After the capture and death of the popular hero, Lord Edward Fitzgerald, the remaining leaders felt compelled to call for an immediate rising, even though this would be before further French aid would have time to arrive.

The secret date was set.

Sir Robert Westbourne joined in mutual accord with his neighbour Sir Richard Kingsley and the other Protestant landowners in the region. Sensing difficult times ahead, they had by now sent their wives and children to England. Sir Robert also hired a band of loyalist Protestant mercenaries, who made their presence felt by riding through the streets of Allanwell or patrolling the bounds of the Westbourne estates. They were well armed. The villagers hated these 'heretics and butchers'; they spat at their feet and cursed them. The hired soldiers showed as little love in return, going so far as to ride down a drunken man who stumbled into their path.

Once the United Irishmen had decided on rebellion, they had to secure the willingness of the people to actively join. Their recruiters went about the country, reaching even remote population centres like Castlerigg, Ballyganna and Allanwell. They held meetings in the meadows, out of the knowledge of the mercenaries. Allanwell men flocked to these gatherings, to be harangued by spokesmen emphasising the financially rewarding aspects of overthrowing the government, asserting that reform would bring a major re-dispersal of property. They implied that republicanism would bring low rents, the dissolution of tithes, and taxes levied only on the rich and slothful rather than the impoverished and hard working.

In the village a torn piece of paper was, clandestinely, going around. Well-thumbed and dirty, it was beginning to crumble at the edges. Few of the villagers could read it, but they all knew what it stated. It was the United Irishmen's doctrine, and it said in part—

'I believe in a revolution founded on the rights of man, in the natural and imprescriptable right of all citizens to the land... As the land and its produce was intended for the use of man it is unfair for fifty or a hundred men to possess what is for the subsistence of near five millions...'

In the minds of the people, revolution became associated with release from poverty. The United Irishmen recruiters swore in many new members.

John Delacey heard from Sir Robert that Lord Leighton, who had spent a month in captivity in the Austrian Netherlands, having been taken prisoner by the French, had returned home as hale as ever, but sizzling with hatred for the foreign foe. It was rumoured he had been ransomed, and his family and friends had been forced to pay an enormous sum to obtain his release. It was also whispered that, deploring his beard, his captors had made him shave it off. Leighton, who appeared publicly in full but somewhat shorter beard, refused to tolerate any mention of his humiliation at the hands of the French. His temper, ever short, had become volcanic. Shortly after his return his second wife died of an accidental overdose of laudanum, to which she had become addicted during the first year of her marriage.

On returning to Ireland, Leighton assembled a band of mercenaries and amused himself by going about the countryside "restoring law and order" as he called it. His men quickly became infamous for their extreme brutality towards prisoners and civilians. They conducted summary executions, torture, and other acts of violence beyond what was considered acceptable even in wartime. They imposed martial law and suspended civil liberties, and they deliberately destroyed homes, farms, and other property.

In the town of Tethring Hill during one particularly bloody week, they expanded their savagery to include the kinfolk of militia members, forcibly evicting wives and children, assaulting and even sometimes killing them.

These outrages led to deep resentment and lasting grudges against Lord Leighton. The Tethring Hill militia, in particular, vowed to be revenged. They swore to pursue a personal vendetta against him all the days of his life, but the earl took this as a badge of honour. He laughed when he heard of their threats, and continued to inflict cruelty upon common people, bringing fear and misery wherever he went.

In Allanwell, sometimes Ilvenna McGinty saw portents in the formations of clouds and the flight of birds. She also possessed some sticks that she used for divining the future. Concerned about the strife that was beginning to tear apart her country, she read them in private. Only to her Ma did she divulge what she had discovered.

Having tossed the sticks on the kitchen floor, Ilvenna knelt beside them to make sense of the way they had fallen and the shapes they formed.

"I see an apple," she said, "a beautiful apple, golden-red on one side and grass-green on the other. And there are three worms bitin' at its core."

Then she exclaimed, "Blessed Lord Jesus! Hold my hand, mother."

Ma did so, crouching beside her daughter. "What is't? What else d'ye see?"

"I've seen far into the future, Ma. Another fifty years, maybe. Half of the apple will rot away entirely, and yet the worms won't leave it alone, even then." She stared blindly into her mother's face. "Ma, tell your grand-children they must leave Ireland before the heart of the new century. A terrible t'ing is going to happen then—a truly terrible t'ing."

"Tell them yourself," said Ma in a brittle voice.

"That, I shall not be able to do," said Ilvenna, "for I shall never meet them."

Silence enveloped the kitchen, except for the whisper of flames in the grate, like the wind rustling through dead leaves.

Ma stood up. Her weather-creased face was puckered with pain.

Leaning down she scooped up the divining sticks and threw them on the fire. "'Tis no good at all that lot was ever doin'," she said angrily. "They was forever crooked."

For fear of betrayal, the leaders of the United Irishmen refused to divulge to the rank and file the date set for the rising to commence. The only clue they gave—and this only to a select few—was that it was to start in Dublin.

"You will learn of the rising in Dublin when the mail coaches cease to arrive," they said, "for we will have stopped them, thus sending a message of triumph to the rest of the country—we have taken Dublin—the fight for freedom has begun! That will be the signal to rise throughout the nation. When that signal comes, rebel units must take the local estates by force, then, when they are secured, we must spread out to surrounding areas, turning out all English and loyalist land-owners from their estates. The French succeeded. So can we."

Early in May, John Delacey had been made lame in his left leg when a horse kicked him. He could place no weight on the limb and was forced to hop about on crutches. In days like these when every man must declare himself on one side or the other, he had—amongst the villagers— declared for the United Irishmen, even though there was little he could do to aid the cause. Sir Robert never asked him which ideology he supported, presuming that as a blue-blood of the gentry,

Delacey would unquestionably side with the loyalists. And John Delacey never volunteered the information, since it would cost him his livelihood.

John Delacey's conscience dictated that he ought to resign from his post as overseer on Sir Robert's estate, but as there was no other way he could put food on his family's table, he was forced to continue.

"Sir Robert will dismiss me soon enough I suppose," he said, "now that I can scarcely get about, I am not much use."

Yet his job was not denied him.

"I give my support to the name of freedom," John Delacey said to the village men, "but I will not support any who seek to take the life of Sir Robert."

With this assertion he fell foul of some of the men. There were those who thirsted eagerly for Protestant blood, especially of the aristocratic kind.

Delacey was kept well informed by his connections in Dublin, and he passed on most of this information to his four daughters—for, as he said, "Knowledge is power, and to be forewarned is to be forearmed."

"There are many who believe a rising is imminent, " he told them. "For my part, I think it is inevitable now. The people are going to revolt against the British with or without help from France. But the leaders of the United Irishmen are drawn from the middle-class. I fear that this fact has already begun their undoing, and because of it they must fail."

"Why, Papa?" asked his eldest daughter Margaret, fear catching in her throat like ashes.

"I do not know whether the leaders have grasped that no system exists to prevent the tradesmen and cottiers from pressing for more than the bourgeois, democratic and separatist aims of the rising."

"I don't understand," said Lizzie, wrinkling her nose.

The youngest sister said nothing. Since her final dream of Keane, Rose spoke rarely, though these days she went often to the church to speak with Father Joseph, and to pray.

John Delacey explained. "The leaders, mostly Protestant, are in fact working only towards Irish self-rule—for complete separation from the English monarchy. But if they are successful, the masses—the men of no property—will want the land redistributed. And many of the leaders are land-owners."

"But the United Irishmen recruiters promised that the land would be re-distributed!" cried Margaret. "I heard Rafferty say so!"

"They may well have said so," said her father gently, "but Maggie, if we still owned Charter Hall, would you willingly divide up our estates and parcel them out to the poor?"

"Yes! No—maybe." Margaret struggled to divine her own feelings.

"Well, what does this mean for the rising?" broke in Katherine, her eyes intently fixed on her father's.

"It means," said John Delacey in anxious despondency, "that it carries in its soul the seeds of its own destruction."

CHAPTER 11

False Dates on the Gravestones

The fateful day arrived; May 23rd, 1798.

In the city of Dublin, the Irish people rose in arms. Thousands of citizens turned out for the rising, but the attempt was rapidly and brutally suppressed, with very little fighting. It was not long before the Dublin rebellion collapsed hopelessly.

Reports of this failure travelled to every corner of the countryside.

"I have heard from my friends in the capital," John Delacey grimly told his family. "They say that Reynolds, one of the informers who betrayed the rising, recanted because he feared his ancestral estates would be confiscated if it did not succeed. You see, it is as I guessed—the class basis of the leadership of the United Irishmen has already begun their dissolution."

The mail coaches, some of which were still managing to ply their routes despite the nation-wide unrest, brought further news. Three days after the rising was initiated, the hierarchy of the Catholic Church had officially issued a statement of loyalty to the English Crown and censure of the rebellion. Despite this proclamation, throughout Ireland most of the Catholic commonalty chose to continue as they had begun, and some individual Catholic priests played important roles in helping to lead them.

After the crushing of the Dublin rising, Irish loyalists and British forces visited further punishment on the rest of the country. In Wicklow and North Wexford more than fifty United Irishmen prisoners were executed. Civilians were murdered, homes were burned.

But the resistance did not flag.

Mail deliveries suddenly ceased. From Allanwell, many who were fit to bear arms had taken their pitchforks, scythes, flails and other armaments of an agrarian nature, and gone off to join the revolt at its most active centres. Others remained, ready to take action closer to home.

Rebellion broke out spasmodically, and without a central plan. A few days after the fiasco at Dublin, a rider came galloping back into the village. He brought word that major risings had occurred in Wexford, and in Antrim and Down in the north. Elsewhere there had been minor skirmishes. Thousands of Catholics and Protestants had turned out and fought side by side in a series of battles, despite the obvious futility of the situation. But in a surprising twist, Wexford had been successfully taken and held by the United Irishmen.

Eager to defuse any sectarianism between the Catholic and Protestant sections of his forces, the leader of the Vinegar Hill Camp, Edward Lough, proclaimed on 7th June: "This is not a war for religion but for liberty."

"Saints in heaven, I never thought I'd live to see the day," the Delacey's servant Mary said joyfully, on hearing these tidings. "Wexford a republic! And thirty thousand Irishmen defending the town from the savage British butchers! Brave souls, God bless them."

"And men of both religions fighting side by side," said Katherine wonderingly. "Could this be a new dawn of tolerance?"

"Not in Wexford, or so I've heard," said her father. "You'll not be forgetting how cruelly the largely Protestant Militia and Yeomanry persecuted Wexford Catholics before the uprising?"

"How could we forget?" said Rose softly. "Sir Robert's mercenaries are saints by comparison."

"They say that Vinegar Hill is the site of a great many executions—three hundred, maybe four hundred men, mostly Protestant," said John Delacey. "In Wexford, Protestants are attending mass as the only means of saving their lives."

"But it is supposed to be a war against the English tyrants," said Lizzie in disgust.

"Sectarian tensions are never far from erupting," her father reminded her.

"Let us hope they will be smoothed in the cause of freedom," Lizzie cried. "Long live the Republic!" She too had been caught up in the heady excitement of success.

Emboldened by the victory in Wexford, United Irishmen sympathisers from Allanwell and outlying areas now rose against Westbourne and the other local Protestants. To the gates of Charter Hall they marched. There they were met by a small band of Sir Robert's hired men.

"We out-number you four to one!" said the rebels. "Open the gates or we will show you no mercy!"

The mercenaries opened the gates.

As the rebels made their way along the sweeping drive-way, the rows of hedges on either side whispered softly, like conspirators. And indeed, they did conceal a secret.

The secret was death, which, when the rebels were half-way along the road, emerged from ambush. Mercenaries had been hiding behind the walls of greenery. Springing out with a roar of smoking musketry and yells of bloodlust, they took great toll amongst the invaders. Victory went to the mercenaries. Several Allanwell men were slain. Wounded or hale, many were taken prisoner.

"You will be escorted to Dublin and tried," said Sir Robert, when they were brought before him.

The hired men treated the prisoners cruelly, but worse was to befall them. On the way to Dublin their wagon was overtaken by Irish loyalists and every prisoner was slain.

In Allanwell, Sir Robert's men went around the village demanding the surrender of any other United Irishmen sympathisers. They demand to know who supported the rebellion—by word, if not by deed—to know who held republican views, whose brothers and sons had gone to join the rebels. Nobody admitted to it. Meeting with no response, the mercenaries threatened torture. Their threats were not empty. Seizing three men who had fallen under suspicion, they wrung names from them under duress. When those named were confronted with their crimes, they begged for mercy, saying they had been forced against their will to side with the rebels.

"You shall be imprisoned until these troubles are over," Sir Robert told them, "and then you will be tried in a court of law."

The accused men were jailed in one of his out-houses. Among them was Rafferty, who was well known for having been outspoken against the English, particularly since his sons had been taken by the press-gang.

That evening as the mists began coagulating in the valley Mrs Rafferty turned up at the doorstep of the McGinty house, in a terrible state, with three small children wailing and clinging to her skirts like burrs that had attached themselves to the plumes of a passing pheasant. She was weeping, tearing out handfuls of her hair and bawling repeatedly, "Ilvenna McGinty! Ilvenna McGinty! Tell me if there will ever be peace in this God-forsaken land!"

Ma and Ilvenna brought her indoors immediately, and tried to soothe the anguished woman with herbal teas and comforting words, but Ilvenna refused to divine the future of Ireland for the sobbing wife. "I will not," she insisted. "I do not want to know and neither should anyone. The future of Ireland is in God's hands and we must have faith in the Lord."

Later, after Ilvenna had returned from escorting Mrs. Rafferty home in a somewhat quieter mood, Ma said to her flatly, "But you have divined it, haven't you."

"That I have," Ilvenna said bleakly. "And there will be peace. Oh yes, there will be peace some day." She lifted her chin to meet her mother's troubled gaze. "But never in our time."

Meanwhile, the collapse of the "Wexford Republic" took place only three weeks after its establishment. The thirty thousand Wexford rebels were, according to their foes, "utterly untrained, practically leaderless and miserably armed." On 21st June 1798 the final major battle of the Wexford Republic was fought at Vinegar Hill. General Gerard Lake, who had savagely disarmed the north in the preceding year, rushed the rebels with twenty thousand British soldiers, defeated them and entered Wexford. Less than a month after the British flag had been torn down in Wexford, Irish resistance to British rule was broken.

Instead of signalling the end of bloodshed, this event heralded the outbreak of further and more widespread violence. A governance of panic and terror ensued. In some regions no sectarian motive could be attached to the massacres, for several of the remaining rebel units slaughtered the families of known loyalists. Many Protestants and Catholics, however, thrust aside the quest for Irish independence regardless of religion, and resumed their ancient hostilities. It was the British army and loyalist forces, nonetheless, that inflicted greater carnage in most parts of the country. Thousands of rebels were killed.

During this savage aftermath, British soldiers and Irish loyalists rampaged all over the countryside. They dragged people out of their houses and beat them to death, or set fire to their homes and burned entire families, sparing neither wives nor daughters nor sons. It seemed they were mad with the lust for blood. In Allanwell Sir Robert's mercenaries, who seemed to take the British victory as a signal that they might now freely inflict vengeance on all who had supported the rebellion, joined the orgy of atrocities.

In August the news arrived that British Admiral Horatio Nelson had wiped out the French fleet at the Battle of the Nile. The tidings dampened the enthusiasm of the rebels—it seemed to indicate that British forces were powerful enough to overcome even the great Napoleon. At the urging of rebel leader Wolfe Tone, the Directory at Paris had sent troops by ship to help the Irish rebels, but by the time the French force arrived in Ireland that same month, it was too late to help the cause.

On August 22nd the French landed at Killala and defeated a number of British contingents. On 15th September, however, they were forced to surrender to General Cornwallis at Ballynamuck in Connaught. The brother of Wolfe Tone was captured and hanged. Tone himself was captured at sea on October 12th. He was thrown into prison and sentenced to death, but on November 19th he—reportedly—slit his own throat with a penknife, and died a week later.

By autumn, the rebellion had been defeated. Some thirty-two United Irishmen had been executed in the North. Tens of thousands of people had been killed, and a reign of terror had spread throughout the country.

Death leaned through every doorway.

The Delacey household survived this dark period, thanks in part to the protection of Sir Robert Westbourne. For the populace of Allanwell, where mercenaries patrolled the streets, daily life eventually returned to a distant semblance of normality. Yet nothing could ever be the same there, or anywhere in Ireland, after that.

In hushed tones, the Delacey sisters discussed politics with their father.

"This country suffers more violence than ever in the aftermath of the rebellion," he told them. "Men are burning down chapels, both Catholic and Protestant. The government is deporting shiploads of suspects to the penal colonies on the other side of the world, in New Holland."

"Dear God!" cried Katherine passionately. "They might as well have saved the trouble of the journey and hanged all those poor creatures in Dublin! New Holland is a death sentence in itself. If the snakes and the boiling sun do not kill them, the crocodiles and flesh-eating spiders will!

"Hush Kate," Margaret reprimanded. Reluctantly, her sister suppressed her emotion.

"In Wexford," their father continued, "the death penalty applies to anyone who was a United Irish officer. It is in the best interests of those who participated in the rising to declare they knew nothing about it, or assert that they were uninformed puppets, or that they were compelled by 'the rebel mob' to have do whatever it was they did. So great is the terror of the families involved that they even go to the lengths of inscribing a false year on the headstones of their relations who were killed during the rising."

"When will it end?" Margaret murmured.

"I cannot foresee any end to it at all," her father replied sadly. "I fear that this reign of terror will continue, even into the next century. You must all take very great care in everything you do and say, for these are uncertain and lawless times. Even the innocent may find themselves in peril."

CHAPTER 12

Christmas at Charter Hall

The winter of 1798 seized Ireland in talons of ice. The landscape, lately running red with gore and slathered with the ashes of pyres, glistened pristine, silvery-white. Frost glittered on naked twigs like diamonds on lace. It was as if the snow had fallen, soft as a virgin's kiss, to deliberately obliterate mankind's misdeeds. Winter tenderly wrapped a burnt and bleeding victim in pristine, freezing finery.

Christmas—otherwise known as Yule—was drawing near when the widower and erstwhile hostage Lord Leighton journeyed to Allanwell. He travelled in a carriage guarded by heavily armed outriders, for the purpose of visiting his acquaintance Sir Robert Westbourne—or conceivably, as some whispered, to distance himself from the gossip and clandestine sneers of several of his urban associates. The Delaceys were bidden, rather than invited, to call on the Westbournes during Leighton's stay.

"With my own girls away in England, there's not a pretty face to brighten the bleak aspect of this godforsaken outpost except those of your own daughters," Sir Robert said to his steward. "Bring them to my house. Let us set differences aside and dine together on Christmas Day! We shall drink to His Majesty's health!" And the steward, who was obliged to his master for many things—not least his livelihood—had no option but to bow and mutter his thanks.

Although households all over the country were going hungry, the Christmas tables at Charter Hall displayed no lack of comestibles. They were arrayed with traditional, rich fare such as roast goose, glazed vegetables, fruit mince pies, shortbreads, butter and cream, brandied plum puddings, and wines as tawny as fire-glow or crimson as juniper-berries. Festoons of ivy and holly decorated the mantelpieces. Energetic flames bounded upwards from hefty logs of timber that had been carted in from Galway. Candle-light glimmered on the silver-gilt dinner service and glanced in tiny rainbows from long-stemmed wine-glasses of Waterford crystal.

Lizzie could not help visualising Mary, faced with a dinner of boiled cabbage and bacon at Mrs Rafferty's house, while the ragged children huddled for warmth around a little peat fire. When she looked from the familiar windows and beheld the snowy yew hedges lining the driveway, she could not suppress recollections of the massacre that had recently occurred in that very spot. Images of blood and death flickered before her inner gaze, and her old home seemed no longer a welcoming place, but a trap.

The Delacey sisters possessed very little finery with which to adorn themselves and please the eyes of the esteemed gentlemen at dinner on Christmas Day. They could only put on their Sunday best. These garments were not the same clothes they had worn at the Charter Hall tea-party four and a half years earlier. Fortunately, since then their father had been able to acquire fresh fabrics from Dublin, and they had all sewed new outfits for themselves. Notwithstanding, the cut and materials of the outfits had already become passé. In the best circles fashion altered rapidly, driven by the couture of the king's court.

It remained a fact, however, that no titivation of lace and spangles could do much to enhance the natural charms of John Delacey's daughters. Together they resembled an extraordinary bouquet of delicately-coloured blossoms, dressed in their gowns of plain muslin, with their dark hair enclosed beneath plain bonnets and falling in ringlets across their shawls. As ever, each sister's mouth was a startling splash of ruby against the ivory-paleness of her skin, each pair of eyes shone limpid blue. As they sat side-by-side at the dinner table, the sisters looked as pretty as sylphs in a painting by any romantic artist.

Leaning back in his chair, Lord Reginald Leighton surveyed them all from his fierce single optic. His head was adorned with a powdered peruke so foppishly curled that Lizzie was hard put to resist giggling at it. His waistcoat strained tightly against the swell of his paunch, the buttons threatening to pop.

"He was right, your Uncle Francis," Leighton said to the girls, leering at them from the depths of his bushy beard. "It was he who informed me that Charter Hall estate harboured not just one, but a veritable herd of fine young fillies. Then and there I decided I must come and see for myself. And he was right! Eh, Westbourne?" The peer laughed loudly and immoderately.

Embarrassed, Lizzie blushed. She saw Katherine's cheeks blazing angrily red, while Margaret's grew pale with mortification. John Delacey set his jaw. Only Rose, as withdrawn as usual, appeared indifferent to the slight.

"And you my dear," Leighton said, turning his attention upon Lizzie, to her utmost consternation, "why you would be quite the belle of the ball if you were to appear in London. You must join us there next season, I insist upon it. One of your sisters can accompany you."

Lizzie visibly shuddered, then jumped as Margaret kicked her in the ankle beneath the table. "You do me too much honour, sir," she said in a small voice, almost fainting with fright.

"Not at all! Not at all! I daresay when you're tarted up with a bit of velvet and a few pearls you'll be worthy of court, young woman!" To the dismay of Lizzie's family, Lord Leighton suddenly leaned forward and chucked her under the chin, as if she were some bold milkmaid or wanton floozy making eyes at him.

John Delacey's hands were shaking. He swallowed, and made an effort to speak in cordial tones as Lizzie gasped and bridled. "Pray tell us, your lordship," he said stiffly, "what tidings of great deeds from the outside world?"

Delacey found himself in a painful plight. He ached to protect his daughters from the boorishness of this buffoon, but on the other hand, much depended upon his fostering cordial relations with these powerful men, especially Sir Robert, from whom he had recently requested clemency for Rafferty, who was currently imprisoned with the other rebels in Galway, awaiting trial.

"At this Christmas season, sir," Delacey had said in a private moment, "to grant the man his freedom on condition of his good behaviour, would that not be a most Christian act? The man's wife and three young children are now destitute, and his older boys were taken by the press gangs. Without their father the little ones will starve."

"He should have thought of that before he joined the rebels," growled Sir Robert. "Why should I show mercy to a fellow who would have murdered me and my family in our beds and stolen our property? Pray do not presume to lecture me, sir." He would not relent, and Delacey dared not say more.

Meanwhile Lord Leighton, clearly rejoicing in his role of boor, swigged a draught of wine, wiped his lips on the back of his lace cuffs and launched into a lengthy discourse. He commenced by railing against the military success of Napoleon Bonaparte during the previous year. The famous French commander had marched through Europe, capturing cities and conquering nation after nation. Ultimately Austria signed the Treaty of Campo-Formio, surrendering the Austrian Netherlands to France.

"It seems no army can stand against the great Bonaparte on land," observed Sir Robert Westbourne, signalling to a butler, who stepped forward to refill his glass.

"Perhaps. But on the seas, sir," Leighton said emphatically, "it is a different story. God save Horatio Nelson, Britannia's God of War! The good Admiral put the wind up Boney; that he did. The Frogs are nothing but peasants, don't you know; a nation of garlic-stinking cheese-eaters with the habits of dogs."

Sir Robert waved his glass of claret in the air. "I have always been of the opinion that France is a country that is much too good for the French," he remarked. "Long live King George." He gulped his drink.

"We'll finish them next year!" Leighton proclaimed. "When Britain has formed alliances with Russia, Austria, and the Ottoman Empire, we'll blow them all to the devil!"

Lizzie glanced across the table at Margaret, who was wincing in discomfort at being confronted by such offensive language. Meanwhile Katherine, fuming with indignation at this uncouth behaviour, opened her mouth and was about to enquire of Lord Reginald whether he had been forced to eat a lot of garlic during his detention by the French, when she caught Margaret's warning glance. With difficulty she reined in the impulse to provoke a conflict she could only lose in any case, and subsided. She spent the rest of her detention at the table concealing various foodstuffs in her voluminous sleeves, so that she might later donate them to the Rafferty children.

"Ah, those Russians!" boomed Leighton. "Now there's a country that knows how to pay homage to its great men. Back in 'twenty-five when their Tsar died, their men-o-war hoisted black sails as a token of mourning. Imagine that! What a sight, a fleet of black-sailed ships! The formidable naval force amassed under the direction of Peter the Great, though in no wise comparable to our own Royal Navy, was nonetheless a source of immense pride and approbation from his countrymen."

"Ah yes, black sails," said Sir Robert. "I understand that the frog-eaters followed the Russian example when Louis XV met his maker in 'seventy-four. French naval ships hoisted black sails and flags in mourning for the supreme leader of their pitiful excuse for a navy."

Leighton replied, "My good friend Admiral Sir Phillip Collingthorpe holds that the fleet of the Royal Navy ought to raise black sails as a sign of respect and honour for officers of high status, upon their demise. He's been trying to get it into the Articles of War, ever since he heard about the Russians."

"It would be a most extraordinary sight, a ship under dark canvas, instead of the usual white," remarked John Delacey. "I have always understood that it is only pirates who carry them. It'd be like seeing a black swan!"

"They have black swans in New Holland!" said Sir Robert, chuckling. "And furred ducks, laughing birds, giant jumping rodents and so forth."

"It's a rarity, yes," said Leighton, "for a mercantile ship or naval vessel to carry black sails. But, unlike the unfortunate dodo, it ain't extinct! The admiral opines that darker sails decrease glare when ships are sailing in the tropics, and at night they make vessels harder to see—thus, less of a target for pirates. He says it would be handy to keep some in reserve as spares, in case the primary white sails were damaged or lost during a voyage."

"But are not black sails more costly than white?" asked John Delacey.

Leighton made an impatient, dismissive gesture. "Hardly at all, man! Hardly at all!"

After dinner the three gentlemen took port and sherry together in the smoking-salon, while the young ladies, on the instructions of Sir Robert, repaired to the Music Room. Attended by the ancient, deaf housekeeper and a stolid footman they sat there in silence, listening to the susurration of voices from beyond closed doors, or attending to their own private thoughts. Later the gentlemen joined them and Leighton and Westbourne, jovial in their cups, insisted that the girls must sing and play to entertain the party. Submissively, without even bothering to voice concerns about their lack of rehearsal, Rose took up her accustomed seat at the harp while her sisters gathered around her.

The Delacey daughters moved like automatons. The gravity of the world's woes was weighing heavily on their spirits— the press-gangs, the wars, the tragic uprising, the loss and grief and destruction, the injustice of it all. They were in no mood for music, but their father exchanged glances with each one in turn, and nodded encouragingly. His look was filled with kindly compassion, which lent them strength, and in a moment they had arrived at a murmured agreement on which piece to perform.

While Katherine carefully re-arranged the folds of her sleeves, Rose grasped the harp's pegs and tuned the somewhat tarnished strings. She let her fingertips trail deftly across the instrument, and a liquid arpeggio rippled forth. Her three sisters began to join in harmony, lifting up their dulcet voices and singing the traditional Christmas carol,

"The Holly and the Ivy when they are both full grown,

Of all the trees that are in the wood, the Holly bears the crown.

Oh the rising of the sun and the running of the deer,

The playing of the merry organ, sweet singing in the choir."

As Lizzie took a breath, ready to sing the next verse, she happened to glance up. She was instantly impaled by the piercing stare of Lord Leighton's eye. He winked—or perhaps blinked, it was impossible to be certain—which so horrified and disconcerted her that she lost the melody for seven bars.

At this season the sun, cool and dim, rose late and set early, never lifting itself high above the horizon. The slopes around Allanwell glittered, lightly dusted with snow. Smoke plumes drifted from the chimney of every cot and bothy, and the breeze bore the sweet fragrance of burning peat. Between icy banks the Oranowin River flowed sluggishly. The low-pitched, sonorous caws of ravens resounded across the valley. It was on the chill and gloomy afternoon of Epiphany, beneath overcast skies that Lizzie muffled herself in warm clothes, braved the slippery, snow-stifled paths and went to visit Ilvenna McGinty in her Ma's cottage.

"He's taken a fancy to me, Ilvenna," she cried, "but I hate him! I beg you to cast a spell or make me some potion to repel that insufferable pig."

The air in the cottage seemed always sweet, tinged with the fragrance of turf-smoke and lavender, no matter the season.

"Pigs have good manners, Miss Elizabet'," Ilvenna reprimanded. "Everyone is forever t'inking they are filt'y because they're kept in sties, but if people were kept in sties they would be filt'y too, themselves."

"Well then, I apologise to pigs for comparing them to that... to that one-eyed, bearded swine," fumed Lizzie, too overwrought to wrestle with epithets. "He's old enough to be my father, Ilvenna! Really, his conduct is simply too coarse for words. Turn him into a slug and let the hens at him."

"If I had such a luxury as ownership of a hen these days I'd not be after giving it indigestion," Ilvenna replied, rolling her eyes. As if to give the lie to her words, a raucous clucking and squawking of chickens arose from the direction of the

McGintys' lean-to coop at the side of the bothy, where Ma was replenishing the nest-straw. Lizzie, however, understood perfectly well that Ilvenna, in the true tradition of the storyteller, had deliberately exaggerated her deficiency of fowls for the sake of a moment's entertainment. "In any case," the young red-haired woman continued, "if the Baron of Muckinrake were a slug I would be grindin' him beneath the heel of me boot, as he and his kind have been grindin' us down for years."

These dire utterings failed to distract Lizzie from her purpose. "Please do something to help me," she pleaded.

"I'll do what I can,' replied the seer, breaking some withered leaves off a bundle of dried herbs, "but I will not make any promises."

"There are some in this village that doubt your magical abilities," Lizzie said fervently, "but I for one have complete faith in you. I think you could work miracles if you had a mind to."

"Ach, miracles!" Ilvenna exclaimed. "Miracles is for saints, not sinners like me." She hesitated for an instant. As an afterthought she added softly, "But as I sometimes say to Ma, I have always believed I might have one miracle in me."

"Ooh, truly?" Lizzie echoed, suddenly astonished and intrigued.

"Aye. Although to make a miracle happen would be a huge t'ing, so huge it might be the very last t'ing I ever do."

Lizzie paused in silence. She habitually regarded Ilvenna with a certain awe, and this arresting statement compounded her respect. Presently she said, "We're in need of quite a few miracles nowadays, quite apart from the greatest miracle of all, which would be peace. Everyone is making themselves disagreeable. Maggie wails that she's unfairly doomed to be an old maid, and Kate is in an insufferable temper because the Dutch East India Company is going bankrupt after nearly two hundred years of trading, and now she thinks she'll never again set eyes on her sailor from that merchant ship, you know, the one with the vegetable lamb."

"Good riddance to the Sasunachs," Ilvenna said under her breath.

"And," Lizzie continued, oblivious of the interruption, "it'll be a marvel if Rose ever gives up her love-lorn moping, and an infinite wonder if the entire village does not turn against my family."

"And why should they be doin' that?" Ilvenna wanted to know. She threw the herbs into a pot of water that was boiling over the fire.

"Well, lately it seems to me that a few of them have become hostile towards us because of our connection with Charter Hall and its inhabitants. It is hard for my family, Ilvenna. We balance upon a political tightrope. We feel as if we have been pushed to the outer edge of every circle. For certain, we belong neither to the sphere of the villagers nor to the realm of the local gentry."

"Pay no heed to any who show ye ill-will, Miss Elizabet'. There is no fault to be laid at the Delaceys' door. There are those in Allanwell who are angry wit' the entire world, and for good reason. They look for somewhere to lay the blame, and choose what's closest at hand. That is all." Ilvenna let fall a pinch of powder into the steaming pot.

"Is that a potion you are making for me, to charm away his lordship?" Lizzie asked, craning forward to peer into the vessel.

"'Tis sage and onion soup for supper," Ilvenna replied briskly, stirring the concoction with a bacon bone on which a few shreds of meat were still clinging. Cocking a shrewd eye at her visitor she appended, "'Twas always one of Flynn's favourites."

Lizzie caught her breath. "Oh, Flynn!" she said, her hands fluttering up distractedly to pat her bonnet and hair. "Have you heard from him, Ilvenna? Is he coming home?"

"We have heard not a t'ing. 'Tis merely that whenever I make this soup I t'ink of him. Now let us talk business. Mind, Miss Lizbet', I cannot do what you are requestin' for less than eightpence ha'penny, but as always, I never accept payment until the customer has obtained the desired results."

"If it works I shall give you a shilling!" Lizzie cried, "and kiss the ground at your feet for good measure!"

"And why should it fail?" Ilvenna demanded, somewhat testily. "My charms always work, if the customer uses them properly."

CHAPTER 13

Papa Falls Ill

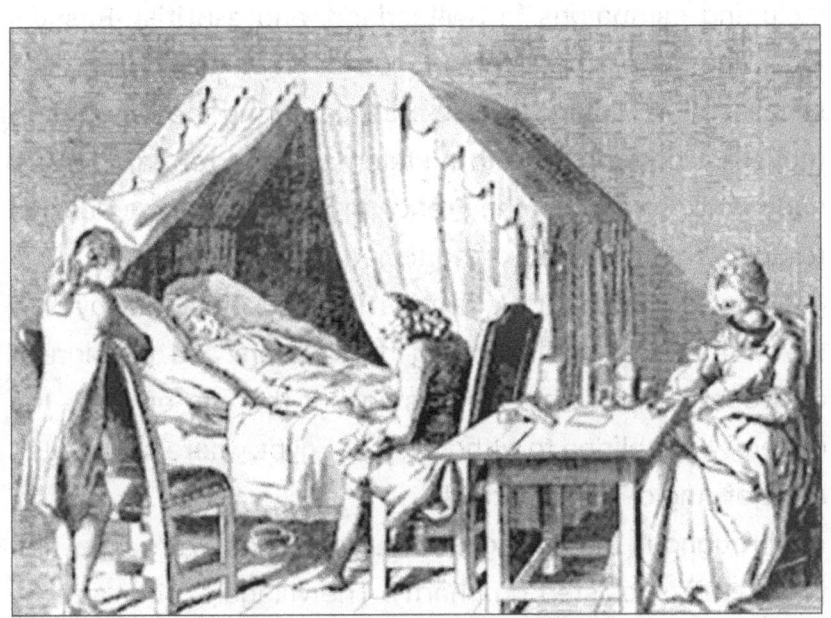

"The Sickbed" (unknown artist)

Irish everyday life carried on in an atmosphere of tension and violence throughout the two years following the rising. Lord Leighton made further visits to Allanwell from time to time, bringing news and displaying a fondness for Lizzie's company that unsettled her to the point of nightmares. Ilvenna's cantrips did not appear to be having the desired effect, although their maker advised Lizzie that she must 'be patient and give them more time'.

As Lord Leighton had proclaimed with such relish, Britain had signed treaties with Russia, Austria, and the Ottoman Empire, forming an alliance against France. In 1799 this "Second Coalition" had set several invasions in motion, including campaigns in Switzerland, and a British-Russian incursion into the Netherlands. The allies were less successful in Holland, where after capturing the Dutch fleet they were confronted with a stalemate, and retreated. After early victories against the French in Switzerland, the Russian troops were completely vanquished.

Napoleon Bonaparte's armies invaded Syria, but by May 1799, with plague rife among his soldiers and no sign of a favourable outcome in his siege of the city of Acre, the general was obliged to withdraw into Egypt, where he repelled a major Anglo-Turkish attack.

Throughout the spring and summer, Rafferty's wife and youngsters subsisted on charity. The villagers, poor as they were, donated as much food, clothing and fuel as they could spare, which was little enough. The Rafferty household was indeed a sorrowful one.

In June 1799 some of the rebels imprisoned after the 1798 uprising were released, and Rafferty was among them. Some were pardoned or had their sentences reduced as part of the government's efforts to restore order and promote reconciliation. Rafferty gained his freedom because of the lack of sufficient evidence against him. He appeared to have aged five years by the time he came home to his family, but the rejoicing throughout Allanwell was tumultuous.

Bonaparte's exploits on foreign soil were destined to come to a temporary halt. When he learned that a political and military crisis was developing in France he abandoned his army, sailed through the British naval blockade and made his way back to the French capital. In Paris, in November 1799, he utilized his enormous popularity and the backing of the armed forces to mount a coup d'état, following which he announced that he had taken on the role of First Consul, the leader of the French government.

As the final years of the 18th century drew to a close, momentous events were afoot right across Europe. In England, food riots began at the end of 1799. Meanwhile in Ireland, with the threat of French invasion and in the the aftermath of the unsuccessful insurrection by Irish nationalists, the burning political issue of the day became whether or not to establish a Union with Great Britain. All members of Irish society contributed to the intense debate. The nation's opinion was divided as to whether Union would bring benefits or disadvantages to the country.

By strict definition, the 19th century would begin on January 1, 1801, not 1800. Most people did not celebrate December 31st, 1799 as the turn of the century, instead waiting for the occasion a year later.

In the end, the vote in favour of uniting Great Britain and Ireland was passed. The Act of Union 1800, would be a significant political and social event, and the Catholic Church marked the occasion by designating 1800 as a Holy Year, an opportunity for reflection, prayer, and special religious activities during this momentous time in both political and religious history.

On 28th March 1800 the terms of the Union were agreed. Ireland was to officially join the United Kingdom, with effect from 1 January 1801.

In the spring of 1800 Sir Robert Westbourne's family returned to Charter Hall. A luncheon was organised to welcome them home. The eldest daughters Georgiana, Henrietta and Alexandrina were not amongst the arrivals; all three had wed aristocratic gentlemen and now resided with their husbands in England. Edwin accompanied his mother and siblings, having resigned his commission with the Royal Rathskillen Dragoon Guards. He had left his three-year-old son in the care of his wife's sister, in England—'for safety'.

During the period since his departure from Ireland, the Westbourne heir had married, achieved fatherhood, and become a widower. His ailing wife had perished from complications following childbirth.

On meeting him again for the first time in five years, the Delacey sisters, who had been prepared to lavish him with comforting kindness, concluded that none of his travails had served to alter his temperament. After expressing their sympathy at his loss they withheld further attempts at consolation, having diagnosed that he appeared scarcely troubled by grief, and remained as condescending, selfish and cocksure as ever. From Mary they found out that the servants had been whispering about his fondness for viewing the bare-knuckle boxing matches held in London, the large amounts he gambled on fights—usually to his betterment— his predilection for nocturnal visits to masked balls in Soho and his attendance at a club of highly questionable morals in Pall Mall, which was infamous for a floor show that included a Tahitian "Love Feast" between a dozen nymphs and a dozen youths. It was wondered how Mr. Westbourne would re-adjust to life in the country after such excitement.

At almost twenty-seven years of age, Edwin Westbourne was still good-looking, although a little extra flesh was accumulating around his jowls, and a slight thickening could be detected about his middle. His eyes remained startlingly golden-brown, and his figure was as tall and strapping as ever. As a wealthy gentleman he owned a large and fashionable wardrobe, and at this initial social gathering he displayed part of it—to the disgust of the Delaceys, who considered that he ought to be still clad in mourning raiment. Square-cut frock coats being considered passé, he was clad in an elegantly cut dark-green silk coat with two tapered tails, which was decorated at the front with two short lapels. His amber waistcoat was embroidered with tiny rosettes. A lace cravat was tied in a large knot at his throat, and his breeches of straw-coloured cashmere fitted in equestrian style, extending down as far as the calves where they were fastened with bows over striped stockings. Low-heeled shoes adorned with bows completed his outfit.

The luncheon room was agleam with the radiance of candles glancing off polished silverware, and pristine daylight reflecting off the snow beyond the French windows. Outside the west wind was blowing hard, spicing the atmosphere with a sea tang. Grey cumulus clouds billowed across the sky, as majestic as warships in full sail. Between breaks in the clouds, shafts of sunshine slanted down like the golden spears of angels. Through the windows, bright splashes of yellow and purple could be glimpsed in the garden. Buried bulbs had quickened, and spring flowers thrust through the hard soil; daffodils, snowdrops, jonquils, irises and hyacinths. Large flocks of migratory birds winged overhead, returning from their winter feeding-grounds.

It was at this luncheon that Rose Delacey discovered another fact about Edwin. After the meal was over he urged her to don her outdoor garments and take a turn with him about the gardens, "for old times' sake". Somewhat reluctantly she allowed him to help her put on her cape. She wrapped her muffler about her neck while he donned his stylish bourdalou—a round hat with a high crown and encircled with a silken cord—and picked up an elegant brass-footed cane with a carved hand-grip. He took her arm politely and escorted her on a stroll through the budding gardens, where he seized the opportunity to inform her that he was still enamoured of her—indeed, that he had never ceased to be so—and to press his suit.

"So soon after your bereavement," Rose murmured in agitation, her eyes flicking back and forth in search of some acceptable means of escape from his presence. The wind plucked at her bonnet, and she wished the millinery would fly off her head so that she might avail herself of the excuse to run after it.

"Mine was not a happy marriage," he told her.

"Please sir, do not speak to me about such intimate matters!"

Ignoring her distress Edwin said, "I note that none of your sisters is yet married. Miss Delacey must be full twenty-five years of age now, is she not? And Miss Katherine is twenty-four? Do they have prospects?"

Rose had to admit they did not.

"In that case, what does the future hold for them? May I speak candidly with you, Miss Rose?" Without waiting for a response Edwin continued intently, "As you know, my family enjoys substantial wealth, and furthermore we have good connections at court, such as the Baron of Maughinray. Marriage to me could only elevate your family's standing in society, and increase their fortune."

"But it would decrease your own," Rose hastily pointed out.

"I am a pauper and could bring you no dowry. I hardly think your parents would approve of such an imprudent match."

"My parents," said Edwin with a smile, "as ever, deny me nothing. They are never happier than when they see me getting what I want."

She recalled, then, that his first wife had left him a fortune. He was wealthier than ever.

He grasped her hand and lifted it up. "I see you still wear that wire loop on your finger. Take it off and I will replace it with a band of red gold and diamonds."

"I have no wish to offend you, Mr. Westbourne," Rose said in a low voice, pulling her hand away, "but I am not in a position to accept your offer. I am pledged to Keane O'Connell and will continue to wear the half-ring.

"How long is it since your blacksmith fellow went away? Five years? Six? He is not coming back, you know. You must face the facts. I do not wish to be cruel, but by now the other half of that ring is rolling at the bottom of the sea."

Rose forced herself to appear calm, unintentionally clenching her fingers so tightly that her knuckles blanched. "Even if that were the case, sir, you and I could never wed. Our religious differences are too great an obstacle."

"I hardly think so, m'dear. You attended the Protestant services in Dublin, did you not? And God never struck you down with a bolt of lightning! You and I could get married in the Church of Ireland."

"That is out of the question. I am a Catholic."

Edwin continued to present reasons why she ought to change her mind, but his arguments, though persuasive, could not sway her.

Shortly after the return of his family to Charter Hall, Sir Robert told John Delacey that he could no longer keep him on as overseer.

"Sorry Delacey, but I need an able-bodied man on the job," he said. "With that game leg of yours you cannot move as spritely as you used, and it's taking you too long to do the rounds. Besides, it disturbs Lady Lavinia to see you limping about on your sticks. Her nerves are damned sensitive you know, and she cannot abide seeing people in obvious pain. It is likely to give her an attack of the vapours." Sir Robert fidgeted and shuffled his feet. "Besides, Edwin has brought it to my attention that you are not a loyalist after all. Is that so?"

"I have declared for the United Irishmen," John Delacey said steadily.

"Good God, sirrah," Sir Robert said, with sudden vehement distaste. "Are you mad? I cannot understand why on earth you would want to associate yourself with those murderous devils."

Delacey made no reply but stood calmly with hands folded, awaiting the pronouncement of his sentence.

"That rather puts the seal of doom on our relationship, I'm afraid," his employer resumed, checking his outburst and reverting to his habitual veneer of civilised restraint. "At dark times like these, I would do better not to associate with you.

111

People become suspicious at the drop of a hat. Furthermore, I think you will agree that I have been putting you in quite a predicament by employing you. The villagers do not approve, did you know? If you work for me much longer, no doubt they'll turn against you on some pretext."

"Sir Robert," John Delacey said, "if you dismiss me, I will have no way of feeding my family."

"Well," the lord of Charter Hall stammered, looking acutely uncomfortable. "Well, perhaps we could come to some arrangement. Rent-free tenancy of your cottage, or something. But I have to do it, you see? I cannot keep you on." He regarded his overseer with an expression that was part beseeching, part defiant, somewhat angry.

John Delacey drew breath. His visage was pale. "Of course," he managed to say. He made a shallow bow. "I am grateful for your patronage, Sir Robert, and remain your humble servant."

"Capital." The landowner turned away, clearly relieved. "Well, that's that, then."

As the snows began to melt, the waters of the Oranowin swelled until they were rushing at full spate. Spring storms came tumbling in from the ocean; fierce disturbances of the atmosphere that caused the sea to rise up in fury and thrash the coastline. High-speed winds careered like roaring dragons down the valley of the Oranowin. Above Madigan's Leap the sea-birds—the fulmars, kittiwakes, petrels and shearwaters—revelled in the challenge, gliding through the flying foam on the lookout for minnows, pilchards and other aquatic animals tossed helplessly by the waves

Early in May, having fretted day and night about how he was going to provide for his family, John Delacey fell ill. He developed a fever and stomach pains.

"You have literally worried yourself sick," Margaret declared as she put her father to bed with a mug of hot saloop. "And there's no need for it. We are doing very nicely, Papa, so banish all troubles from your mind." As she spoke, she whipped her free hand behind her back and crossed her fingers, to avoid being jinxed for lying.

For her father was very ill indeed.

CHAPTER 14

Just like an angel weeping,
On the rock sighs every day

Keeping Watch from the Cliffs
"Girl Carrying a Basket" by Winslow Homer

"There was thirteen on the press-gang, they did my love surround,
And four of that accursed gang went bleeding to the ground.
My love was overpowered, though he fought most manfully,
They dragged him through the dark, wet streets towards the Victory.

Your ship she lay in harbour just ready to set sail.
May heaven be your guardian, love, till you come home from the sea.
Just like an angel weeping, on the rock sighs every day
Awaiting for my own true love returning home from sea.

From 'The Victory' (Traditional)

Sweating and shivering John Delacey lay abed, while his daughters looked after him, serving him gruel and clear soups and arrowroot puddings. Their meagre savings dwindled.

Rose, when she was not tending her father, or busy at needlepoint, or helping Mary with the housework, returned to her habit of lingering atop Madigan's Leap, peering into the hazy distance to discover whether any sail could be espied on the horizon. In the evenings before she went to her repose she would take out the piece of paper upon which Lizzie had drawn "The Face", and look long and lovingly upon the image, and sometimes kiss it, very carefully, so as not to smudge it.

"Of course, the fact that you don't dream of him any more means nothing," Lizzie would tell Rose with unconvincing sincerity. "I am certain he still lives, and will come back to you. It is only that he is so far away, the dreams cannot reach you."

Wanting to believe her sister's words of solace, Rose would nod and smile. Yet her heart was as hollow as a conch shell cast up by the waves at the foot of Madigan's Leap. None of Ilvenna McGinty's charms or potions seemed to have any effect; no matter what they tried, Keane did not come back.

"Well what do you expect?" Katherine said disparagingly to Rose, when they were alone together. "Ilvenna's hocus-pocus is nothing but make-believe. Why, she could even brew a potion to make her chosen man love her."

Rose shot her a scandalized look. "Of course not! " She cried. "Ilvenna would never try such a trick, for she has too much respect for him! And who would want such a hollow love? Besides, it's my opinion that he already loved her from the moment he saw her."

Neither of them mentioned their names, but Ryan O'Connell and Flynn McGinty were very much in their thoughts. They had not been seen for many a long day.

Edwin Westbourne persisted in protesting his love to Rose during the weeks following his reappearance in Allanwell. Steadfastly she continued to refuse him, yet she could not but ponder on the material benefits he could bring to her and her family, if he so desired. Summoning all her resolve and pushing aside her self-respect, she seized the opportunity to beg him to ask Sir Robert if he would re-employ her father, even if it were on a small wage. Her suitor told her that he was unable to exert influence upon his sire in this matter.

With a brief flare of annoyance, Rose asked, "Did you not inform me that your parents take delight in pleasing you?"

"Indeed, but the decision to dismiss your Papa was made purely on financial grounds. Your father is a cripple and cannot work as he once did. Surely you must understand I cannot ask my own father to run the estate at a loss! Your Papa was paid a handsome wage during his term of employment, and my father is generously allowing him use of the cottage rent-free, but we are operating a business, not a charitable institution. Believe me, I wish I could help, but there is no more that can be done."

Rose was unable to stop herself from blurting, "But why now? Why should Sir Robert terminate my father's employment at this particular time, just after you and your family have returned?"

"I have no idea," said Edwin, pursing his lips and tapping his cane against his boot. "Miss Rose, surely you are not accusing me of foul play."

"No, not at all," she replied, fearful lest she strain the relationship and put her family in danger of losing their dwelling.

"There is no ill feeling between my family and yours," Edwin said mildly. "Quite the contrary, as I have so frequently made plain."

Rose smiled wanly and nodded, concealing the fact that she was unable to believe him.

The fortunes of the Delaceys dipped to an unprecedented nadir.

To make matters worse the local gentry, having learned of John Delacey's declared allegiance, would have nothing more to do with the Delacey family. Margaret and Katherine lost their jobs as governesses with the Kingsleys, and were obliged to turn their hands to embroidering more ladies' handkerchiefs.

Burdened by care, Rose's father tormented himself with self-reproach for the family's difficult situation. His health, already fragile, took a turn for the worse.

"If ever we were in need of your miracle," Lizzie said to Ilvenna McGinty, "it is now." The young wise-woman's remedies, however, seemed unable to cure the patient's afflictions, though she administered an extract of willow bark, which eased his pain.

"It seems the time for my miracle has not yet come," Ilvenna said, "but do not lose hope yourself, Miss Elizabet'."

In a gesture of acknowledgement towards one who—formally, at least—occupied a niche in his own social stratum, Sir Robert sent his surgeon from Dublin to attend the patient.

Dr. Conway was an earnest, bespectacled gentleman of slight build, in his early forties. He arrived in Sir Robert's landaulet, well dressed and accompanied by an assistant carrying a large black bag. Margaret ushered the visitors into her father's bedchamber. After examining John Delacey the doctor and his man left the half-insensible patient in the care of Mary and entered the kitchen, where the four sisters waited. Without delay Conway revealed his prognosis, which was not altogether optimistic.

"Nevertheless there are remedies worth trying," he said, as his aide placed the bag on the kitchen table.

"You are not going to bleed him, are you sir?" Rose cried.

"No, my dear. I only bleed patients in emergencies."

Rose sighed with relief and performed a small, abashed curtsey.

Conway addressed Margaret. "New medical treatments have lately been developed, Miss Delacey," he said. "Chirurgical theory is perhaps too complicated for the delicate mind of a woman to really grasp, but I shall try to make it clear for you. In Edinburgh the well-known author and lecturer John Brown has set forth his opinion that fundamentally, only two diseases exist; sthenic and asthenic, or strong and weak. Correspondingly there are two treatments, stimulant and sedative; alcohol for stimulation and opium for sedation. In your father's case treatment requires rest and the administration of carefully measured doses of Godfrey's Cordial, a patent and trusted sedative. In addition, you must make up a quantity of Fever Mixture. Ridley will copy down the recipe for you." The assistant produced a notebook and pencil and began scribbling, while the sisters looked on in silent awe.

Dr. Conway opened his bag, extricated a flat-topped conical vial with steep-pitched sides, and set it on the table. Its label read, in flowing script, 'Godfrey's Cordial'.

"Oh, and you might also give Mr. Delacey fresh milk to speed his recovery," the doctor murmured, as he snapped shut the black case. "When I was a boy my old nurse used to dole it out to me if I was poorly in the stomach, and it did me the world of good."

The sisters thanked the learned physician and, after his departure, consulted the recipe.

"Mix a drachm of powdered nitre," Katherine read aloud, "two drachms of carbonated potash, two teaspoonsful of antimonial wine, and a tablespoonful of sweet spirits of nitre in half a pint of water. Maggie, do we have all of those ingredients in the house?"

"Ilvenna says Godfrey's Cordial is dangerous," said Lizzie.

"Rubbish! It can be given to babies! Mothers and nurses use it when their infants will not go to sleep," Margaret snapped.

"All medicines can be dangerous if you do not use them properly," Katherine pontificated.

"We have some of the ingredients," Margaret went on, "but not all. I will send to Dublin for the rest."

"Do we have enough money?" Katherine asked dubiously.

"No, but the apothecary will surely extend credit to us. In the past we have always paid our bills on time."

"In the past..." Lizzie broke off and never finished her sentence.

The Delaceys were able to purchase a daily half-pail of fresh milk from the Murphy family, who had recently bought a new and highly productive milch-cow. Mrs. Murphy had given birth to twins, but was unable to nurse them adequately, as 'she had not enough milk for two'. Over the following week, on the diet of sweet, creamy milk and doses of unpalatable medicine, John Delacey began to get well. His fever abated and his stomach ceased to ache. He even got out of bed and sat in a chair by the fire.

Just as his daughters were at last allowing themselves to believe he would recover, the fever returned with a vengeance. Strange lumps swelled in his neck, and he complained of chest pain. He started coughing up mucus and sputum, and the flesh seemed to melt from his bones. He was sicker than ever. The sisters were at a loss as to why, until they learned that the Murphy twins were afflicted with the same sickness, whereupon they understood that the disease must be something to do with the milch-cow. Sure enough, when the cow was examined she was found to possess all the symptoms of scrofula.

Ma and Ilvenna McGinty confirmed the diagnosis, naming the affliction "The King's Evil". They did what they could to help, but John Delacey's health continued to deteriorate. Dr. Conway made a second visit, and unwittingly agreed with the wise women.

"Unfortunately your father has contracted scrofula," he told the sisters, who had gathered in the kitchen to hear the doctor's verdict after his examination of the patient, "a form of consumption affecting the lights and the glands, especially of the neck. It is most common in children and is chiefly spread by milk from infected cows. It is also known as The King's Evil'. Your father's condition is serious. It is necessary for me to bleed him."

"Oh Lord, no!" Katherine blurted. "I pray you sir, do not! Surely there is some other method—"

"I beg your pardon ma'am," Conway said coldly. "I am sorry to hear you doubt that a professional gentleman with twenty years' experience in the field knows his own business. Ridley, put everything away." The doctor's aide began to replace tongue depressors and a six inch Allbutt clinical thermometer in the doctor's huge silk-padded portmanteau, alongside such items as surgical knives, suture needles, tweezers, forceps, probes, lancets, an array of tubes, a speculum, a trephine, linen bandages and a spool of catgut.

"Wait!" cried Margaret. "I apologise, sir, if any offence has been given. Pray forgive us, and understand that, distracted by our anxiety, we perhaps say things we do not mean."

Katherine opened her mouth to object, but Lizzie's elbow furtively jabbed her in the ribs and she subsided.

"Very well then," the doctor relented. " I shall treat the patient, but mind, I shall brook no interference. I invite you, Miss Delacey, to remain at your father's bedside, during the procedure, but no others. You are not the swooning kind, are you?"

The sisters submitted to the doctor's rule, since there seemed no other choice if their father was to receive treatment.

It was with leaden feet and burdened hearts that the younger three banished themselves from the cottage for the duration of the ordeal. Margaret, sick at the thought of what was to eventuate, forced herself to wait passively for instructions.

"Now sir, you must sit up," Dr. Conway was saying to her father at his bedside, "for when a patient is bled he should always be in the standing or sitting position. If he should happen to faint he can in most cases be brought to by being placed flat on his back while the doctor stops the bleeding."

Too ill to do anything other than submit, John Delacey heaved himself upright with the help of the doctor's aide. Margaret packed the pillows around his back and shoulders to keep him in position, after which the assistant tied a tape about the patient's right arm, three or four inches above the elbow. "Open and shut your hand, sir," he murmured to Delacey, "constantly and quickly".

Below the tape John Delacey's veins could be seen to swell and stand out like purple worms resting beneath his pale skin. Margaret turned her head away, but not before she had seen Dr. Conway's fingers tracing a vein which passed up the middle of the forearm and, just below the bend of the elbow, sent a branch inwards and outwards. Presently, unable to bear the silence and thinking that her own imagination was probably conjuring images more gruesome than reality could ever provide, she turned back to observe the procedure.

The doctor took a lancet in his right hand, between the thumb and first finger, then placed the thumb of his left hand on the outer branch of the vein. Just above his thumb he gently he thrust the tip of the lancet into the vein and, taking care not to push too deeply, cut the flesh in a crescent shape and brought the implement out, point upwards, about half an inch from the original incision. The vein, having been severed lengthways, began to spurt dark blood, which the assistant caught in a kidney-shaped dish. When Dr. Conway judged that sufficient blood had been taken he removed the bandage from above the elbow and placed the thumb of his left hand firmly over the cut until the bleeding ceased. The assistant then placed a small pad of lint over the wound, with a larger pad over it, keeping the two in their places by means of a linen roller bound tightly over them and around the arm. John Delacey was assisted to lie down again, and Margaret re-arranged the pillows.

The extreme whiteness of her father's face made the bleached pillowcases look cream-coloured by comparison, and the young woman fought to keep the nauseous darkness hovering at the edges of her sight from closing in. Her father shut his eyes and lay very still.

"That is all that can be done for now," the doctor announced briskly, as his aide collected the implements. "Keep him warm, Miss Delacey, and continue to administer the treatments I have prescribed, including the hemlock and chamomile fomentations for that cold-abscess of the neck. I will look in again tonight. I am staying at Charter Hall if you need to send a message."

CHAPTER 15

St Mungo's Well

December 31st, 1800 was treated as the end of one century and start of a new one, marked by celebrations and reflection on the passing of the 1700s.

To observe the end of the Holy Year and to celebrate the turn of the century, special masses and ceremonies were held. The more lavish celebrations were confined to major cities like Dublin and Cork. In rural areas, it was seen as just another New Year's Eve.

Whether Dr. Conway's attentions would have benefited them or not, the Murphy twins in their cold and cheerless hovel did not survive long. On hearing the sorrowful news of the infants' passing, and observing that their father's condition was worsening the Delacey daughters, in desperation, got their hands on a printed broadside that one of the Murphy boys, aged thirteen had brought from Dublin. The lad could not read, but he knew that this pamphlet conveyed important information about a new "patent medicine", a miracle cure, and he had brought it for his mother—alas, too late.

The publication was a forty-six page brochure by a promoter named Robert Turlington, and it asserted that the "Author of Nature" provided "a Remedy for every Malady," which "Men of Learning and Genius" have "ransack'd" the "Animal, Mineral, and Vegetable World" to discover. Turlington declared that his search had led to the Balsam of Life, "a perfect Friend to Nature." The medicine, he claimed, "vivifies and enlivens the Spirits, mixes with the Juices and Fluids of the Body, and gently infuses its kindly Influence into those Parts that are most in Disorder." By so doing it cured a vast range of maladies, from croup to epilepsy. Its efficacy, Turlington declared, was proved by numerous expressions of appreciation from patients who were now cured.

Most of these recommendations were from plain folk—a porter, the wife of a gardener, a hostler, a bodice-maker— but some enjoyed higher status, including a "Mathematical Instrument-Maker" and the doorkeeper of the East India Company.

The testimonials ranged all the way to the New World. One endorsement was issued by "a sailor before the mast, on board the ship Britannia in the New York trade", while another quoted "a Philadelphian woman". Everyone who attested to the medicine's extraordinary potency was overjoyed at being cured.

"For the cure of Scrofula, King's Evil," Margaret read aloud, "White Swellings, Ulcers, Tumours, Mercurial and

Syphilitic Affections, Rheumatism, Gout, Scurvy, Neuralgia, Cancer, Goitre, Enlargements of the Bones, Joints, Glands, or Ligaments or of the Ovaries, Liver, Spleen, Kidneys, etc. All the various Diseases of the Skin, Dyspepsia and Liver Complaint, Jaundice and Nervous Diseases, Dropsical Swelling, Constitutional Disorders, and diseases originating from a depraved or impure state of the Blood or other fluids of the body."

"My goodness, will you look at the picture of the bottle," said Lizzie. "Violin-shaped, with sloping shoulders and all that embossing. I have never seen such an odd-shaped thing."

"That is so that shysters cannot copy it," said Margaret, "and put their own labels on and pretend its Turlington's."

"Well why should this Turlington's Balsam be any better than anyone else's?" Katherine wanted to know. "It is very dear at thirty-six shillings a dozen bottles. Daffy's Elixir, for example, sells for only fifteen."

"It says in the pamphlet that it contains the very best ingredients, and rare ones too, that's why," said Margaret.

"Daffy's does not work," said Lizzie. "Anyone knows that."

"I think we ought to send for one of those American remedies," said Katherine, "Dr. Kilmer's Swamp-Root Tonic, or Kickapoo Indian Sagwa."

"Why?" asked Lizzie.

"They are made out of herbs used for centuries by the native Indians."

"And why should that be a good thing?" Margaret enquired.

"Because the Indians are noble savages, that is why. They live in harmony with Mother Nature, and have inherited centuries' worth of recipes for herbal nostrums."

"If it is expensive to import medicines from Britain it would be twice as costly to bring them in from America," Margaret snapped. "Besides, I do not hold with that 'noble savage' nonsense. This Turlington's Balsam is British, and scientific, and that is good enough for me. Look here, the pamphlet says, 'What may seem almost incredible is that many diseases hitherto considered hopelessly incurable are frequently cured in a few days or weeks and we cheerfully invite the investigations of the liberal minded and scientific to cures which have no parallel at the present day.'

"Mrs. E. Farnsworth of Sussex says about Turlington's, 'Dear Sir, Your Balsam of Life has made one of the most remarkable Cures. A woman near me has been suffering with Scrofula for six weeks. At times her Suffering was so great that she was expected to die. A month ago she went to Bath for Treatment but in a short time she was as bad as before the Treatment, so much so that her friends said that she would never leave her Bed again. After she read of the wonderful Cures your Balsam has made, her mother purchased a Bottle for her. Before she had taken the whole Contents of the Bottle she walked to my home. She has taken about three Bottles of your Balsam and says she is quite as well as she ever was.' And Mr. E. Hartwell of Hemel Hempstead says, 'It is always effectual and never fails to perform the cure speedily. It also kills or drives away all sorts of lice.'"

"Let us get some for Papa, then," said Katherine. "Clearly Conway's methods are doing no good. I declare, after all this bleeding Papa looks sicker than ever. That dreadful cold-abscess continues to grow. And it is Conway's fault he got the scrofula in the first place."

"Only money can buy this remedy," said Margaret, "And money is what we do not have."

By scrimping on food and—what seemed far worse—cutting off their hair and selling it for wigs, the sisters managed to save enough to purchase the miraculous nostrum. Their father seemed to rally for a day or two after he started taking it, but once again he fell back into the downward spiral.

"The stuff does not work," Margaret was forced to admit, bitterly. "It is like all the others; a waste of money."

"What about Dr. Jayne's Alternative?" Lizzie asked. "That elixir sounded quite marvellous in the last broadside. It cures everything from—"

"Please!" Margaret cried. "No more of those quackeries! Really, Lizzie, you can be too gullible for words."

Crestfallen, Lizzie made no reply. After a while she timidly said, "One thing we have not tried yet. Ilvenna suggested it."

"Not drying the hind leg of a toad and getting Papa to wear it round his neck in a silken bag," said Margaret scornfully.

"No," said Lizzie, "that only works for people who live in Devonshire. I mean the laying on of hands."

"Oh, I suppose you mean the king's hands?"

"Indeed I do. The royal touch is definitely able to cure the King's Evil."

"And naturally the king would be overjoyed to oblige us. How are we supposed to get the king to come and see Papa?"

"Papa must go to the king."

"He is hardly fit enough to travel!"

"There is another treatment," said Rose. They all turned to look at her, since she contributed so rarely to discussions. "Ilvenna suggested this one, too, and I have also read about it in Mrs. Fiennes' 'The Northern Journey and the Tour of Kent', in which that lady writes of her travels around England. It is, I daresay, more feasible than a visit from the king, though not an easy feat to attempt. Papa must make a trip to England, to take the waters of Harrogate and St. Mungo's Well."

"For heaven's sake Rose, what are you saying? A long journey like that would—" Margaret lowered her voice—"would kill him!" She added, "Even if we could afford it!"

"Maggie," said Rose, "do you think he's not dying already? Would it not be better for him at least to be given some hope in his last days?"

Margaret pondered. "What's so wonderful about these wells?" she asked grudgingly, whereupon Rose fetched her booklet and read aloud from it.

"'From Harragate to Cockgrave is six mile, where is a Spring of an exceeding cold water called St Mongers Well, the Story is of a Child that was laid out in the cold for the parishes care and when the Church Wardens found it they took care of it, a new born Infant, and when it was baptised they gave it the name of Amongust because they said the Child must be kept among them; and as the papist sayes he was an ingenious Child and so attained learning and was a very religious gentleman and used this spring to wash himself; after sometymes that he had gotten prefferrment and so grew rich he walled the Spring about and did many cures on diseased bodies by batheing in it, which caused after his death people to frequent the Well which was an inconveniency to the owners of the ground and so they forbad people coming and stopped up the Well and, the Story sayes, on that severall judgments came on the owners of the ground and the Spring broke up all about his ground which forced him to open it again and render it usefull to all that would come to washe in it—thus farre of the fable—

'Setting aside the Papists fancyes of it I cannot but think it is a very good Spring, being remarkably cold, and just at the head of the Spring so its fresh which must needs be very strengthning, it shutts up the pores of the body immeadiately so fortifyes from cold, you cannot bear the coldness of it above two or three minutes and then you come out and walke round the pavement and then in againe, and so three or four or six or seven as many tymes as you please; you go in and out in Linnen Garments, some go in flannell, I used my Bath garments and so pulled them off and put on flannell when I came out to go into the bed, which is best; but some came at a distance, so did I, and did not go into bed but some will keep on their wet

Garments and let them drye to them and say its more beneficial, but I did not venture it; I dipp'd my head quite over every tyme I went in and found it eased a great pain I used to have in my head, and I was not so apt to catch Cold so much as before, which I imputed to the exceeding coldness of the Spring that shutts up the pores of the body; it is thought it runns off of some very cold Spring and from Clay, some of the Papists I saw there had so much Zeale as to continue a quarter of an hour on their knees at their prayers in the Well, but none else could well endure it so long at a tyme; I went in seven severall seasons and seven tymes every season and would have gone in oftener could we have staid longer.'"

Rose finished reading and looked up expectantly at her audience.

"This St. Mungo 'did many cures on diseased bodies by bathing in it'!" cried Katherine. "I daresay the water does possess some unusual healing quality."

"If Catholics are forever praying around the well," said Lizzie, "there must be quite a lot of goodness going into it."

When the sisters described these regimens to their father he said, "My dears, I have no faith in the magical power of the royal touch, least of all the touch of the King of England. If any gentleman were to own that divine power, surely it would be His Holiness the Pope. The other suggestion, however, sounds more scientific—the curative waters of these English wells. Those I would be willing to try, though it would take all my last remaining strength to endure such a long journey.

In any case, travel is out of the question while we remain in our current pecuniary circumstances." He managed a wry smile. "If any of you should happen to spy a leprechaun in the hedges, make sure you grab him and hold him tightly. We could do with a crock of gold."

His daughters laughed dutifully, though their eyes filled with tears.

The first of June was a sunny day. Dr. Conway was long gone; he had returned to his practice in Dublin. John Delacey had now been ill for almost six weeks. His condition had stabilised since the doctor's departure, but so weak and gaunt was he that although he was getting no worse, he was getting no better either. He spent most of his time in bed, occasionally allowing Mary and the girls to help him outdoors into the sunshine, where he would sit in a wicker chair with blankets wrapped around his bowed shoulders, and watch the bees darting in and out of the apple blossoms.

That day Edwin Westbourne came to visit Rose at the cottage.

He brought his two bodyguards with him, as he always did when travelling in the village. Ever since the Rising, the people of Allanwell had hated the Westbournes with a deadly passion. Indeed, the squire's family now employed watchmen and guards to patrol their estate, ensuring the protection of their property and deterring any potential trespassers or intruders.

After conversing briefly with Rose's father, Edwin took her aside. Together they walked in the garden, stepping around the pecking hens, while Mary watched from the window, her face as sour as unripe blackberries. Rose dreaded being in Edwin's company, for he never failed to harass her with questions and demand to know when she would acquiesce to his wishes. This occasion was no different in that respect—however, he had a new tactic at his disposal.

"How many years is it," Edwin asked as they passed the vegetable patch where rows of potatoes were sprouting, "since your blacksmith departed?"

"More than six," said Rose, not suspecting a trap.

Her escort smiled. "In legal terms," he said conversationally, "if a person is missing for seven years they are presumed to be gone forever."

"Is that so?" Rose was on her guard now.

"It is indeed. Soon your blacksmith will be legally dead."

"Legal terms make no difference to me."

"Perhaps not, but if you and I were wed, you could send your father to London to be presented to the king. My family has some influence in high circles. Every so often a chosen group of high-born invalids gains audience with King George. His Majesty is generous enough to place his own hand upon them. It is a most efficacious remedy for many ills, they say."

Rose found herself infused with hope and despair simultaneously. "I have seen," she said in a low voice, "in a book written by a physician to the Paris court, a copperplate engraving made in 1609, depicting King Henry IV of France touching a number of sufferers of scrofula who are gathered about him in a circle. But I have heard that the King of England refuses to touch Catholics, he does despise them so, and that in any case he avows that the beliefs attached to 'the royal touch' are naught but superstition. Similarly my father dismisses the royal touch as nonsense, but he does hold out some hope for the curative waters of certain wells in Yorkshire."

"I, too, have viewed the engraving," said Edwin, "and I have heard of the Yorkshire waters. You hold the key to your father's cure, Miss Rose. The key to his cure and to my heart. I have spoken to your father just now and he gave me his blessing in my enterprise. He said he would bless any man who made you happy. Seven years is a long time, dear girl."

"I say again, Mr. Westbourne, I could not have a Protestant wedding!"

"What if I agreed to have a Catholic wedding as well as a Protestant one?"

Hanging her head, on the brink of giving up all resistance in the face of unrelenting assault, Rose murmured, "Perhaps..." She glimpsed her father through a gap between the nodding leaves of the blackcurrant bushes and one of the elderberries. He was hunched over in his chair, his face, pale and sunken, turned towards the sun, and his dearly loved form, once upright and strong, looked as shrunken and fragile as a child's. With a single word she could change his fortune, could pour balm upon his suffering.

Suddenly she could bear her own agony no longer. "Very well," she said, stopping in her tracks and tilting her head up to Edwin, who halted in surprise. "I will pledge myself to you on two conditions."

"Dearest! I am happy beyond words. Name them!"

"Your family must finance a trip to England for my father. That is the first."

"But of course! And the second?"

"If Keane O'Connell returns before the wedding day, the pledge will be immediately annulled."

"Agreed!" Shouting his triumph, Edwin swept Rose off her feet and swung her around. As soon as he put her down she backed away, her eyes wide with consternation. "Pray sir, do not treat me with such familiarity. We are not man and wife, and may never be..."

"We shall be wed, Rose. We shall!" Edwin cried joyfully. "Mark my words! Now let us go and proclaim the news to the world!"

The wedding day was planned for the following year, 1801, the first of the nineteenth century. The date, the fourteenth of April, would be exactly seven years after Keane was taken. It would also be Rose's twenty-first birthday.

Mindful of the fact that her father would withdraw his consent for the union should he discover that she had only accepted Edwin's hand under duress, Rose feigned happiness. Had her father not been so ill, he might have taken her by the hand, looked into her eyes and asked her earnestly if she had really forsaken hope of seeing Keane

O'Connell again, and if she really loved Edwin Westbourne. He was, however, in no fit condition to think clearly.

It cost his youngest daughter dearly to feign joy when her heart was breaking. Only in the company of her sisters, or when she was alone on Madigan's Leap, could she drop the facade and privately weep.

After the betrothal had been formally acknowledged, Sir Robert Westbourne exerted his influence to arrange transport and accommodation for his erstwhile steward all the way from Dublin to Holyhead, through Wales to Manchester, from Manchester to Leeds and thence to the well of St. Mungo before coming all the way back—a distance of around five hundred and forty miles. It would be no easy excursion, even for the halest of men.

In October 1800 John Delacey set off for Dublin in the company of his eldest daughter Margaret. The three remaining sisters were left behind, penniless and despondent. The feelings of Katherine and Lizzie were lacerated by the anguish of knowing that Rose had agreed to marry, against all her deepest feelings, simply to help her family. All of them held serious doubts that their father would survive the journey.

As for Rose herself, she knew she could not avoid her fate now. Furthermore, she would be forced to marry in a Protestant ceremony, since Edwin had "changed his mind" about the Catholic one.

Wedding preparations commenced.

Ireland officially joined the United Kingdom on the first of January 1801. The country no longer had a parliament of its own, so Protestant Irish MPs such as Lord Leighton sat in London's Westminster Parliament. The Union Jack was adopted as the national flag of the new United Kingdom of Great Britain and Ireland, and in Belfast the Unionists sang,

'We'll join hand in hand, all Party shall cease
And glass after glass shall our Union increase.
In the cause of Old England we'll drink down the sun,
Then toast Little Ireland and drink down the Moon.'

Legislative union meant the same laws applied to both countries, and emancipation for the Irish—allowing Catholic gentlemen to sit in Parliament—was supposed to follow. King George III, however, refused to make concessions to Roman Catholics, and by February the British Prime Minister William Pitt the Younger had resigned from office in protest.

After the Union the various factions in Ireland began to realign according to religious beliefs. Little by little, the hearts of Protestants turned to England once more. The terms "Protestant" and "Unionist" became practically interchangeable as the old rifts between Protestant and Catholic widened and deepened. The situation became "the Orange versus the Green". As of old, sectarianism was the great Irish divider.

CHAPTER 16

'It will not be long, love, till our wedding day.'

"Waiting"

In Sight at Last
Drawn and engraved by Herbert Dicksee.

John Delacey returned to Allanwell with Margaret in March 1801, his health fully restored. He exhibited only a slight limp as a trophy of his troubles. As tribute to the Westbournes, who had financed the trip, he did not disagree—yea, he maintained, that it was bathing in the waters of St. Mungo's Well that had healed him.

"Truth to tell," he confided to his family, "it was not the sulphur-stinking water of those wells that cured me. I believe it was the change of air, for I began to feel better soon after we landed at Holyhead."

Their letters had preceded them by the post-coach. In these epistles father and daughter had described their experiences in England and their general impressions of the denizens of that country. They had not, however, told the whole story, for they were prudent enough to refrain from committing to record their dismay at hearing about King George's latest bout of madness, and their contempt for the thirty-eight-year-old Prince of Wales whose pasty, bejewelled hand they had glimpsed once, in a carriage window, as he went on his way to a soirée given by a Lady Hertford at Temple Newsam in Leeds.

"A fat oaf," Delacey said to his daughters. "He may well be known as the 'First Gentleman of Europe' and considered a great wit, but by all accounts, he is an arrogant drunken buffoon; a corseted, self-indulgent wastrel. Even the English poke fun at their mad monarch and their spoiled crown prince, lampooning them mercilessly in popular broadsheets and songs."

These opinions and more were voiced, and stories were recounted, and Mary kept repeating that it was a miracle that her employer had been cured, and no doubt the blessed Lord looked kindly on him for his goodness. It was a time of happiness in the Delacey household, though the sisters' joy was tinged with sorrow at Rose's unvoiced sacrifice. Even Katherine, who envied such a good match, pitied her sister.

They invited all their friends among the villagers to celebrate the homecoming at the cottage, knowing it would probably be the last time they could ever do so; soon, with Rose married to a Westbourne, they would be shunned by the people of Allanwell, who hated the Westbournes since the Rising and refused to have anything to do with them unless compelled by law. They disapproved of Rose's betrothal and believed she had accepted the young Westbourne for her family's sake, so that the Delaceys would receive financial support from their new in-laws. While they understood this motive, not everyone believed she had acted appropriately.

Day by day, Rose's distraction amplified. Her promise to Keane had meant the world to her, and she would have honoured it even to her grave, had it not been for her father's illness. Wretched and despairing, she could barely eat anything, and only forced herself to nibble a crust of bread or drink the occasional sip of water to prevent swooning. She did her best to conceal her desolation from her sisters, but they knew. They knew, and tried to aid her in her game, for, as

Margaret said, "sometimes it is the outward show that holds us up like a framework and sustains us through hardship."

She spent all her spare time on her knees, praying, atop Madigan's Leap. When at dusk her anxious sisters braved the haunted place to look for her, they would find her curled up on the turf, fast asleep and as cold as marble.

Of spare time, however, she had very little, because Lady Westbourne demanded her presence for the fitting of the wedding gown and trousseau. Heavy-eyed and always sleepy, Rose obeyed. Ever paler and more taciturn she grew, wasting away, until even Edwin chided her for her slenderness.

"Too slight to be a China doll," he said, frowning. "You need some padding. I shall take a shooting party out onto the uplands, for I am in need of some sport, and I will bring you a brace of pheasants."

Roasted bird, nonetheless, failed to tempt her.

The day of Rose's twenty-first birthday dawned, and still there was no sign of her sweetheart; no word, not even any rumour. Nobody knew whether Keane O'Connell still walked the earth. In the eyes of the law he was gone forever. Rose had made a promise, and the marriage must take place that afternoon at St George's Church on Whitethorn Hill.

And so it did.

On her wedding night Rose lay silently awaiting the arrival of her husband. She could hear, whenever the wind gusted, the sound of Tom O'Grady, ancient as parchment and withered as a weed in winter, playing a wistful whistle-tune up on Madigan's Leap.

She had sent away the lady's maid Lady Westbourne had hired for her.

"I can prepare to retire without your help," she said. The maid's eyes twinkled with a fatuous knowingness as she curtseyed and left the bedchamber. Rose despised the girl for her silliness. She had no wish to entice her bridegroom by letting him undress her. Quite the contrary. She wished she might stay trussed up for the rest of her life in the billowing vision of glittering gems and snowy silk that was her wedding gown.

Weak from weariness and lack of nourishment—for she had been able to eat nothing at the wedding feast—she lay down on the great, silk-canopied marriage bed. Although she closed her eyes to shut out the sight of it, she could not eclipse the sounds of celebration from downstairs, where her bridegroom's friends hoisted him high on their brawny shoulders and paraded him round and round, cheering and jesting as he laughed and protested and hiccuped all the while. They were singing,

"Beauing, belling, dancing, drinking,
Breaking windows, cursing, sinking
Every raking, never thinking,
Live the Rakes of Mallow!

One time naught but claret drinking,
Then like politicians, thinking

To raise the sinking funds when sinking.
Live the Rakes of Mallow!

Living short but merry lives,
Going where the devil drives,
Having sweethearts, but no wives,
Live the rakes of Mallow.

Racking tenants, stewards teasing,
Swiftly spending, slowly raising,
Wishing to spend all their days in
Raking as at Mallow!"

In silent despair, Rose prayed that they might keep him from her forever.

Tom O'Grady was playing one of the most haunting tunes on earth—"She Moved Through the Fair". The words of this traditional song were well-known, and as if to drown out the bellowing from below stairs Rose began to sing them, very softly as she lay,

"My young love said to me, 'My mother won't mind
And my father won't slight you for your lack of kind.'
And she stepped away from me and this she did say,
'It will not be long, love, till our wedding day.'

"She stepped away from me and she moved through
the fair
And fondly I watched her move here and move there,

And then she turned homeward with one star awake,
Like the swan in the evening moves over the lake.

"The people were saying, 'No two e'er were wed
But one had a sorrow that never was said.'
And I smiled as she passed with her goods and her gear,
And that was the last that I saw of my dear.

"Last night she came to me, my dead love came in
So softly she came that her feet made no din,
And she laid her hand on me and this she did say:
'It will not be long, love, 'til our wedding day.'"

A sudden noise, right there in the chamber, startled the lamenting bride. Her lids flew open.

There at the foot of the bed stood a man.

Her gaze, incredulous, took him in from head to toe. The intruder was not her bridegroom. Nor was he any of the wedding guests, eight hours early for the shivaree. Too startled even to think of danger, she scrutinised him.

He looked like some weather-beaten sea-captain... a ghost from a shipwreck...

A bushy beard half-obscured his face and his hat concealed his brow but even before he approached her, holding out the other half of the ring, all at once she knew him. Amazement paralysed her, but only for an instant. Springing from the bed in a lather of milky sheets and silky skirts she dived into his arms and they clung together, wordless.

Then she, sobbing: "Oh, why did you come too late? For I am married this very afternoon!"

For a moment he did not—could not speak.

At last he said, in a voice made rasping with emotion, "Only come with me. . . "

When the door crashed open twenty minutes later and Edwin was thrust, sweating and wine-drenched, into the room, he stood aghast. For he found the bed empty and the window open, the shutters flapping in the breeze, and to his ears there came only the plaintive sound of a tin whistle, and a ghostly suggestion of swift horse's hooves galloping into the distance...

CHAPTER 17

May the Lord Have Mercy on Them

for Their Sad Cruelty

Mitglieder der Commune. (1793–1794.)

'Sans-culottes', circa 1799

As I was a-walking along Ratcliffe Highway
A recruiting party came a-beating my way.
They enlisted me and treated me till I did not know
And to the Queen's barracks they forced me to go.

When first I deserted, I thought myself free
Until my cruel comrade informed against me.
I was quickly followed after and brought back with
speed,
I was handcuffed and guarded; heavy irons put on me.

Court martial, court martial, they held upon me
And the sentence passed upon me: three-hundred-
and-three.
May the Lord have mercy on them for their sad cruelty,
For now the Queen's duty lies heavy on me.

Selected verses from THE DESERTER (Traditional)

XV. Deserting to an enemy: Every person in or
belonging to the fleet, who shall desert to the enemy,
pirate, or rebel . . . being convicted of any such
offence by the sentence of the court martial, shall
suffer death."

The Royal Navy's Articles of War, established 25th of December 1749.

For Keane O'Connell the deserter, trapped in a leafy lane on a dark September night back in 1797, a yellow glare flowered in the darkness. With a crash, the world tilted upside down and he fell into the sky; into a void so lightless that it annihilated existence.

Next thing he knew, he was lying on his back on the road, looking up. Someone was slapping his face hard, presumably to bring him back to consciousness. The silhouettes of two men blocked out the stars and moon. He had awakened to an aching and a spinning in his skull, a red-hot searing around his wrists where they were roped together behind his back, the stench of a filthy rag tied across his mouth. The men roughly pulled him to his feet, speaking in a language that was neither English nor Irish. With gruff commands and hearty shoves his captors forced him to stumble along the country road, goading him with blows from the butts of their muskets.

In about half a mile, they arrived at a barn set back among a grove of trees. Upon entering, Keane was pushed to the floor, and the gag torn from his mouth. He lay sprawled on the dirty straw gasping the words, "Water, for the love of God".

A hand picked up a jug from a wooden trestle and dashed its contents in his face. Gratefully he licked the water droplets from his lips. The man who had doused him stood over him, hands on hips, legs apart. Stocky and of medium height, he looked to be little more than thirty years old. He was wearing ragged brown trousers, a striped double-breasted waistcoat with several buttons missing, a dirty neckerchief and a blue jacket with white turnbacks piped red. The fellow appeared to be their captain, for the other men obeyed him. His wild mane of greasy black hair was topped by red phrygian cap with a tricolour cockade. Though he had never beheld such an emblem, Keane recognised it at once. It was the symbol of the French Revolution.

Piercing brown eyes in a weather-beaten face regarded the Irishman with astonishment and contempt. The captain barked an order, and two ruffians began to search the captive's clothing, delving into his pockets, pulling off his boots and tearing the lining of his jacket. Keane protested and struggled.

"Be still or die, Anglais," one of the men hissed in his ear, in English.

The hissing fellow pulled the slender ring from the hidden pocket of Keane's waistcoat, where he had secreted it while aboard the sailing ship, and handed it to the man in the phrygian cap, who began to examine it closely. At that, the Irishman began to struggle again, violently, and one of his captors booted him in the ribs.

"Arrête ça," the captain said peremptorily, and the pummelling ceased. He scowled at the captive. "'ow you call yourself?" he enquired in heavily accented English.

"I am Keane O'Connell."

"Give to me reason why we not keel you, Monsieur O'Connell. Your joli looks, zey are not sufficient."

The Irishman was quick to grasp any chance for survival. "I can help you," he hazarded, by way of exploration.

The wild-haired man threw back his head and laughed. "'elp us eh, Monsieur O'Connell! 'ow you sink you can do zat?"

From the corner of his eye, Keane noted a large assemblage of other men standing or sitting about, watching him closely. They were dressed in an assortment of uniforms and civilian clothes. Those in white uniforms and tarleton helmets were, had he known it, veterans from France's ancien régime period. Others, clad in in shirts and breeches, were fédéré Garde Nationale troops—men with jackets dyed purple, pink, green, red, orange or blue, all in varying states of repair and cleanliness. Some were cleaning muskets, others were re-bandaging wounds or playing at dice. Pikes, pitchforks and scythes leaned against the walls. One fellow, who was seated in a corner skinning a rabbit, caught the Irishman's eye and spat on the floor.

"I can give you information that will further your cause," said Keane.

"You can tell lies, oui, sailor-boy?" responded the captain, grinning.

"I tell the truth. I've knowledge that will be useful to you, but you must act wit'out delay. I know the plans of the British. While aboard their ship, I overheard the officers discussin' reports that reached the vessel by letter and signal."

"And you sink we believe your admiral tells you 'is secrets?" the Frenchman said with a sneer.

"The officers openly discussed politics and the latest reports," Keane said quickly. "'Tis little fear they have of the men overhearin', because we never got the chance to go ashore and spread the news. Even when talkin' of confidential matters they were uncautious about keepin' their voices down, and in cramped quarters there is very little said by anyone that is not, in time, relayed to everyone else."

Keane's interlocutor leaned close; so close that his garlicky breath caused the young man to retch. "Say now what you know. And if you lie, Monsieur O'Connell, you die."

"A treaty is to be signed next mont'," came the reply. "Bonaparte intends to force the Austrians to accept his terms and put an end to the Coalition[6] that's trying to crush your republic."

"Zis is no secret," said the captain, glaring.

"There is an English gentleman," continued Keane, "by the name of Lord Reginald Leighton. He is soon to be leavin' England and travellin' across the continent in disguise, on commission from the English king. He will be bound for a secret audience in Salzburg with Franz the Second of Austria and Count Ludwig von Cobenzl. His mission is to persuade Austria not to sign the treaty."

"Austria", vowed Captain Fournier, "must never be part of an alliance against France with Prussia, Spain, and—" he turned his head aside to spit on the ground—"Bretagne! Where will he come, and when?" he demanded. "By what equipage does 'e travel, and 'ow many guards? Tell us of zis disguise!"

"'Tis at Oostende he will be landin' within a fortnight of

6   The first attempt to crush the French Republic came in 1792 when Austria, the Kingdom of Sardinia, the Kingdom of Naples, Prussia, Spain, and the Kingdom of Great Britain formed the First Coalition. (Wikipedia)

today, dressed as the Italian cardinal Francisco Antonio de Lorenzana, the appointed envoy extraordinary from Spain to Austria. He's to travel in a private carriage, with changes of horses along the way, and his entourage will be small, so as to attract as little attention as possible."

The captain laughed again. "Maybe, maybe," he said, nodding his tousled head. Glancing aside he gave an order in French, and one of his patchwork soldiers brought a tankard of watery ale, tipping it to the captive's lips. Keane gulped thirstily. "Now Monsieur," the Frenchman continued, "you see we be gentle to you. You come with us to Oostende and we learn if you spik truths."

"I speak it as I heard it," said Keane. "Whether the plans have changed since then, I cannot say."

"If ze Eengleesh plans 'ave, as you say, changed, then you will die," the captain said with a shrug.

"I could fight alongside you better as a livin' man than as a ghost," said Keane.

"Fight? You wish to join us? Faugh! I despise your attempts to save your 'ide, Monsieur O'Connell. You are a deserter, and now you would be a turncoat into ze bargain! By your own words you betray your country. We will 'ave no traitors in our midst!"

The rabbit-skinner was by now standing beside his captain, staring down at Keane with a look of hatred. He was remarkably ill-favoured, with a crooked nose, sunken eyes that were exceedingly close together, and a mouthful of blackened teeth. "No doubt you 'ave killed Frenchmen, preety Eengleesh garçon," he said. "You should pay for zat with your life, no matter if you speak truth. We should 'ave left you to the mercy of ze men zat 'unted you. Ze punishment for desertion is death."

Keane's expression hardened. "I have killed no Frenchmen and I am no Englishman. Neither am I disloyal, for I am as patriotic as any other Irishman. I was pressed into the service of the Royal Navy against my will."

"Irish, eh? Sacré bleu!" The captain's demeanour changed instantly, as did that of those men who had overheard Keane's comment. They stopped what they were doing and moved in closer to hear what was being said, the Irish being allies of the French. "Is it so?" the captain demanded.

"Ze Eengleesh coward tries to save 'is life," said the rabbit-skinner disbelievingly.

"Fermez la bouche, Livron," the captain ordered, whereupon Livron slouched away, scowling. Keane laid his head on the dusty ground and closed his eyes, snatching a few moments' rest while the captain conferred with a couple of his seconds. Presently one of them approached him and squatted on his haunches. The Irishman sat up, still with bound hands, and strove to focus his attention while the man proceeded to ask, in broken and barely intelligible Gaeilge, where he was born, who his father was, and many other questions pertaining to his Irish background. When the questions had been answered, the interrogator stood up and nodded to his leader, who remained expressionless save for the flick of an eyebrow.

Presently the captain gave a curt order and the Gaeilge speaker untied the ropes that had been cutting into the wrists of the captive. The Irishman rose to his feet.

"Gallou, 'e says you 'ave convinced 'im," said the captain. "Zis is not so much a difficult thing," he added drily. "Gallou, 'e is a Breton. What does 'e know, eh?"

The Gaeilge speaker made a rude gesture at his superior which, in the Royal Navy, would have resulted in a flogging. "Fournier, 'e think Breton is no difference to Irish Gaeilge," he said. "Nossing is more wronger. 'e 'as jealousy because I speak more languages to 'im."

The captain laughed good-humouredly and slapped his second on the back. To Keane he said, "We take a chance on you, Monsieur O'Connell, because you are a good fighter. We saw you fight ze marines. Now we 'ave saved your life from them, and for payment you must promise zat life to le Republique. Swear your loyalty to ze service of la France, alors, and you join ze fraternité of Capitaine Jules Fournier; Huitième Compagnie, Troisième Bataillon, Trente-septième Demi-brigade d'infanterie légère."

The Irishman had heard of the French light infantry demi-brigades. Formed from soldiers who had shown skill in marksmanship, these units were used for skirmishing in front of the main force. They typically lacked uniformity in either weapons or equipment, which explained the strange assortment of clothing worn by the fusiliers of Huitième Compagnie—Eighth Company—and the bizarre variety of weapons they bore.

"But we 'ave no weapon to give at you excepting a stick of ze tree," said Captain Jules Fournier.

"I am well used to wieldin' a shillelagh," said Keane, "and soon I hope to capture meself a sword of English steel."

"Ha! Zat is what we like to 'ear!" exclaimed Fournier. The gold half-ring still lay in his grimy hand. He tossed it upwards; it glittered and spun. Keane, with quick reflexes, snatched it out of the air before it fell.

"Keep your trinket," said the captain with a wry grin. "It is only aristos zat I take of their treasures."

So it happened that in September 1797 Keane O'Connell had to swear an oath of loyalty to France, and join her cause in the country then known as the Austrian Netherlands.

CHAPTER 18

A Yellow Flame Blossomed

Eventually, the men of Eighth Company told him that they had been patrolling the coast when they spied the British landing-party. Swiftly they set up an ambush. Concealed by darkness and thick foliage, they watched the British boats come to shore. They had witnessed it all—his escape, the fight—and Captain Fournier had immediately assessed the situation.

They saw the deserter stumble. At the moment he fell, one of the fusiliers had fired his flintlock musket from their hiding places in the hedges. Whether the ball was meant for him, and who had fired it, Keane O'Connell never asked. In any event the missile had whistled over his head as he crumpled onto the ground. His head chanced to knock against a stone, rendering him unconscious. The British pursuers halted, alarmed by the gun's report, whereupon the French fired on them and they quickly retreated from the unseen foe.

When the coast was clear the fusiliers ran across to

examine the man lying senseless in the road. Contemptuous of deserters, they tied him up and gagged him. After roughly slapping him awake they heaved him upright and forced him to stagger along with them. Two of them took him to the company's temporary headquarters, a barn. The rest chased after the sailors, who jumped into their boats in great haste and put out to sea. The fusiliers fired at them from the shore as they rowed, and at least one seaman was killed before they reached the ship, while others howled as musket balls tore through their flesh.

Eighth Company's motley band of about a hundred soldiers was not altogether well-disciplined. Captain Fournier, however, was an experienced and canny leader, one of the few seasoned veterans of the Revolutionary Army, and he knew how to bring out the best in his men.

The company could operate without orders from above, and their leader, having hearkened to Keane O'Connell's revelation of Lord Leighton's mission, was bent on hunting down the English aristocrat. To increase their chances of intercepting Leighton and his entourage they decided that they would not make for Oostende but for Ghent, where they would waylay their enemy. For that, they needed horses.

As the fusiliers travelled swiftly and furtively along the lanes and byroads, commandeering or bartering for horses wherever they could, Keane grabbed handfuls of blackberries from roadside hedges and consumed them, whether unripe or ripe. It was natural for a seaman to be attracted to fresh fruit and vegetables, having been short of them for three and a half years. It was autumn, and the countryside was filled with wild fruits of the wayside such as hazelnuts, berries and dandelion greens. The French laughed at the Irishman, chaffing him for eating what they called weeds. They preferred to slaughter lambs or chickens stolen from farms as they passed, and roast them over their camp fires.

The Irishman, deep in thought, spoke rarely as he rode with his companions. Night after night, lying beside a camp-fire or in some barn, he would drift asleep in the hope of a dream-glimpse of his sweetheart. Alas, after the blow to his head, the visions of Rose had ceased. His mourning for this loss was a dark river, flowing mutely beneath the surface of his composure. Could she still see him in her dreams? If not, perhaps she would think he no longer lived. And then what would she do?

His longing for his sweetheart was as relentless and piercing as a winter's gale. To compound the pain, he also missed his brother. He and Ryan had been inseparable all their lives, and a gap yawned at his shoulder where that amiable young man used to walk.

He asked his comrades if it were possible to write to "his family in Ireland", at least, to tell them he was alive. In no uncertain terms, they communicated that such an undertaking was quite unfeasible. Even if a man could get hold of pen and ink and paper, who would carry a letter to a port on his behalf? Besides, no shipping company operated mail packet services between the Austrian Netherlands and Ireland; even the Thames and General Steam Navigation Company only carried mail as far as London. From there another carrier, such as the Dublin Steam Packet Company, would take over. And all along this perilous and uncertain route, customs officials would be slitting open envelopes, reading the mail, searching it for coded messages from spies or rebels, noting, in their ledgers, the addresses to which the letters were directed, and forming suspicions about those who dwelled at the addresses.

No, a letter seemed out of the question.

The fusiliers asked the newest member of the company if he was glad to be able to practise the "true religion" again, after being repressed by the Protestant heretics. He silenced them with a curt nod, but the more perceptive among them guessed that in his heart, after all that he had endured, it was likely he eschewed religion, as did some other men made cynical by the horrors of war. Sensing the brooding darkness within him, most of them left him alone.

Adjudant Pierre Livron, however—he of the blackened teeth—made no attempt to conceal his distrust of the newcomer, and his envy of his growing friendship with the captain of the fusiliers. His biting comments revealed the extent of his jealousy. "Your angelic looks are per'aps your only virtue, Preety Boy, though I wonder if eet is more a curse zan a blessing."

"You talk enough for two, Adjutant," Keane replied. "'Tis a shame that neither has anything of interest to say." Generally, however, he ignored the man's barbs.

By contrast, Keane came to hold Captain Fournier in high regard. Despite his rough exterior and loud, abrasive voice, the leader of Eighth Company was a soldier with a strong sense of justice who had the welfare of his men at heart. The men of his company knew he would never order them to undertake any mission he himself would not attempt. In addition to being resourceful and courageous, he was surprisingly well-educated.

Indeed, Fournier appeared to warm to the Irishman in return. There were moments beside the campfires at nights, as the men were rolling themselves in blankets ready for sleep, when the captain would seat himself near the newest recruit, puffing on an evil-smelling cigar.

The two men would converse companionably for a while.

Once, Fournier asked him about the tiny compass rose tattooed on his upper arm. "For your sweetheart, mon ami?"

"Quite so. And for luck."

The Frenchman nodded.

"And you, mon capitaine," said Keane, "that mark of a star on your own shoulder?"

"Ah, zis my lucky star. Eet protects my secrets." The captain blew a cloud of blue smoke from his nostrils. "For every man 'as secrets, no?" He chuckled. Bestowing a piercing glance on Keane he rose to his feet and walked away to join his lieutenants.

Keane's determination to return to his beloved in Ireland grew stronger than ever, though it was difficult to see how that goal could ever be realised. He had given his word to his captain, and as a man of honour there was almost no circumstance under which he would break his pledge. He would, however, shatter any vow for Rose's sake. More formidable barriers were the large stretches of water that separated him from his sweetheart—the English Channel and the Irish Sea. In his favour, however—he believed at first—was the fact that least he was on land and somewhat more liberated than he had been in the British Navy.

That sense of relative freedom was not to last. Soon it became clear that he was no more of a volunteer to the French than to the English. It seemed that everywhere he went, men sought to appropriate the use of his strength and youth in order to wage their wars.

Lord Leighton's carriage carried him from London to Ramsgate. Having donned his disguise, the robes of a cardinal, he voyaged with his bodyguards across the English Channel to Oostende, before setting off by post chaise through the Austrian Netherlands towards Brussels. His plan was to travel through Germany, via Munich, to Salzburg. There he intended to meet with the king of Austria, upon whom he would use all his powers of privilege, wealth and eloquence to persuade him to stand firm against Bonaparte at the signing of the treaty.

The fusiliers on horseback, made good speed, and were soon rapidly approaching Ghent. Their spies and scouts, sent on ahead, returned with the news that the supposed Italian envoy, Cardinal de Lorenzana, was expected to put up at the Court St George, the town's most salubrious coaching inn. Coaching inns stood scattered along the turnpikes. As well as serving coach travellers, these hostelries offered stabling, and a place to change the horses.

By this time, Keane O'Connell had managed to obtain some tattered clothing that made him look less like a British sailor and more like part of the French Revolutionary Army. Due to supply issues and rapid changes in government and military organization, the concept of a standard uniform was not always strictly adhered to, so almost anything was acceptable. He bartered for a white—or a grime-stained approximation of white—shirt, waistcoat and breeches, a long-tailed coat of dark blue wool with a high collar, and gaiters that reached up to the knee. Upon his mane of hair he wore a black tricorne hat.

Now that the information about Leighton was verified, Fournier entrusted him with weapons— a somewhat rusty and unpredictable musket, a sword and a cutlass. He had left behind his own skian at O'Sullivan's smithy when the Royal Navy had impressed him in the middle of the night. There was also a cartridge box, a bayonet, and a haversack for carrying rations. A battered scabbard, a bag of musket balls and two powder horns now depended from the Irishman's belt. Privately, he would have felt more comfortable armed with a shillelagh, but he was as ready as anyone to do his part in the forthcoming skirmish.

"We ambush eem before 'e reaches town," said the captain to his men. "We take 'is mercenaries by surprise. 'e 'ave not many. You were right, Irish, ze aristo travels with a small escort to escape attention. Ah, but 'ze dog 'as gained my attention!"

He gave orders for the horses to be tethered beside a stream in a small woodland, not far from the road.

At a well-chosen bend in the turnpike, dense thickets of elderberry, beech and hornbeam overhung the deeply-rutted thoroughfare. Here, concealed amongst green-gold autumnal foliage, the captain's chosen men crouched, waiting, with, their flintlocks loaded and primed, and bayonets fixed. Keane O'Connell was among them.

A feeble breeze rustled the leaves.

The call of a wood-pigeon sounded close at hand. It was a signal from one of the scouts, alerting them to the approach of the post-chaise with its outriders. Hoofbeats sounded, growing louder. As the equipage rattled around the bend, Fournier's chosen men sprang out from both sides of the road, in front and behind. Crack! Crack! Sparks and puffs of smoke flared from their muskets. They shot at the guards before they had a chance to draw their own firearms.

Crack! The postilion plunged sideways out of his saddle and the harnessed team of four frightened horses slewed to an abrupt halt.

One outrider toppled from his mount, while the seven who remained in their saddles wheeled and rode at the attackers with swords drawn. The riderless horse reared and squealed in alarm. Acrid and sulfuric scarfs of smoke floated in the air.

Keane O'Connell braced himself, standing shoulder to shoulder with his Breton comrade Gallou as they held their ground against the rider who charged at them. The guard leaned down, swinging his sword in a slicing motion. The Irishman moved with the speed and grace of a lion. Dodging the blow by a hair's breadth, he grabbed the man's sword-arm and hauled hard, dislodging him from his seat. A moment later Gallou joined in, helping to drag the rider off his steed.

The Breton struck the fallen man's head with the butt of his musket, knocking him out. Keane glanced up, noting that in the confusion, Captain Fournier had become cut off from the main melee. Standing alone, he now faced off against two horsemen simultaneously.

The Irishman ran towards Fournier, his movements fluid and calculated, using his bayonet to fend off the horsemen's blades. The riders were caught off guard by this sudden attack, giving the captain the opportunity to strike a decisive blow. More fusiliers rushed in behind the Irishman, and the fight was soon over.

"Merci mon ami," said Fournier, his breath coming in short gasps. He wiped his brow with a filthy hand. "You saved my life."

Keane nodded acknowledgment. "I swore an oath."

"Ha ha! To le Republique, but not to me, mon frere. I do

not forget what you have done. Come, let us see our prize!" the captain added with a grim smile, striding towards the stationary carriage.

Two fusiliers wrenched open the doors of the post-chaise, springing backwards immediately in case the occupants starting firing at them, which indeed they did. Leighton's bodyguard burst forth, both arms extended. A yellow flame blossomed from each hand, as he fired a flintlock belt pistol from one, and a pocket pistol from the other.

One! Two! Both shots went wide of their marks, and in the next instant rough hands seized the man and hurled him to the ground. The fusiliers summarily dragged Lord Leighton from his refuge and frogmarched him to the feet of their captain. Keane, together with a handful of his comrades, ransacked the coach, discovering a hefty purse filled with coins. Meanwhile, Gallou and several others had taken charge of the frenzied coach team. After calming the horses, they began to release them from their harness.

"This is monstrous!" Leighton shouted hoarsely at Fournier, struggling against his captors. "You will pay for this, you French scum. Unhand me! I am—I am a man of the cloth!"

"Mais oui, of course you are your worship!" said the captain dryly. "Such a holy cloth sack of potatoes."

Leighton spluttered, speechless with rage. His powdered periwig had tilted sideways, but still clung to his balding head. During the struggle his eye-patch had fallen off, revealing a sunken button-hole of flesh in the empty socket. His glance flicked away from Fournier and lit upon Keane, who had just arrived at his captain's side carrying the nobleman's pillaged purse. For one long moment the Englishman stared at the Irishman balefully, full in the face, glaring with outrage. His single anger-reddened eye seemed to glow with a fiery resentment from the pits of hell, and a kind of vitriolic cunning.

"You, all of you—" he had recovered his voice at last— "you will pay. You will rue the day you crossed me."

"Enlève ce miserable!" commanded Fournier, and the prisoner was dragged off to be bound, gagged and tied across a horse.

Five guards died, that day, while four were made prisoner. The victors led away the horses, all unscathed. The occupants of the carriage were taken prisoner also, and all their possessions confiscated.

That famed Protestant, Lord Frederick Leighton, never reached Salzburg.

Fournier's fusiliers were not gentle in their treatment of him. They took no small delight in humiliating their enemy. They were careful, nonetheless, not to damage him excessively, or take his life, for they intended to deliver him to the President of the National Convention, who would ransom him for a princely sum.

Adjutant Levin's loathing of the Irishman reached new heights after he saved the captain's life.

"'ere comes ze 'ero!" he would say with a scowl and a mocking bow.

He was the only man in Eighth Company who failed to like and respect Keane O'Connell. The rest came to know they could count on him in challenging situations. He was a courageous fighter who shirked no duty. He was generous and fair. Besides, he could also tell a good story at the end of the day, and make them laugh.

CHAPTER 19

There is Lights in the Cliff-top
When the Boats are Home-bound.

A cutter in a swell. Date unknown.
Attributed to Thomas Buttersworth (1768–1842).

O my true love's a smuggler and sails upon the sea,
And I would I were a seaman to go along with he;
To go along with he for the satins and the wine,
And run the tubs at Slapton when the stars do shine.

O Hollands is a good drink when the nights are cold,
And Brandy is a good drink for them as grows old,
There is lights in the cliff-top when the boats are
home-bound,
And we run the tubs at Slapton when the word goes
round.

The King he is a proud man in his grand red coat,
But I do love a smuggler in his little fishing-boat,
For he runs the Mallins lace and he spends his money
free,
And I would I were a seaman to go along with he.

"The Smuggler". From "A Sailor's Garland", selected and edited by
John Masefield. New York: Macmillan, 1906.
NB: Slapton is a small village just south west of Dartmouth in Devon.
To 'run the tubs' was to unload the small barrels (tubs) of contraband
liquor and transport them away from the coast.

Now that the Irishman had proved himself a worthy member of the company he was no longer closely watched. Consequently there was greater chance that he might escape and make his way back to Ireland.

One moonless night, when all were asleep except the guards on watch, he moved noiselessly out of the barn in which the men of Eighth Company were currently billeted. Carrying on his shoulder a small knapsack of provisions, he glided into the darkness like a wraith.

He had not progressed far, however, when there came the distinct sounds of pursuit. Hoofbeats thrummed through the ground beneath his feet, rising in volume. Riders galloped on his trail.

Throwing down the knapsack he broke into a run, but the horses, at full speed, were faster. The pursuing fusiliers swooped on their prey and dragged him back to the barn to face the captain.

At the edge of the glare of lantern light, Keane spied Adjutant Levin's triumphant leer. It was he who had led the hunt.

"Deserter!" the Frenchman cried. "'ave 'im flogged!" Leaning close to Keane's ear he muttered, "You will get your punishment, pretty boy. I will make sure of it."

Keane wrestled mightily with his captors, but he was outnumbered.

"Be still or die!" shouted Levin.

"Is that your favourite proverb?" Keane retorted, without letting up.

"Ta guile, Levin," said Fournier, bleary-eyed and only half-awake. "I am captain 'ere. Let 'im go!"

The fusiliers who had been holding the Irishman's arms released him. Their sullenness indicated they wished they'd not been obliged to restrain their comrade.

" Alors, Irish," Fournier continued, turning his gaze on Keane, "Deserting? But you not do that, n'est-ce pas? You swore an oath to ze army of Le Republique. You'd not break your oath, would you?" He bestowed upon the Irishman a look imbued with meaning.

Taking his cue from this look, Keane said, "Of course not, mon capitaine."

Levin screamed, "I was watching you, scum! Saw you steal ze food today. Saw you creep away in the dark, like an animal."

Said the captain, "Ze Irish is no fool. 'e knows he does not get far without papers. In zis country every able-bodied man 'as been conscripted. 'e will be stopped, searched, demanded for 'is papers. 'e has none. Not even forgeries. Zey put 'im in jail and give 'im to ze firing squad."

Papers!

In Keane's eagerness to be free, he had overlooked this point. He would not have got far without genuine documentation—or an excellent forgery thereof—proving he was a civilian and a free man.

"You were instead going to a tryst with ze farmer's daughter, Irish, no?" said Fournier, raising one eyebrow. "Sly dog! Ha ha!"

Keane hesitated. It was well-known that he despised falsehoods, and he was torn between honour and good sense. Conceivably at that moment he asked himself whether he really owed these men the truth—these men who had forced him to join their army to risk his life for their cause.

"Irish," said Fournier, "eet is either confess to that or be manacled and flogged for desertion. And you will be useless to me with your skin 'anging in bloody rags from your back, so speak up now."

Keane hesitated no longer. Carelessly he said, "Aye, you have the right of it, mon capitaine. A fair wench she is, and no mistake."

Fournier slapped him on the back.

"That Nicola would bewitch any man, but I warn you, Irish, never do it again!"

"'e stole food", interrupted Levin. "Search 'is knapsack!"

Fournier rounded on the fusilier. "Will you shut up? I know what 'e did. Do you take me for a fool?"

"Non, mon capitain. . ."

"Hors de ma vue!"

The adjutant scuttled away.

"A man must face punishment for stealing food, Irish," said the captain to Keane O'Connell, "as an example to ze others."

Keane nodded to signify his acceptance of this pronouncement.

"I could 'ave you imprisoned."

The French cachots and maisons d'arrêt were dirty, dark, damp and ill-ventilated. Prisoners inevitably emerged from them in poor health, if they survived at all. Imprisonment was close to a death sentence.

"Alors," Fournier continued, "zey need more men for building ze border fortifications to keep out ze British invaders. Your punishment will not be imprisonment but 'ard labour."

Hard labour, though an ordeal in itself, was indeed a preferable price to pay.

Without further ado Keane was packed off to the border with a working party, to perform back-breaking work digging redoubts, trenches, and other earthworks. As he departed, Levin laughed at his humiliation. Keane longed to knock him down, as he knew he could, but to beat the man must only humiliate him and increase his vindictiveness, so he ignored the fellow.

When his stint of hard labour was over and he returned to Eighth Company, Adjutant Levin made use of every opportunity to make life difficult for him in petty ways. Eventually Keane had had his fill. One evening, following one of Levin's pranks, he grabbed the man by the front of his shirt, thrusting his face so close that the Frenchman's stale stench made him gag. "Vex me once more, soldat, and believe me, you will regret it."

That was all it took! It was the last time Levin troubled him with small annoyances. Instead, he turned to inflicting his sly and petty harassments on weaker members of the company.

Keane made no more attempts to desert, but the longing to be with Rose gnawed at him, day after day. He thought of her, tried to imagine what she might be doing, and wondered whether the dreams of her reality would ever return.

Fournier's successful kidnapping of the English lord—in addition to the simultaneous acquisition of a weighty purse of gold—brought him to the attention of his superior officers. In fact, it marked the beginning of his swift rise through the ranks of the Revolutionary Army. He was soon promoted to the rank of commandant and transferred to another unit. A younger officer replaced him as captain of Eighth Company.

"Bonne chance, mon capitaine," Keane said to Fournier as they parted with a firm handshake.

"I saved your 'ide, and you saved mine, Irish," Fournier murmured confidentially. "You bear some secret sorrow maybe, and I know you want to go back to your 'ome. But you kept your word, and zat is what counts. If you need me, seek me out."

Keane said, "That I will, to be sure."

The exiled Irishman spent the snowy winter of the year 1797 and the entirety of the following year in Holland with the French army, though he despised being part of an occupying force.

Eighth Company joined forces with the other companies of the Third Battalion to launch attacks against the British and defend the ground they had taken. They moved constantly about the countryside, finding shelter in towns and villages.

During this time Keane O'Connell, who had no previous military training, learned a great deal about army practices and protocol. Such an adept fighter was he, and so calm in the face of danger, that he rose through the ranks to become a lieutenant.

He had no real desire for military rank, but accepted it, as it provided some benefits. Life, for him, was merely a matter of survival, until he could find some way to return home. At nights, his sleep was dreamless.

He learned much about the men who lived and fought alongside him. The Breton, Gallou, owned a small linen bag which he took with him wherever he went. When asked why he carried it, he explained that it was filled with flower seeds from his mother's garden.

"If I fall in battle, zose seeds will be buried with me. The flowers will spring up, and my grave will become a tiny piece of Brittany, where I will lie forever in my mother's garden."

They were superstitious, these men, no less than the sailors of the Royal Navy.

One soldier, more pious than the rest was known to his comrades as "Holy Joe", for he prayed every night and every morning. Every time the company went into battle he saw—so he claimed—arising between the two armies, serried ranks of diaphanous phantoms clad in white, with light shining around them, each with one arm outstretched and the other drawn back, letting fly burning arrows from their longbows.

"Ze angels," avowed Holy Joe with unshakable faith, "with flaming bows and arrows, zey are protecting us. Ze angels, zey are on our side!"

Many of the men laughed at him, but after a while others started seeing the archers, too. Word went around that supernatural forces were miraculously intervening to help the French at key turning-points in each battle. This boosted the confidence of the whole battalion, and Eighth Company's new captain encouraged it.

It seemed that an opportunity for Keane to return to Rose in Ireland would never arise. To desert from the French army would involve enormous risk, with small chance of success. How was he to traverse this war-torn land where he stood out as a foreigner, with no papers, and with his limited grasp of their languages? And if he made it to a port, how was he to cross the sea? And even if he did, by some miracle, maneuver a return to his native land, he would face further peril there, for the Royal Navy had him marked as a deserter.

Meanwhile his comrades crowed in triumph, assuring him that he was lucky to be with the French, on the winning side.

Nonetheless, in 1799 Britain, under the Duke of York, drove the French out of the Batavian Republic. On 9th November of that same year, Napoleon took over the government of France.

In the new year the tide turned again when General Moreau led the French against Britain at Hohenlinden in Bavaria, and defeated the British.

Throughout the year 1800, Keane O'Connell remained as a lieutenant with the Eighth Company. He never sighted Fournier, though it was rumoured that he still lived, and that Napoleon had promoted him to the rank of Chef de Brigade, the equivalent of a British colonel. Now and then he made attempts to discover the whereabouts of his erstwhile captain, but with most of western Europe in upheaval, and the French forces moving frequently from place to place, it proved an impossible task.

The treaty of Lunéville was signed on February 9, 1801. This peace agreement between France and Austria confirmed French dominance in Italian territories and parts of Germany, and weakened the Holy Roman Empire. Thus ended the continental conflict—though not the broader conflict. It meant that only the British were still at war with France.

At this time the men of Eighth Company found themselves quartered in a small village near Bruges, which was now part of the French Republic. During the period of exhausted peace that followed the treaty's signing, they were given leave to celebrate at the local inn.

Keane's comrades called him "le sombre," the somber one, for he never joined in with their carousing. They had not known him in the days of laughter and song, before his exile. Leaning back against the wall in a corner of the tavern, a half-tankard of Flemish ale on the table in front of him, he watched with detached amusement as the other fusiliers bellowed out songs and indulged in high jinks.

Gossip from the next table reached him through the hubbub. He had picked up enough French to decipher the news that a Chef de Brigade had arrived in that locality the day before, accompanied by his staff. He had set up his headquarters close by in a château-ferme, or fortified farmhouse, near Bruges.

"This officer, Fournier, 'e was once a captain of Eighth Company," the fusiliers remarked with some pride.

On hearing this, Keane determined to seek out his erstwhile captain, for old times' sake, and because Fournier was the only man in this country that he considered a true friend.

He took a draught of ale and returned his attention to his surroundings. One of the barmaids was a particularly pretty young woman. She was well-respected in the village, for it was said she possessed benevolent powers, apparently bestowed upon her by the Blessed Mary, Queen of Heaven. Marie was her name, and Adjutant Levin seemed intent on harassing her.

Late in the evening, when most of the other men were too drunk to notice, Levin demanded that Marie bring up a bottle of the tavern's rarest wine from the cellar. She entered the back room, kindled a flame in a lantern and, holding aloft the light, began to descend the stairs. Levin followed her.

On seeing this, Keane arose and went after them.

At the foot of the stairs, in the dank, shadowy confines of the cellar, Marie's lantern lay on the floor, its yellow flame sputtering. Levin had clamped his hand across the mouth of the struggling woman and pushed her against a wall.

Keane vaulted lightly down from the middle of the staircase. He grasped the assailant by the shoulders and pulled him away, thrusting him bodily into a rack of wine bottles, which smashed as the man hurtled into them, scattering glass shards. It happened so quickly, in the dimness, that Levin never even glimpsed his face.

"Come," said Keane, picking up the lantern and guiding the dazed girl by the elbow.

They ran upstairs to where, in all the commotion of uproarious capering and revelry, nobody had noticed anything amiss.

"Tu vas bien?" asked the Irishman, as they stood for a moment together in the back room.

"Oui, monsieur." The young woman trembled, but lifted her chin bravely. "Je vous dois. Je maudis ce voyou, mais je te bénis avec ton souhait le plus cher."

Which he took to mean, "I am unharmed. I am in your debt. I curse that thug, but I bless you with your dearest wish."

And her pale hands fluttered like doves as she made the sign of the cross.

"Merci!" he replied with a bow. He departed like a shadow.

That night, it seemed to Keane O'Connell that two signs augured it was time for him to make a break for home. First, there was the lull in the fighting, brought about by the treaty. Second, Marie's blessing—for surely it was potent and would deliver luck!

He made the decision. There would be no better time to take his chance. He could endure the parting from Rose no longer, and he yearned, too, to know how Ryan fared.

Somehow, he must return to Ireland, or die in the attempt. He would simply trust to fate and make a desperate flight across the country to some port, where—if fortune favoured him—he might find a vessel to carry him home.

There was one action, however, that he wanted to perform before he took his life in his hands. He would bid farewell to his old captain, Fournier.

CHAPTER 20

I place my fate in your hands.

The Irishman took advantage of a few days' leave to seek the now-famous Chef de Brigade. On arriving at the sprawling château-ferme, he was escorted into a shabby but spacious salon. A fire, piled up like crimson glass shards smashed from some cathedral window, burned in the cavernous hearth, and two bulldogs sprawled in front of it—the battalion's mascots. They jumped up with tails wagging and greeted the Irishman affably as he entered, before returning to the hearthrug.

A group of officers, deep in conversation pored over a large table, across whose surface was strewn a number of well-thumbed maps. Men of lower ranks scurried to and fro carrying ledgers; members of brigade staff engaged on administrative tasks. When they glanced at the newcomer their surprise was evident. Their gazes lingered on his countenance, which remained exceedingly comely by any standards, being of perfect symmetry and unmarked by pox or scar or blemish of any kind, and thus a rarity.

On a large oaken desk by an open window, the white plume of a bicorne hat waved lazily in the breeze. Sunlight limned an ink-pot and two quill pens, an oil lamp, a carafe of red wine, a box of cigars and three Venetian drinking glasses. Fournier was sitting at this desk, giving orders to an officer who acknowledged with a formal gesture, turned on his heel and marched off.

As Keane O'Connell approached, Fournier stood up, smothering a cough. He was resplendent in a blue coat with red and white details, brass buttons, and gold lace. The two stars on his gold epaulettes indicated his rank. He was now sporting a large, bushy moustache, and clearly he was living well, for he displayed a fuller, more robust shape beneath his tight-stretched waistcoat.

Crisply, Keane raised his right hand with palm facing forward, until his fingers touched the edge of his hat. His eyes met those of his superior officer in an exchange of mutual respect, before he swiftly brought his hand back down to his side and stood at attention.

"Repos!" After returning the salute, the Frenchman greeted his visitor with a friendly grin and a hearty slap on the shoulder. "Salut, Lieutenant O'Connell! I was not so surprised to receive a message you come to see me. Seat yourself! Take some wine! Ze vintage of Bourgogne, she's not a bad drop."

Fournier looked older of course, his mane of coarse hair more grizzled, his face weathered, engraved with deep furrows. O'Connell might have wondered how he himself must look, after years of fighting, and sleeping rough. In fact, now that the maturity of manhood was on him and he looked less of a boy, his full grace and power and masculine beauty was intensely apparent, though he himself was unaware of it. Even clad in a melange of well-worn garments—the eggshell-white breeches, the threadbare waistcoat, the dark blue coat—his tall, lithe form was a drawn bow, poised and powerful. An ink-spill of raven hair tumbled from beneath his tricorne hat, falling across his shoulders.

"Sláinte, Mon Colonel!" The Irishman raised his glass to his friend and the two men seated themselves. Keane swung one leg over the other, resting his booted foot atop his knee.

"You are fortunate you arrive at zis time," said the Chef de Brigade, "for if you turned up much later, I would be gone. Ze brigade, she is departing for Spain next week."

Companionably they discussed old times, while the harsh sounds of shouted orders drifted in through the window. In the courtyard beyond, soldiers were being drilled.

At length Fournier said abruptly, "Why did you come to me, Irish?"

Keane held his gaze steadily, openly. "To bid you farewell."

"Farewell! Humph!" Fournier poured more wine. "Evidently you place great faith in me, to confess such treasonous intentions."

"Aye, that is the truth. I place my fate in your hands."

"Eet is my duty to persuade you away from such a foolish course. If you abscond, ze French will 'ang you as a deserter. If you go back to Ireland, and ze British catch you, zey will 'ang you as a deserter. And you know, n'est-ce pas? —zat also your homeland is a dangerous place for you, after ze 1798 uprising and all ze troubles. Ze Irish might well 'ang you for no particular reason!" He coughed explosively, and took a gulp of wine.

"I have that knowledge,' said Keane, "but it makes no difference. I must return. Aye, 'tis dangerous, but I must go back to—I have people there—"

Fournier observed him shrewdly.

"Back to your sweet'eart," he said with a chuckle. "Of course! You sink she will be still waiting for you after all zis time? Maybe not, no?"

"If you knew her, Mon Colonel, you would not say that," said Keane gravely. "The leavin' is on me. I will take for myself a false name and a disguise. I must find her, and when I do, I will marry her."

"Ah, so zat is how eet is, eh?" Fournier shrugged. "Mon dieu, after all, your friend Le Chef de Brigade 'as a soft 'eart. In my opinion, life is too short for two lovers to be apart. Oui, your old friend is sympathique. Alors, you 'ave done your part as a soldier, my Irish. Ze war is over, or so zey say. I 'ave in my power to grant you a discharge, though to be honest you never really enlisted in the first place. Eh, mon ami? Ha ha!"

A discharge! Sweet mother of divine! Keane O'Connell turned his head aside for a moment, to hide his emotion.

If Fournier gave him those official papers, there would be no need to travel secretly across the countryside, constantly in mortal danger. "Merci, Mon Colonel," he murmured somewhat hoarsely. "You'll be doin' me a great favour, and that's the truth."

"Ha ha! Now you see, I 'ave many decorations on my shoulders. Bonaparte himself recommends me. I 'ave some power in these parts, and I can do more for you," said Fournier, winking. Peremptorily he summoned his chief-of-staff to his side and issued some instructions. Keane had learned enough of the French tongue to comprehend that his mentor was telling his assistant to make ready his discharge papers.

The officer, making notes on a leaf of paper, asked upon what grounds Lieutenant Keane O'Connell was to be discharged.

Fournier acerbically demanded whether he was expected to think of everything, and asserted that he didn't know; perhaps it was the white plague or something. Growing more confident in this idea he added that yes, now that he thought on it, he was certain his personal physician had examined the lieutenant and discovered he had the white plague.

The chief-of-staff asked what that meant, and Fournier replied that some called the disease "consumption", whereupon the officer glanced warily at O'Connell—who smiled guilelessly at him—and took a step backwards. Fournier, with the air of a schoolmaster chastising a wayward student, told his subordinate that only idiots did not know that the treatment for consumption was to get fresh air and exercise, and to eat good food, which was why the lieutenant was to be discharged from the army, where the air was foul and the food was worse.

"Prepare ze discharge papers. And instruct ze apothecary to concoct a vial of herbal medicine for ze lieutenant to carry upon 'is person."

"Oui, Mon Colonel."

As the clerk hastened away, Fournier addressed the Irishman. "I advise you, lieutenant, as soon as you 'ave ze discharge papers in your 'ands, depart immediately! Just in case my physician Monsieur Mallard 'ears of your sickness and insists on bleeding you. 'e believes that draining a sick man's blood can cure diseases. 'e might prescribe ze tobacco for you, too, and it is an expensive cure, believe me. 'e persuades me that the cigars will ease my cough." He coughed again. "I smoke of zem every day, but still it gets worse. I suspect Mallard is a quack." He chuckled at some private joke, but the laughter turned into a bout of coughing. When he had recovered, he said, "Now follow me."

The Chef de Brigade led the way out of the salon, through a heavy door and into the courtyard. The overcast sky clamped down lie an iron lid, and a bitter February wind shook the bare branches of an ancient chestnut tree that grew beside the well, with a sound like rattling bones. A tall watchtower with narrow windows and a rooftop parapet cast its shadow across the buttressed walls, and the vanilla scent of hay wafted from the nearby stables.

The two men halted in a secluded corner of the courtyard, where the shouts of a drill sergeant drowned out their words and their conversation could not be overheard.

"Too many listening ears in that chambre," said Fournier jerking his chin in the direction of the salon. He placed his boot upon the edge of a stone horse-trough and leaned upon his knee. "What I tell you, nobody else must 'ear." In a low voice, almost a whisper, he continued, "You must travel north to ze Batavian Republique, a port called Scheveningen. Seek a ship's captain by the name of Doyle. When 'e knows you are my friend, 'e give you voyage to your country. Doyle, 'e is a smuggler, and 'e will smuggle you. 'e knows 'ow to dodge ze navy patrols, ze revenue cutters. Zere will be no customs officers to plague you with questions when you arrive."

"Many t'anks, my friend. I will repay you if I can."

"Repay me? You saved my life. Eet is for me to repay you, which is what I do now!"

Keane O'Connell smiled his white flash of a smile. "How shall I prove my identity to Captain Doyle?"

"I tell you a passphrase. No letters, no papers. Eet is too dangerous to be carrying zem in case you are stopped and searched on your way north. Besides, Doyle, 'e cannot read or write."

Fournier told Keane what the captain looked like, and how he might identify him. "Eef you sink you find ze right man, say to him, 'For every door, there is a key.' Eef it is Doyle, he will reply, 'And every darkness, its dawn to meet.' This is ze smugglers' way to know a stranger is no enemy." Having finished this speech, he pressed a grubby handkerchief to his mouth, suppressing a splutter.

Keane said, "I will offer to work my passage, for 'tis little money I have in my pockets, and I would rather not spend it on a fare."

"Pah! Money!" said Fournier with a snort. "Doyle, 'e owes me many favours. When 'e comprehends eet is moi, Le Chef de Brigade that sent you, you will pay nothing. Maintenant, if the British do not shoot or 'ang you as soon as you set foot in Irlande, and if you find your sweet'eart, where do you go?"

"I have no home," said the Irishman. "'Tis in her father's house she dwells, but I will not be stoppin' there. 'Tis danger to her family my presence would be bringin'. I will find somewhere safe, and when I am settled, I will take her there."

Fournier rolled his eyes and raised his palms skywards as if pleading with the clouds. "Irish! Irish! No home, no money, n'est-ce pas? Lord 'ave mercy on you."

"I have my strength," replied O'Connell with quiet dignity. "I will have my true-love. We will make a life for ourselves."

Fournier groaned. "Ingenu! One more favour I will do for you. But in return you must make me a promise."

"If 'tis in my power, I will do so."

The Frenchman lowered his voice again, so that Keane could barely hear him. "One day, God forbid, I might need your 'elp. If zat day comes, I will send you a message, and you must do as I bid you in ze message. I do not ask this . . . 'ow they say? Bon gré mal gré? Sans raison valable . . . sauf si c'est une question de vie ou de mort. . . ."

Keane understood, and nodded. Fournier would never call upon his help except in dire need.

"You see, mon ami, ze price you pay for being an honest man, is zat other men maybe want your services. I trust you as I trust only two other souls living on zis earth. Maybe never will I call upon you. At most, once only. You swear?"

"I swear," said Keane, and the look of affection in his eyes touched the Frenchman to the heart. Fournier felt it a good reward for his generosity.

"Bon! Now, let us return indoors and take some more wine, while I write to my friend in London. 'e is a man of some influence. Come!"

Seating himself at his desk in the salon, Fournier pulled a sheet of paper towards him, dipped a quill in an ink bottle and began to scribble.

Presently he sprinkled the page with pounce to absorb excess ink, and set his quill upright in the ink bottle.

"Now for ze pièce de résistance!" he said.

Keane watched with interest, as the Frenchman summoned a junior member of his staff and spoke into his ear. The man trotted away and presently returned with a portable lap desk. Fournier unlocked it with an ornate brass key depending from his belt. He subtracted a fresh sheet of paper, a bottle of liquid that resembled water, and a small artist's paintbrush. With these tools, he began again to write.

After some time, he showed Keane the paper on which he had been exercising the little brush. The Irishman shot him an inquiring look. "It appears to be blank!"

"As you know, sending letters in zese times is risky," said the Frenchman, waving the sheet in the air to let it dry. "When ze mail packets arrive in port, all papers are seized and read by ze customs officers. Zey scrutinise ze addresses. Men 'oo are discovered to be communicating with ze enemy are flogged, imprisoned or 'anged.

"Voila!" He indicated the first page, which he had inscribed with black India-ink. "I send an innocent letter of greeting to my London friend, discussing maybe the weather. But ze true message is not in ze letter. Eet is on the inside of ze enclosing paper." And he pointed to the sheet that seemed vacant.

Fournier explained that he had written on the inside of the envelope with invisible ink, a clear solution that was the result of mixing green vitriol with water. When the invisible writing was exposed to heat, or painted with a "réactif", it turned black and became legible.

With the admonition, "Keep this safe!" he gave a small bottle of réactif to his Irish lieutenant, in case he, Fournier, should ever need to write secretly to him.

The Frenchman folded the letter inside the paper inscribed with the green vitriol solution, and closed it with a blob of red wax and his personal seal. He told his assistant to place the missive in a leather satchel and expedite its delivery to the port of Oostende.

"Zis letter will voyage speedily to England on a mail vessel of ze Imperial and Royal Post Office of Austria, and next by road to London by way of someone I trust as much as you, Irish."

"To London! But why should Englishmen help you or me?"

"My London contacts, zey are no Anglaise, but French. Aristos. Escaped from ze guillotine. Tell no-one!"

In answer to Keane's inquiring look, he added in a murmur, "Aristos, yes. I detest them, most of them, but these are family. If you breathe a word of zis to a living soul, I will deny it. And never trust you again." He tapped the tattooed symbol on his forearm. "My lucky star protects me."

"Upon my honour, your secret is safe with me," the young man assured him.

"Irish, you must commit to memory what I now tell you. Write down nothing. Keep it all in your 'ead."

The general leaned in close to the Irishman, so that his mouth was almost brushing his ear. In a low murmur, he proceeded to divulge a longwinded set of instructions regarding what he must do to secure a safe refuge in Ireland.

"And you must choose a new name for yourself," he said. "What will you 'ave?"

"Driscoll. 'Tis as good a name as any. Conor Driscoll."

The chief-of-staff marched up, saluted his chef de brigade and presented him with a wad of papers. Fournier riffled through the pages, running his eye over the contents, then handed them to his lieutenant. "Your discharge documents."

Soon afterwards, Keane took his leave of his friend.

195

From that day, Keane O'Connell ceased to touch his face with a blade. His jaw darkened, and whiskers sprouted. As he made his way north towards the Batavian Republic, he grew a luxuriant beard, so thick that it made his face almost unrecognisable. At Scheveningen, calling himself by the name of "Driscoll", he boarded the smugglers' cutter Skylark, a small fore and aft rigged sloop with two headsails, a vertical stem, and a long bowsprit. These small, fast sailboats were often used by bootleggers, and also by the authorities who were sent out to catch them.

The Skylark's crew carried small arms, and the ship herself was armed with a carriage gun loaded with lead. Her cargo was 366 casks of cheap brandy, 31 bags of snuff, and two bags of tobacco.

Smugglers' cutters usually took a route from the Batavian Republic to Ireland that followed the prevailing winds and currents. The most direct path was across the North Sea, around the northern coast of Scotland, and then south along the west coast of Ireland, but, as Keane O'Connell learned, this way was also the most dangerous, as it passed through heavily patrolled waters and was prone to storms and rough seas.

That was why Captain Doyle charted an alternative course, sailing south through the English Channel, past the coast of France, and then west across the Atlantic to Ireland. This route was longer but also less hazardous, as it avoided the vigilantly monitored waters of the North Sea and the English Channel.

"A free trader's course is not guaranteed, Mr. Driscoll," the Skylark's bo'sun told him. "We have to use our brains. We might change course or alter our plans at any time, to avoid detection and make the most profit."

The ocean journey as a free man was utterly unlike the Irishman's experience aboard the naval vessel. Indeed, it afforded the usual discomfort associated with sea voyaging, but it gave him a sense of wonder and joy. He felt at liberty, at last, to think only of Rose, to picture their imminent meeting, to imagine her in his arms.

As the cutter crossed the Atlantic, he braced his feet against the rolling of the deck, tasting the salt spray in the air and looking out across the vast expanse of the ocean. The constant motion threw him slightly off balance, as the Skylark rose and fell with the waves. Sometimes his body would thrill with a sensation of weightlessness.

There was no land in sight. The endless monotony of the waves was broken only by the occasional sighting of a pod of dolphins, schools of fish jumping out of the water, or a bird soaring above. The sound of the waves crashing against the hull was a constant backdrop to the voyage, accompanying the creaks and groans of the wooden vessel as it navigated the rough waters. Occasionally, the sound of the captain or first mate shouting orders, the clang of metal against wood, or the snap of wind-tautened canvas overlaid the sounds of the sea. Below deck, the cramped quarters were hot and humid, stinking of unwashed bodies, bilge and slightly stagnant drinking water.

High above on the topgallant mast, the lookout in the cross-trees scanned the horizon. He was keeping watch for naval or revenue vessels, in particular a famous cutter called Swallow, owned by the British Customs and Excise service, famous for intercepting and capturing smugglers.

The bo'sun joined Keane as he leaned on the taffrail

"Cap'n's aiming to make landfall at Selkie Cove," he commented. "'Tis wild and remote, a divil of a dangerous place to anchor with all dem rocks, but safer for us than the main ports with dem cursed revenuers. Bejasus, but the ports ain't what they used to be."

"What's your meanin'?"

"There's more folk a-bustlin' there than I ever seen afore."

The seaman described his last sight of Wexford Harbour, where, under a louring sky, rows of tall ships stood alongside the docks. Small water-craft plied to and fro. On the wharf, crowds of men, women and children dodged among carts, horses, donkeys, dogs, barrels, crates and bales. Stevedores and longshoremen contributed to the commotion, shouting orders as cargo was loaded and unloaded. Many of the people on the quay were clad in rags. They were poverty-stricken families waiting to board the ships, embarking on a one-way voyage to foreign lands.

"They're leavin'," said the bo'sun softly. "From every main port. There's a great leavin' on us."

The cutter approached the coast of Ireland—a dark line scrawling itself across the horizon, representing the cliffs and green hills rising out of the ocean. This glimpse of his homeland made Keane pace the deck restlessly, like a pent-up wild horse sensing open country and eager to break free.

He was, by this time, half-delirious from lack of sleep. The wind had been blustering, and the sea had been rough during the last part of the voyage. All the past night and day, choppy waves tossed the Skylark up and down and sideways. When the young man eventually fell into a light doze, he had dreamed about Rose—not as before, when she had appeared so real, but as a barely-substantial phantom figure forever out of reach, her arms stretched beseechingly towards him.

With the crew members, he took a tot of rum as the evening sun touched the horizon and sent burning clouds drifting across the sky. The cutter hugged the coastline, limned by that low, ruby-amber radiance. O'Connell looked out from his position at the taffrail. Tiny islands of rock jutted from the sea, and upon them rested a number of figures.

The golden light bathed their limbs and hair.

"By all that's holy!" he exclaimed, and hearing this, the bo'sun hastened to join him. Together they leaned over the rail, straining towards the vision.

Was it a company of young women they saw there, reclining on the rocks? They appeared to be quite unconcerned by the surge and swell and boom of the ocean all around them. Great, powerful waves crashed against the perpendicular sides of the craggy skerries, and hurled a white smoke of spray into the air. Among this surging, seething tumult of oceanic power, they sat or lay down, combing their hair or bending their lovely heads towards each other as if in conversation.

Near them lay strewn some gleaming, silver-grey garments.

"Do you see that?" the bo'sun gasped, his arm outstretched.

Other crewmen hurried to cluster at the rail, gaping.

"Aye," replied Keane, shaking his head in wonderment.

"'Tis only the lucky few who gets to see the selkies," said the bo'sun.

The man in the cross-trees gave a sudden shout, and the young women on the rocks—if that is what they were—glanced sharply towards the ship. Next instant they had seized hold of the lustrous coats, slipped them on and dived from their perch into the roiling water.

And in the instant their bodies speared into the sea, they no longer looked like women, but sleek grey seals, vanishing beneath the thundering waves.

Afterwards, many of the sailors scoffed at the notion they had observed anything but seals. Then it came to Keane that he had been fooled by a trick of the light, and the rum, and his weariness. He came to doubt the vision, but he never forgot it.

When the Skylark neared her destination she hung back from the coast, out of sight, until nightfall. Soon after sunset, the first mate flashed a signal lamp. Watchers on the beach sent forth a light in reply. Under cover of darkness the cutter sailed into the cove.

By the time she dropped anchor, the watchers had sent for the carriers. Horses and carts stood ready. The crew loaded small rowboats to goods, to transport them from the ship to the shore, where men loaded them on the carts, ready for transport to a safe inland location.

Light, misty rain began to fall as Keane helped unload the smuggled goods, then bade farewell to his shipmates.

He had arrived at last, and the Emerald Isle was where he wanted to be. Charged with a sense of purpose the Irishman hoisted his knapsack on his back, climbed out of the rocky inlet to the cliff top and started along a faint track that led inland, raindrops running down his coat and the breeze lifting his black hair. Suddenly, on impulse—and to the astonishment of a passing hare—he kneeled to kiss the green turf of his native land. Then, he set his face against the wind and struck out for Allanwell.

CHAPTER 21

One Half of the Ring is Still Here With Me.

Emigrants Leave Ireland by Henry Doyle 1868

I'm bidding you a long farewell, my Mary kind and true
But I'll not forget you, darling, in the land I'm going to
They say there's bread and work for all, and the sun shines always there
But I'll ne'er forget old Ireland, were it fifty times as fair.

Verse from "The Irish Emigrant"
Published by Robert McIntosh of Glasgow.
Probable period of publication: 1860-1890

Ireland was still in a state of turmoil following the rebellion, the passing of the Act of Union, the abolition of the Irish Parliament, and the subsequent stirring of resistance and resentment among many Irish people, who wanted greater independence from Britain. Nationalism, republicanism, and sectarianism were on the rise.

Across the country, some rebels continued to fight against British rule and oppose the Act of Union. They formed secret societies, staged sporadic attacks on British forces and loyalists, and sought support from France, Spain and America for their cause.

The British government tried to suppress Irish dissent and rebellion by imposing martial law, curfews, censorship and harsh punishments. They deployed a large army of regulars and militia to patrol and garrison the country, and used informers, spies and agents provocateurs to infiltrate and undermine rebel groups.

To escape from political oppression and economic hardship, a portion of the Irish population emigrated to far-off countries, while others joined the British army or navy as soldiers or sailors. Some young Irishmen joined the armies of countries such as France or Spain, who were fighting against Britain. Other groups tried to achieve political reform within the framework of the Act of Union, advocating for parliamentary reform to reduce corruption and increase accountability in government.

Into this seething crucible of upheaval and crisis Keane O'Connell came striding—tall and proud of bearing, aged five-and-twenty years, but with a wealth of experience. His handsome face was partly concealed by a thick beard, his hat was pulled down over his forehead, and to a casual observer, he would be almost unrecognisable as the youth who had been impressed into the Royal Navy almost exactly seven years earlier.

During his journey overland to the port of Scheveningen he had traded the quasi-uniform of the French demi-brigades for civilian attire.

A motley array of unfashionable garments clothed him, much patched and mended, collected from a variety of sources. His feet were thrust into buckled leather boots with durable wooden soles, which could withstand long hours of walking. The corduroy breeches that covered his long legs were buttoned at the knee, and he wore a dull russet waistcoat over his linen shirt. Concealed beneath his clothing was a slim French dagger, the only weapon he had brought with him on the voyage. The Irish were still forbidden to bear weapons, so he could not risk carrying anything more obvious such as a pistol, a musket, or a sword.

Aboard the smuggler's cutter he had bartered with the bo'sun for his waterproof canvas coat. Double-breasted, the jacket reached to mid-thigh and was fastened with brass buttons. This, he had shrugged on over his other clothes to keep out the fine mist of rain that was now falling. The fabric stretched tightly across the breadth of his shoulders. His long dark hair, tied in a bunch with a black ribbon, hung down his back from beneath his woollen cap.

Scarcely stopping to eat or sleep, he sped towards Allanwell with a single purpose.

The month of April was opening like a flower. A foam of delicate white hawthorn and blackthorn blossoms bedecked the roadside hedges, but the landscape through which he now passed after seven years seemed strange to his eyes. In places, it appeared half-deserted. Lawlessness reigned. In some villages the cottages stood abandoned, or only the blackened stumps of buildings, with tottering chimneys, remained. The muddy road, by contrast, was busy with traffic. Ragged families trudged along, pushing handcarts filled with their belongings. From time to time, accompanied by the thunder of hooves, troops of British cavalrymen would come pelting along, scattering everyone in their path.

It was a perilous road for a lone wayfarer, but Keane O'Connell overtook a wagon-procession of Travellers that was passing in the same direction, and struck up a friendship with them. They were glad of his company, for he entertained them with stories of the foibles of the Flemish, the Dutch and the French—mostly invented, and embroidered for diverting effect—and he was strong, and marvellously well-favoured, and willing to help with heavy work.

The young Traveller women flashed their dark eyes at him, and teasingly pulled his beard, and asked if he was wed. They grabbed his hand and begged to divine his future by reading his palm, but he would have none of it, and gently rebuffed their advances.

"Stay with us, Callan Driscoll," the Travellers said. "Be part of our tribe."

But he smiled and shook his head.

Along the road, whenever he and his companions encountered wayfarers coming from the opposite direction, he asked them for news of Allanwell. The closer they drew to that village, the more news he gathered. Thus he became aware of a forthcoming event much talked-about in these parts—the wedding of the squire's son, Edwin Westbourne, in two days' time, on the 14th of April.

"And who is to be the bride?" he enquired conversationally.

"Why, none other than the beauty of the county, Mistress Rose Delacey."

The old farmer who spoke these words saw the demeanour of his questioner change instantly, like the sudden darkness of a summer storm. The young man seemed at once captivated by unimaginable grief and rage, as if some appalling chaos of desolation threatened to engulf him. The farmer drew back uncertainly, and as he did so he heard the young man murmur, "I will not believe it! Can it be possible? After seven long years, will I be too late by a few hours?"

He spoke not again to the informant, but broke into a run and soon disappeared from view.

From the instant he heard the news, Keane ceased to take rest or sleep. He left the Travellers far behind and struck out alone. Through the entire night he ran, or walked—for no man could run continuously so far, for so long, and not burst his heart—stopping only for a draught of water now and then, and he pushed on all through the next day.

No person he encountered recognised him, although most regarded him with suspicion. Why should a young man of such fine form and handsome countenance appear so distraught, so haunted? What was he running from? Why did he travel so swiftly, so madly along the roads? Had his family been slain, his village burned? Or was he a spy? A thief? But then, the whole countryside was riddled with itinerant strangers those days—people passing through on their way to the ports, or seeking shelter from undisciplined mobs, or gangs of looters, or rebels.

As dusk was drawing in and a gusty wind rising, he arrived at the village, heart pounding, and made for the Delacey cottage.

Aside from the wind's moan, all was quiet in the house and yard. The shuttered windows had a look of blindness. He knocked at the door and nobody answered, save for the clucking chickens in the backyard coop, and a couple of goats, who, for a while, set up a bleating.

Clouds obscured the moon and stars. A streamer of air-currents scored the atmosphere with the sharp, salt tang of the sea. When the wind veered, it carried to Keane O'Connell's ears the sound of someone playing a plaintive whistle-tune up on Madigan's Leap.

A small yellow topaz of light was approaching through the gloom. The young man narrowed his eyes, and presently descried the holder of the lantern. It was Ilvenna McGinty.

She advanced, and halted before him. For a long moment she regarded him steadily, and then she pronounced his name, as if she had been expecting him.

"You know me!" he exclaimed in a voice like rusted iron.

"Indeed," replied the self-proclaimed wise-woman, "but most would not, for yer face is half-hidden. The Sight is with me, so it is. And I've been seekin' yer all day. I had the knowledge you were on your way here, for this pure mornin' at home there came a knock at the door, but not a soul was there when I opened it. 'Tis a sure sign a visitor will arrive soon. I felt in me bones that the visitor would be you, for I niver 'ad such a knock at the door this last seven years, save when yer man came back."

"Ryan? He is here? He is well?" Keane O'Connell spoke urgently.

Ilvenna nodded. "Aye. He didn't believe me when I told 'im yer was comin'."

"Where is she?" he demanded then, somewhat brusquely, for having satisfied himself as to his brother's well-being, he sensed that time was slipping away.

Ilvenna held the lantern closer to his face and inspected him. "Rough is your tone to me, Keane O'Connell," she said, "but I see by your looks that you're sufferin'. A man in pain has small power for politeness." She gestured in the direction of Whitethorn Hill. "Yer one is at the grand house. She was married this afternoon. 'Tis celebratin' they are now, all those grand folk, so they are."

At this news, Keane grew pale and a look of outrage passed over his handsome countenance like a shadow. Ilvenna reached out her hand to steady him. Earnestly, intently, she stared up at his face.

"You will not be lettin' a t'ing like a weddin' get in the way of what's right and true, if I know you, Keane O'Connell," she said. "You must fetch her away. Bring her to me at my place, and I will help you. Go to her! You are her last chance. Go to her! And may the song of the angels enfold the both of you."

The young man bowed to Ilvenna, then ran, as swift as thought, up the hill towards the great house, as if the heavy knapsack on his shoulders was as weightless as a dandelion puff.

Watchmen patrolled the perimeter of the Charter Hall estate, but whether due to Ilvenna's benison, or to neglect of duty, or whether they had indulged in too much of the "water of life" in honour of the wedding, he was able to elude them and slip through their cordon unseen.

The windows of the great house blazed with light. Raucous sounds of merrymaking spilled forth. After vaulting over a low stone fence, Keane kept to the shadows of the garden topiaries, his quiet footsteps unheard against the din.

Where would Rose be? How could he find her?

He twisted the warm metal of the half-ring on his finger, tapped his left hand against the upper part of his right arm, where the lucky tattoo of the compass rose resided. "Guide me now," he whispered.

The moon sailed out from behind the clouds, and stars stabbed forth. In the half-light, the second-story balcony could clearly be distinguished. Rose had spoken of this balcony, a favourite vantage point of her mother's. It was outside the main bedchamber, and could be reached by way of the external staircase.

And she would be there.

Lightly he ascended the stair and ran across the flagstones.

Tall French doors stood before him. Celestial radiance slanted in through their expensive glass panes. His searching gaze followed the silver arrows of starlight and found her.

Like an angel she appeared, lying on the great silk-canopied bed against the pillow, eyes closed. She was still clad in her wedding gown, a cloud of whiteness billowing about her, with hand-sewn pearls and crystals glinting like diamonds, and layers of organza and silk floating like overblown flower petals.

Keane pushed on one of the doors. It gave before the pressure, gliding aside on its hinges. In a few strides he stood at the foot of the bed.

Rose opened her eyes.

She took a sudden, small breath; held it.

Her incredulous gaze took him in from head to toe. The intruder was not her bridegroom. Nor was he any of the wedding guests, eight hours early for the shivaree. Too startled even to think of danger, she studied him.

He looked like some weather-beaten sea-captain... a ghost from a shipwreck...

The bushy beard half-obscured his face and his hat concealed his brow, but even before he approached her, holding out the other half of the ring, abruptly she knew him. Amazement paralysed her, but only for an instant. Springing from the bed in a lather of milky fabric she rushed into his arms and they clung together, wordless.

Then she, sobbing: "Oh, why did you come too late? For I am married this very afternoon!"

For a moment he did not—could not speak.

And then he said, into the inky cloud of her hair, and the pearl-stitched wedding veil she still wore, "My darlin'. Come with me. . . "

It was as if some power made them invisible.

Like a spectre in her palely glimmering wedding dress, hand in hand with her true love, Rose passed unseen with him down the stair and away from the house that glowed with firelight and candlelight. Down Whitethorn Hill they went, into the dark countryside, together at last, he with his knapsack on his shoulder.

And none spied them.

They were like two ghosts. Perhaps it was magic that protected them that night.

Or maybe it was the fact that Ilvenna McGinty had strewn pungent herbs on the footprints of their flight, to confuse the senses of the hounds.

Even when the hue and cry had been raised, no bloodhound could sniff out their trail, and no man or woman or child in Allanwell confessed to having seen them.

Rose disappeared, and the Westbournes could not find her.

Day after day, Edwin Westbourne sought his bride. He and his family spared no expense, sending out search parties and demanding the help of local villagers. They looked high and low in Allanwell and across the countryside, but found no trace of her. Every town and village within a day's ride they scoured—south to Castlerigg, and north to Ballyganna—but she remained elusive. There was no clue as to where she might be

The despairing bridegroom could hardly eat or sleep, being plagued by utter perplexity, anger, indignation and desperation. Though he explored every corner of the estate, and beyond, it was to no avail. The very landscape seemed as hollow and empty as a great iron bell. The mystery of the vanished bride grew ever more confounding with each passing day.

As days turned into weeks, and weeks to months, Edwin's fury and bitterness only amplified. Haunted by memories, he never gave up hope of finding Rose again.

CHAPTER 22

The Fairy Mountain

Wild, windswept and remote are the uplands on the west coast, dominated by rolling hills and rocky outcrops, with towering cliffs that plunge down to the sea. Wild deer and foxes roam there, and the muted greenery of heather and bracken is studded with the vibrant colours of tiny wildflowers.

There rises Slieve Sidhe, the Fairy Mountain, its heights clothed in rugged beauty. Birds of prey find sanctuary among the most dizzying crags, hard against the sky. The weather is notoriously unpredictable. Sudden gusts of wind and driving rain may lash the land's shoulders at any time.

Half-hidden amidst this bleak beauty crouched an old house, weather-beaten and sturdy. Moss and lichen embroidered the thin crevices of its stone walls. Over the years, the building had withstood the fiercest of storms. When the wind howled across the slate roof and the rain beat against the many-paned windows, it remained a haven of warmth and shelter.

Here, in chaste secrecy, dwelled Rose Westbourne and Keane O'Connell.

Their flight from Charter Hall had paused at the McGinty cottage. As in many of the Allanwell houses, a priest-hide existed under the floor, accessed by a trapdoor. It was in this cramped dungeon, six feet underground, that the couple concealed themselves when men of Squire Westbourne's private militia came galloping to the cottage, swung themselves off their steeds and hammered at the door.

It was as dark as a grave in that windowless pit, and as cold, and as silent, but they cared not. And although cramped, it was long enough for Keane to stretch out his legs. In the darkness, the fugitives dared not even murmur to each other in case they betrayed their presence, but they caressed each other's faces, "seeing" with their fingers, and Rose lightly brushed her lips against the cascade of her sweetheart's hair; that hair so black, even in the darkness, that it seemed to absorb light.

When the search parties went away, the couple emerged.

And what a joyous reunion followed!

In the tiny, smoke-scented kitchen, lit only by the pale flickering of the hearth-fire, Keane and Rose and Ilvenna crowded together with Flynn and Ma McGinty, Keane's own brother Ryan and Flynn's young dog, Senan.

Even the goat Gallytrot, very old and cantankerous and relegated to outdoors, butted her head against the shuttered windows.

In the dim light, Rose and Keane stared wonderingly at each other. They spoke no word, but their looks were saying, "Is it you? I hardly dare to believe it!"

Presently Ma McGinty commanded them to be seated, and offered them hot nettle tea. While they sipped, she stirred a cauldron of porridge that was hanging on a hook over the fire.

There were congratulations and handshakes all round. Keane, pressed close to Rose's side, his arm about her waist, asked after the health of the Delacey family, and all his old acquaintances.

"Ryan is my partner in the business," said Flynn. "Since he returned from sea he lives with us, sleeps in the loft over the stable."

Keane shot his brother a considering look, but made no comment. "I have much to tell you all," he said, "but it will have to wait. The British call me a deserter. You are harbouring me, and for that there is a terrible penalty. Besides, I have no doubt the Westbournes would consider me a kidnapper into the bargain. I cannot stay in this house, endangering my friends."

"I will not be parted from you," declared Rose, wrapping her arms around him. "Where you go, there I go too. Despite—" she broke off and shook her head.

Keane kissed her lightly on her forehead. "Of course! A safe place awaits us, but we must travel far. On the slopes of Slieve Sidhe stands a lonely house where we can find shelter.

McGinty, can you smuggle us past the squire's henchmen to the uplands?"

His friends asked no questions. "Aye," said Flynn. "I can arrange a wain filled with hay, but with a wicker cage stowed beneath the load." The moonshiner was a master at transporting hidden goods.

"That will serve well for Rose, but I'll not hide in the hay like a frightened rabbit," declared Keane. "I will drive the wain."

"Don't be an eejit, mo mhac," said Ryan. "Weariness has addled your brain. What good will it do for Rose if you are recognised? And how do you propose to restore the wain to us here, after deliverin' the cargo?"

Keane had to accept the good sense of his reasoning. With a wry smile he relented. "Ach! Well then, it is the hay for me, too."

"You'll be in fair company," said Ryan.

"I reckon those thick-headed gobdaws will be lookin' for Rose for at least twenty miles around Allanwell," said Ilvenna. "You must stay hidden, the two of yez. Lie low beneat' the hay until you reach the next village, and the next."

"After that," added Ryan, "when you are far beyond us, adopt false names."

Keane rummaged in his knapsack and subtracted a small bag of coins, which he handed to Flynn.

"McGinty, this purse holds our fare. Take as much as you need to hire a wagon and any other sundries."

Flynn subtracted some coins and handed back the clinking bag. "All right, if ye insist. But in return I'll t'ank ye to swap them wooden abominations on yer feet for the spare pair of dacent boots hangin' in me work room."

"You strike a hard bargain," said Keane.

Ma said, "There will be no hidin' in hay wains until you get your strength back, Keane O'Connell. Look at ye! Ye've eyes on you like a scuttered owl. Have ye slept at all this past fortnight? Yez look ill, the both of yez. You'll need to be nursed back to health. Get some porridge into yez, then lie down on the bed. Sleep! We'll keep watch and awaken you if the squire's divils return."

Knowing themselves safe and together at last, Rose and Keane fell asleep in each other's arms as if in some enchanted swoon.

Meanwhile Ma threw some bundles of dried willow-withies into the stream to let them soak. On returning to the kitchen, she mixed some health-giving herbal potions. Ilvenna devoted herself to walking around the cottage, surrounding it with protective "charms". Her brother and Ryan drove the cart over to the neighbour's place to buy some hay with Keane's silver, for Kevin O'Flaherty was the owner of a sizeable haystack.

Once or twice, the Westbourne search parties returned. Senan and Gallytrot noisily alerted the women long before the riders arrived at their door, so there was ample time for Ma to rouse the sleepers and hurry them down into their subterranean place of concealment—the grave that, ironically, sheltered the living.

That afternoon, Rose shed her wedding gown. Standing in her petticoats, she handed the foaming curds of lace and silk to Ilvenna. "I have no use for this," she said. "It's sewn all over with gewgaws of some value, I believe. Take them, please, my dear friend. Take the entire gown. Its the least I can do to thank you for shielding us at your own peril."

Ilvenna held the dress in her two hands and ran her gaze over it speculatively.

"So you won't be returnin' it to the toffs on the hill?" Her tone was half serious, half sardonic.

"No. It was their gift to me, and it's mine to do with as I please. Besides I want no further association with them, even indirectly. If I am wrong in this, may God forgive me."

"I can unpick this rag," Ilvenna said. "I'll separate it into bolts of silk and lace, and smooth them with the flatiron, and sell them at the market. I'll sell those little pearls and gems, too. Together they should fetch a pretty penny. 'Tis is a generous gift."

"I never want to see it again," said Rose with a shudder.

"I have no clothes to offer you in return, except my Sunday best," said Ilvenna. "You are welcome to borrow those. They are not worth a fraction of the cost of this creetur."

So Rose exchanged her wedding dress, temporarily, for Ilvenna's practical attire.

CHAPTER 23

The McGintys' Cottage

Ma was sitting on a stool outside the front door weaving willow withies and the O'Connell brothers had just come in from the stable when Gallytrot began to bleat beneath the apple tree. Ilvenna jumped up and ran to the window, while Keane and Rose unlidded the trapdoor in the kitchen floor.

Ma put her head in at the door. "Wait!" she called to the couple, who stood poised to descend into their living grave once more. "Miss Rose, 'tis your father and your sister, coming down the path with Flynn."

Flynn opened the door. In stepped John Delacey and his daughter Elizabeth. To an unenlightened observer, they might have appeared to be simply paying their respects to the McGintys, or bringing clothes to be mended, or carrying a round, ripe cheese in a basket, as payment for some remedy.

Rose and Lizzie flew into each other's arms while Delacey quietly stood aside. Presently Rose embraced her father, resting her head against his chest. Tears fell.

"Dear one! Dear one!" he cried, overcome with emotion. He bent his grizzled head towards her. "You are safe! Oh, heaven be praised! I am overjoyed to see you safe and well. I cannot begin to describe the distress we felt last night, your sisters and I, when we heard you were missing. We all joined the searchers, not waiting to change out of our wedding finery, traipsing over the hills getting snagged on the gorse and briars. At last we went home and sought our beds, exhausted. This morning, who should come softly to our door but Master McGinty, with a happy message. And here we are."

As he mentioned Flynn's name, Lizzie turned away to stare fixedly at the fire on Ma's hearth, and began twirling a loose strand of hair around her finger.

Obliviously, her father continued, "But Rosie, why did you run away last night? I cannot understand it. We were all so jolly at the wedding feast!"

"Dear Papa," Rose said, "I am glad you never guessed the truth. But now is the time for you to know."

And she told him the whole story of how Edwin had persuaded her to accept his hand in marriage in return for financing his journey to the Well of St Mungo to be healed.

"I never wanted to marry Edwin," she said in conclusion. "But he said that he would help you, and he told me my betrothed was dead."

222

As she spoke, John Delacey's face shrank in on itself until it appeared grey and deep-graven, like weathered basalt. He looked aghast as he fumbled dazedly for a stool and lowered himself into it.

Ma poured a tot of Flynn's whiskey and thumped it down on the table in front of him, but he waved it away.

"No thank you, Mrs McGinty. I need my wits." He shook his head. "I needed my wits a long time ago. How could I have been so blind?"

"It's not that you were blind, Papa," said Rose, "it's that I hid the truth from you. From everyone except my sisters, Ilvenna and Ma! They kept my secret. No one else knew why I was getting married, though some may have suspected."

"You kept your secret well, my dear," he said despondently. "I had no idea you were unhappy. Indeed, I felt that you were changed, quieter and more contemplative—but I deemed it was the significance of your forthcoming wedding that wrought this effect on you. I thought it only natural for nerves to affect a bride-to-be. How misguided was I, how ill-judged. How inadequately I know my own daughter. I see now that I have brought terrible sorrow upon you, my dear. Had I known that you agreed to your wedding only to obtain my treatment, I would have forbidden the match."

"That is why I kept it from you."

"And to think I believed the Westbournes paid my fares out of kindness! The truth is, my life has been bought at the expense of yours."

"Never say that, dear Papa! What's done is done, and you are hale again."

John Delacey continued, "Somehow I must compensate you. But for now, Katherine and Margaret are impatient to see you, Rose my dear, and so is Mary, but Master McGinty advised them not to come at all. The whole family visiting together, or even separately in one day, would attract too much attention, and Westbourne's men are still searching, you know."

"They will search for a long time." The voice that spoke from the shadows was deep and musical.

John Delacey looked around blinking, as if seeing the kitchen and its occupants for the first time. His gaze lit on a tall figure leaning upon the water-barrel at Rose's back.

"And who is this gentleman visiting your house, Mrs McGinty? A stranger, I think?" Delacey eyed the young man a little warily.

Rose said, "It is my love! He lives!"

Delacey jumped to his feet with an exclamation. "Good God. O'Connell! Is it you indeed? Why, I did not know you beneath those whiskers!"

With a radiant smile he extended his hand warmly towards Keane, and who grasped it firmly in token of friendship.

"The whiskers do not suit him," commented Ryan. "He used to be pretty. Now he looks like a bear."

His banter caused a ripple of laughter among the gathering.

"They're itchy," said Keane with a smile. "I'd fain shave them."

Noting the way Rose clung to the young man, and the tender looks they exchanged, Delacey grasped the depth of the love that existed between them; a love that had outlasted seven years of separation.

"My darling saved me," said Rose, smiling up at her sweetheart.

"You have done well, young man," Delacey said to Keane. "Though alas, I fear 'tis too late. She's another man's wife."

"In name only," said Keane.

"In the sight of God and the law," Delacey replied heavily. "And that means something."

"It means Edwin Westbourne can be my jailer," said Rose, with an edge of both fear and defiance in her tone, "if he catches me."

Everyone was aware of the rights all men exercised over their wives from the instant they were married. As Rose's husband, Edwin Westbourne now had the legal right to control her personal freedoms. She would require his permission to leave home, travel, buy or sell any property or visit her friends and relations. He even had the right to beat her, if he so chose.

"I cared little about losing my freedom when I thought I had lost you forever, my love," she said to Keane, "but now everything has changed! I hope never to see that gentleman again."

Ilvenna broke in, "Rose darlin', have you considered, you could get the marriage annulled that is, if—" she broke off awkwardly.

"That gentleman never laid a finger on me," Rose said calmly, showing no embarrassment. "The marriage has not been consummated."

Her father's face lit up. "Ah yes, an annulment!" he exclaimed. Then his face fell again and he added, "Yet if we claimed an annulment and Westbourne chose to contest it, he has the wealth to hire the most expensive and powerful lawyers in the land. We would be unable to find one to match them. He would most probably win."

"How likely is it, Rosie," said Lizzie, "that he would want to keep you as his wife?"

Rose could not help laughing. "Oh, you mean after I have been so cold and disagreeable to him all this time? Only you could say such a thing, Lizzie." She enveloped her sister in an affectionate embrace. "I'll warrant the squire's family views me as damaged goods now. He might well want to be rid of me! Perhaps there is hope after all!"

"Then yez don't know the Westbournes," said Ma McGinty grimly. "That Edwin can seem a charmer, but he's like his father—a gentleman who will not be stopped when he sets his heart on getting' somet'in'. And when he gets it, he will not let it go. He will try to keep you, Rose, without payin' attention to your transgressions, as he sees it. But beware, for if he does get you back in his clutches, maybe he'll seek revenge."

226

"I think Master Edwin would not harm you, Rosie," ventured Lizzie. "I think he really loves you."

Ma gave her a black look. "They're not capable of love, dem Sasunachs."

"There must be no talk of Rose goin' back," said Keane. "Pray accept this gift, sir." He placed in John Delacey's hands the same coin-filled purse he had offered Flynn. "In the employ of the French army I saved some silver. It will provide a few comforts for your family. Nay!" he added with a smile, noting Rose's frown. "Tis no bride-price! I would not have ye bought and sold!"

John gently returned the bag. "Have no fear, Mr O'Connell, we do not need your silver, though I am grateful for the offer. Since you've been away I have been working as a land agent, managing properties and collecting rents on behalf of some of the large landowners around here. Some might say it's a job beneath my station, but it puts food on the table."

"Yet," said Keane, "when the Westbournes cease treating you as family, 'tis likely ye will need financial help."

John Delacey shook his head. "Now that we are officially connected to the Westbournes by marriage it behoves them to ensure we are well clothed and fed, even if the bride is no longer living beneath their roof. If by marriage a husband gains rights over a wife, he also gains obligations to her family. I believe the squire will not shirk these responsibilities and risk his social standing. They will consider themselves obliged to look after us."

"Your opinion of them is higher than mine, sir," said Keane accepting the return of the purse. "My offer of help remains, nonetheless, if ever you need it."

Delacey nodded his head.

"We brought some of your clothes for you, Rosie," said Lizzie. From her basket she produced a brown, ankle-length skirt made of wool, paired with a loose-fitting linen blouse. The blouse had a simple, modest neckline, and the sleeves were gathered at the wrist. There was also a sleeveless woollen vest and a green shawl fastened with a pin. Rose thanked her sister with a kiss.

"What are your plans?" John Delacey asked Keane.

The young man hesitated, scanning the faces that surrounded him in the dim recesses of the small chamber—his brother Ryan, Ilvenna, weaving a tiny four armed cross from rushes, Flynn, Ma, John Delacey and Lizzie.

He said, "I am about to put a secret in your company that is capable of endangerin' the man who made this reunion possible. This story must not go further than the walls o' this house. Agreed?"

All those present undertook to keep the secret, whereupon, in as few words as possible, Keane described his last meeting with his mentor, Jules Fournier, a Chef de Brigade in the French Revolutionary Army. The scene was vivid before his mind's eye, and the voice of the Frenchman lucid in his ears.

"When you find your girl in Ireland and marry 'er," Fournier had said, "then you travel discreetly together to—'ow they say—the Irish 'igh country. Tell your destination only to the most loyal few! It is a mountain called Sleeve She."

"Slieve Sidhe? The Fairy Mountain?" Keane O'Connell had interjected.

"Oui, oui. That sounds right. Mon dieu you Irish, your language is unpronounceable."

The Frenchman went on to explain that in order to reach a secure habitation, far from pursuers, Keane and his companion must follow a dusty, winding road called the Green Lane that ascended this mountain. It led to a remote estate, where stood a house that was almost deserted.

By the time they arrived there, the house's steward should have in his hands a message from Fournier's London contacts, the owners of the mountain estate, ordering him to give shelter to the fugitives.

"You will be safe in zat place, as long as you are careful not to give away your secrets!"

O'Connell thanked his benefactor with enthusiasm, until Fournier waved his hand dismissively. "Enough! You give me too much credit. You sink I 'elp you for nossing? One day maybe I call on you to return the favour. Favours, zat is 'ow we live these days. Nossing is really free."

In the firelit kitchen Ma McGinty clapped her hands softly. "That Frenchman is a grand fellow indeed, so he is!" she exclaimed, and all those present concurred.

"We will go there in secret," said Keane. "No one else must be knowin' where we are bound."

"It sounds a splendid plan," said Delacey. "Are you happy with it, Rose?"

She nodded, smiling.

"And this vacant house, does it have a name?" her father enquired of Keane.

"Certainly, sir," was the reply. "Heatherhill, it is called."

"Heatherhill!" exclaimed Ilvenna, startling Flynn's dog who lay on the hearthrug. "But that is the most haunted house in Ireland!"

Keane shrugged. "Maybe that it is," he said. "But if fear is on folk before that place, 'tis a boon for us, because there is no soul dwellin' there except for one old Scottish steward and a housekeeper."

He returned his attention to Rose's father. "Sir, to put your heart at ease, let me assure you that Rose will live honourably in that place! We will be respectful of her marriage vows. She and I will not live as man and wife, that I vow. There will be, no doubt, some outbuildin' where I can lay my head. I am not sayin' 'twill be easy to live in that manner, but at least if she is safe, I will be content, that I will."

Rose blinked away a tear. "Papa, I promised Mama never to lie with any man but my husband. You can believe it. I will honour her last wish!"

Overcome with emotion, Delacey could not look at her. He merely folded his daughter in his arms.

Rose asked Ma McGinty for some paper so that she could write letters to Katherine, Margaret and Mary, but Flynn advised against it. "Put not'in' in writing, Mistress Rose. Tell your father and sister what you wish to say, and they can deliver your messages."

Rose saw the sense in that, and complied.

By the time night fell, despite all precautions, word of unusual doings had spread around Allanwell. Everyone wanted to know where Flynn and Ryan had found the money to buy a cartload of hay from O'Flaherty, and what they intended to do with it.

The villagers knew something was afoot, and suspected it related to the sudden disappearance of the squire's son's bride. Squire Westbourne had put it abut that she had been forcibly abducted, but they preferred the conjecture that she had run away. The notion that the squire's son had been rejected delighted them. They revelled in the discomfort of their enemies.

They'd not breathe a word to outsiders about their suspicions that the McGintys were somehow involved in the scandal. They were used to secrets, and this was merely another one they pledged to keep. For, said they, they must stay loyal to each other, standing shoulder to shoulder against the common foe.

CHAPTER 24

Flight

On that last evening, still keeping an ear cocked for intruders, Rose and Keane sat with the McGintys by the kitchen hearth, taking their supper. Keane described his life during the past seven years, and Ryan spoke of his own adventures.

It was in April 1794 that Ryan had left Allanwell in search of his brother taken by the Royal Navy. In an attempt to track down the ship H.M.S. Conqueror, he had joined the Irish merchant navy. Hindsight revealed that his decision had been misguided, but at the time he could conjecture no other way to follow Keane across the high seas. His search turned out to be fruitless but in the course of it he travelled far, to exotic lands.

As part of the Empire, Ireland's ports were an important part of the British shipping network. Ryan crewed a merchant vessel that voyaged back and forth between the United

Kingdom and South America carrying cargoes such as tobacco, sugar, coffee, precious metals, spices and indigo. For five years he sailed the oceans of the world and, over time, he accumulated a pocketful of gold and silver coins.

"I lived hard but well for five years, and at the end I never found my brother but at least I had something to show for my work," he said. "I've no doubt this charm played a part in it." He smiled at Ilvenna and touched the amber talisman that lay upon his breastbone, depending from a slim metal chain around his neck.

"I was glad to see you hadn't lost it," she said.

In 1799 Ryan gave up hope of finding Keane. Acting on the assumption that if his brother were still living he would one day find his way back to Allanwell, he returned to the village and rejoined Flynn in his clandestine distilling operations, his lavender-growing, and his market-trading. He even learned the rudiments of shoe-making.

"We was doin' well," said Ilvenna. "Plenty of payin' customers, and food on the table. But himself"—she glanced at Ryan—"he was never really happy. I could tell, in spite of what he said. We used to see him up on Madigan's Leap of an evenin', all alone, lookin' out to sea."

"Not always alone," said Ryan. "Others sometimes get the courage to go up there—those who lost boys to the impress men. Mrs Rafferty is up there every second day. As if starin' could bring anyone back."

"All three Rafferty boys are still at sea, then?" asked Keane.

"Not so," his brother replied, "for the elder two were released after five years of service. They disembarked at the port o' Dublin and had to find their own way back here, but they arrived wit' two years of navy pay in their pockets, for the Admiralty wit'held it from them until the last day, to discourage desertion. Ye should have seen the faces on their Ma and Pa when them two lads came saunterin' down the main street."

"Why didn't Colm come back wit' them?"

"Well, he survived the navy, and he stepped off at Dublin too, but in that harbour a well-regarded merchant captain was huntin' for seasoned hands, and he offerin' a damn sight better pay than the Sasunach Navy, so Colm signed up and sailed off. Ye'd think he'd had his fill of the briny, but no, he said it suited him. Told his brothers to pass his regards to his parents and tell 'em he'd come home with a bag of gold one day. So Mrs Rafferty sometimes trots up on the Leap to see if any likely-looking ships are comin' in. To tell ye the trut', I reckon she's gone a bit touched after all the trials she's been through."

"I prefer to keep me distance from Madigan's Leap meself," said Ma, who was knitting a scarf as she listened to the conversation. "Too many spooks and bogles for me taste."

"Some folk have heard keenin' coming from up there," murmured Flynn, winding up some yarn for his mother, "and Aileen Rafferty swears she saw a young lass walkin' along

235

the cliff edge, holdin' a babe in her arms, only she could see right through the bot' of them to the sky beyond."

"That's as may be," said Ilvenna briskly. "Speakin' o' ghosts, take these charms, you two, and keep them wit' you always. I wove them meself, wit' rushes from our own stream." She showed Rose and Keane two amulets, each in the shape of a four-armed cross. "These'll shield ye against fire, lightnin', and evil spirits. At Heatherhill yez'll be needin' charms that ward off ghosts, and these are as powerful as I can craft them, for I wove spells into 'em."

"Thank you," said Rose, accepting the gifts, "though I'll admit, I only half believe in ghosts, and Keane declares they do not frit him at all!"

Ilvenna and her mother were expert basket-weavers. They were used to making willow coffins for Allanwell's dead—wood being quite costly—and the frame for a wicker cage was not much different, only the weave was far more open, to allow the free flow of air for the living. The cage was shaped like a wide sarcophagus, with a flat base and a low hooped vault of a ceiling. It was wide enough for two, or even three people to lie down in, with space enough to move around a little.

Flynn and Keane laid the wicker frame on a bed of hay on the cart's floor.

Next morning, just before dawn, Ma lined the cage with a swathe of drugget. She placed into it a parcel of food and drink, and a simple linen bonnet for Rose. The two fugitives crawled inside with their few belongings, and Flynn covered the framework with hay to hide the occupants from prying eyes.

"Tight as a pair of bugs in a rug," said Ilvenna with satisfaction.

Only she, Ryan and Ma watched them depart. Too large a gathering could attract the wrong kind of attention—the squire's hired men were still scouring the village and its surroundings, hunting for Rose.

About a mile out of Allenwell, Flynn's cart rounded a bend in the hedge-lined lane and there, blocking its path, milled a band of horsemen, muskets bristling threateningly from their hands.

"Halt!" a voice rang out.

Flynn whistled to Clover and pulled gently on the reins, bringing her to a halt. He knew these riders at once by their navy blue livery and tricorne hats—Westbourne's henchmen, in pursuit of quarry.

CHAPTER 25

The Roadblock

Tipping his cap politely to the armed men, Flynn arranged his mouth into an affable, slightly vacant grin. "Top o' the mornin' to ye, gentlemen," he said, deliberately employing an expression nobody but eejits ever used.

"What have you got there, fellow?" the captain demanded, walking his mount closer to the cart.

"Hay."

"Really?" the rider looked both contemptuous and disbelieving. "Why are you carting hay at this time of year? And where are you going? It's not haymaking season, is it?"

"Well now, yer honour, it's always a good time to be prepared, isn't it?" said Flynn in a humble and rather half-witted manner. "Ye're right enough, of course, beggin' yer honour's pardon, but the winter months have been cruel. Now that spring's here the cattle are headin' out to the fresh grass, but there's not enough new growt' yet, so we must bring 'em some of the stored hay."

He plucked up a dry straw that chanced to lie near him on the seat, placed it between his lips and began to chew, in the hope that he might more closely resemble an ignorant clod-hopper.

"What's your name, fellow?"

"Pogue Mahoney, yer honour," lied Flynn.

"Have you passed any strangers on the road?"

"No sir."

"Are you certain?"

"Yes sir."

The men, grim-faced, continued to point their muskets at the rustic driver, while their captain rode slowly around the body of the cart, prodding at the hay with his sword.

Flynn's lips did not move, and the reins hung loosely in his hands. He gave no sign that he was, in fact, silently praying.

Presently the captain trotted back to his men and shouted an order. The riders parted, drawing back to either side of the road, and the captain waved his sword to indicate that Flynn might pass.

"All right," he said, though with no less suspicion in his tone. "Drive on."

Flynn forced himself not to turn his head to look behind as he drove down the road, but the back of his neck prickled, and the effort riveted his shoulders to iron.

An hour later he deemed it safe enough to stop the vehicle beside a stream to allow Clover to drink. The fugitives emerged to stretch their legs, and it was then that Flynn saw the line of red embroidery stitched down the side of Keane's face.

"'Tis but a scratch," said Keane, wiping the blood with his fingers. "A blade penetrated the hay, but thanks be to Our Lady, Rose is unscathed."

On trundled the wain. They travelled slowly, for Flynn was ever aware of his passengers' comfort and did his best to keep the cart steady on the pot-holed roads. When it rained, he drew a canvas sheet over the load. At nights he pulled the cart to the roadside and they all crawled in beneath the cover to sleep, while Clover stood tethered. They dared not stop at any inn or tavern.

At the foot of Slieve Sidhe they passed through a straggling village that seemed permeated with a mildly disturbing air of smugness. From there, the road steeply ascended the mountainside, and they began to climb with it. At last, after a laborious two-week journey on the rutted roads, they were approaching their potential sanctuary.

CHAPTER 26

Heatherhill House

As they ascended the rugged and winding way called the Green Lane, the air cooled and the greenery of the lowlands gave way to low-growing juniper, bog-myrtle, heather, gorse and bilberry.

Clover was hard put to haul the wain up that steep incline, so Keane and Rose alighted and walked alongside. They trusted that it was safe enough, now, to show their faces. For many miles the only other travellers they had encountered beneath that wind-raked sky were hedgehogs, grouse and ptarmigans. Falcons wheeled overhead.

The unpaved road was narrow and quite perilous, clinging vertiginously to the mountainside. On one hand the land fell away in a sheer drop, while to on the other a steep cliff wall rose. Spectacular views spread out as far as the eye could see—rolling hills blanketed in heather and studded with weathered rocks; far-off peaks thrusting up like jagged pillars supporting the sky, girt by swathes of mist and cloud.

To the west, the afternoon sun rinsed the hills in a sanguine glow. Shadows lengthened across the valleys. Far below, nestled into the foothills, the cottages of Drumnaveen looked like miniature toys, their white-washed walls and thatched roofs barely visible from this height.

A high stone wall loomed at the roadside. In it, a black iron gate all wrought with lilies.

Two stunted yews grew on either side of this gate, the foliage of the trees being as dark as the spaces between stars. As the visitors approached, a hullabaloo of barking and yapping erupted. Four brawny Irish wolfhounds lunged at the ironmongery, shaking and rattling the gate on its hinges. A harsh voice rang out in command, and the dogs fell silent, though through the railings they could be seen to remain alert, fixated on the newcomers, and panting. A figure materialised from the shadows beside them; a tall, gaunt man, pale and rather stooped, with a hawk's bill nose and glittering eyes.

"Fa are ye?" this man enquired sourly.

Keane O'Connell strode forward. He introduced himself and his companions and explained their business.

The gatekeeper of Heatherhill House was a suitably dour-faced Scotsman whose gaze seemed perpetually disapproving. Clearly blind to the remarkable comeliness of Keane and the intense scrutiny of Flynn, he stared censoriously at Rose's hay-speckled dress and disheveled hair, but made no comment.

"Hamish MacTavish is my name," he announced. After some further conversation the steward bade the hounds stand aside, and permitted the newcomers to enter.

The house, sturdy and imposing, had gathered about itself a large, ill-tended garden within a low wall of hewn stones. Frugal windows squinted from high up beneath the eaves. A cobbled courtyard and blocky stables adjoined the house, and the weed-infested roof of a small cottage peeped from behind. On the slope rising at the rear, a pair of donkeys could be seen grazing in a field.

Flynn McGinty led Clover to the stables to unharness her and rub her down, while Keane and Rose followed MacTavish indoors.

The houses's elaborate decor might have been fashionable early in the last century but years of use had frayed and abraded it. Richly patterned papers—unevenly faded—and threadbare tapestries adorned the walls. Moulting rugs and animal skins lay scattered on floors of polished wood or flagstones.

When Flynn came in from the stables, MacTavish bade the three newcomers seat themselves at a long dining-table in a spacious chamber. Ornaments and knick-knacks cluttered the mantel over a cavernous fireplace, in which a small fire flickered brightly but failed to emit much heat.

A small, dark woman appeared and served the guests with plates of shepherd's pie. Apparently as impervious as the steward to any notable characteristics of the guests, she wordlessly nodded in acknowledgment of them before vanishing through a hitherto unnoticed doorway.

The steward named the retreating woman as the housekeeper, Nest Priddy.

"'Tis anely the twaa o' us here," intoned the Scot. He stood watching his guests as they dined, his hands behind his back, in the manner of a clergyman observing his flock. "Anely the twa. "Aat is, if ye dinna coont th' hounds 'n' th' donkeys." As an afterthought he added, "And the wee ghosties."

"Ah yes," said Rose, scooping mashed potato into her spoon. She glanced sideways at Keane, with mirthful skepticism. "We have heard that Heatherhill is the most haunted house in Ireland."

"That is whit folk say, aye," said the steward.

"But they do not trouble ye and Mrs Priddy?" Flynn asked.

He scowled. "Nay. They dinnae trouble th' likes o' us. They ken wur friends o' th' hoose. Mind, if ye're no' a friend o' th' hoose they'll trouble ye reet enough."

Rose brushed her fingertips against the four-armed St Brigid's cross on its leather lace, dangling at her throat, Ilvenna's charm against malign forces.

"Be warned," intoned MacTavish as he showed his guests around the premises after dinner, holding up a candlestick in his pale claw to light their path in the dim and echoing spaces. "'Tis is easy tae lose yer way. Ower th' decades, Heatherhill's owners hae added muckle rooms, some hidden 'n' secret."

The house's two floors were connected by staircases in unexpected places, tucked away in corners, or hidden behind doors. MacTavish informed the guests that the number of staircases was hard to measure, because each time anyone counted them, the result was different. The rooms were well-furnished, with large tables, chairs, and cabinets of dark wood, and adorned with elaborate carvings. A few family portraits hung on the walls, in addition to various dilapidated hunting trophies—animal heads, or antlers. There was even a small chapel for private worship. It was hard to locate, being at the heart of the house's labyrinthine ways.

The steward pointed out a low door. "Behind this wee postern is th' arsenal. It is yin o' mah duties tae maintain th' weapons. Th' exterior doors and windaes o' this hoose ur kept locked 'n' barred at a' times."

He evidently derived much satisfaction from his unsettling pronouncements.

Large four-poster beds occupied the bedchambers, furnished with feather mattresses and piled high with blankets and quilts. MacTavish designated a small one for Flynn, with which he was greatly pleased, it being bigger than any room he'd ever occupied.

"This bedroom is duin fur ye." MacTavish shoved open another heavy door. He made as if to enter a larger chamber, then suddenly spun on his heel, throwing a soft glare of candle-light into the eyes of his guests. Peering searchingly at Rose and Keane he demanded, "Ye'r man and guidwife then, ur ye? The chevalier wrote in his letter that ye wur merrit."

"We are not," said Keane O'Connell.

MacTavish looked down his long nose, drew himself up to his full height and took a deep breath. "I'll hae na—" he began.

Keane interjected, "We will not be livin' as man and wife, Mr MacTavish. Pray, do not distress yourself. I will occupy the room furthest from Mistress Rose, or even a separate residence. The stables maybe, or that cottage at the rear of the house, if 'tis vacant."

The steward's shoulders relaxed.

"Weel," he said, peering at Keane condemningly from beneath his bushy eyebrows, "If ye'll want th' auld gamekeeper's cottage you can stay there, though 'tis riddled wi' foosty 'n' spiders 'n' haunted tae boot."

"It sounds like just the place," said Keane.

The following day, Keane and Flynn unloaded the cart, after which the latter departed for Allanwell. Rose and Keane stood at the iron gate watching him as he climbed up to the driver's seat and whistled to Clover. The mare started forward down the hill, and soon the cart disappeared around a bend in the road.

Careless of what the future might bring, the young couple settled down to life at Heatherhill, she in the house, he in the old gamekeeper's cottage. Their happiness, despite their situation, was boundless. They were in each other's company, and that, for the moment, was the only matter of consequence.

The servant Nest Priddy, made a foray into the house's large wardrobes and emerged with a number of garments for Rose to try.

"They be out o' fashion by now, Oi shouldn't wonder," she said, holding up a gown, "but they be clothes just roight for a gen'lewoman to wear, be'er than that 'ere farm frock ye're in. Choose two or three sets, if 'n' ye see fit. No one wears 'em any more. Oi believe that Ma'am de Mandeville 'as clean forgot about 'em. Oi've no doubt that if 'n' she remembered, she'd order me to get rid of 'em."

Rose was delighted to select two chemise gowns—one of pale blue cotton, the other of creamy linen—with fitted bodices, small bustles, and full skirts raised at the sides into a polonaise puff. The sleeves were also puffed at the shoulders. There was an apricot-coloured cape for outdoor wear, and two pairs of high-fronted shoes that fastened at the arch. To pin upon her hair there was a choice of seven day-caps of white linen and lace.

MacTavish gave Keane some of his old, much-mended clothes. "I suppose, sin ye've come 'ere with naught but the sark on yer back I'd better be a guid Christian 'n' clothe ye."

"I'm obliged to ye Mr MacTavish," said Keane. "I'll repay ye with any work you choose to give me."

Night and day, high altitude winds moaned and sighed around the house and its outbuildings, poking their invisible fingers into every cranny, causing doors to creak and bang, keening in the hollows of the chimneys and rattling the window frames. On odd occasions, low murmurings that resembled the chattering of voices seemed to arise from the kitchen, and sometimes, when the night held its breath, a shrill, high-pitched note drilled through the darkness like the scream of a child. Perhaps Rose and Keane were oblivious of these phenomena as they basked in their freedom together, for at nights their sleep was profound.

Keane set to work clearing the weeds off the slate roof of the gamekeeper's cottage, and repairing the gaps where rain water trickled in. Rose took a broom to the place, sweeping out the dust and spiders. The guard dogs, now accepting them as friends, gamboled and frisked around them as they went about their tasks.

April passed, and May, and June. Visitors rarely ventured to Heatherhill. Once a fortnight a cart, laden with supplies, wended its way up the Green Lane from the straggling, smug village of Drumnaveen at the foot of the mountain. Foley, the driver, was the keeper of the local inn, and his spindly young lad sat at his side.

MacTavish had made desultory attempts to grow vegetables in the windswept gardens surrounding the house, resulting in large crops of weeds and potatoes, and not much else.

"Would ye be wantin' some help in the garden Mr MacTavish?" Keane asked.

"Aye," was the gruff reply.

The young man pulled out handfuls of dock, thistles and nettles. He drove posts into the ground and wove willow hurdles, fashioning a wicker fence as a buffer against the mountain winds. He planted hawthorn bushes, so that when the thorn hedges grew tall and the hurdles weathered away to dust, there would be a living barrier to protect the plants. He and Rose sowed seeds of herbs and vegetables, which sprouted and burgeoned. The garden began to flourish. Rose enjoyed working outdoors at his side every day in the cool mountain air. Their happiness was so intense that they frequently gave voice to it with song, their voices weaving ballads or sea shanties into the mountain wind.

In summer's heat, Keane worked shirtless, dripping with sweat, the sun's rays sprinkling cinnamon on his arms. It was thus that Rose noted the compass rose tattoo at his shoulder.

"'Tis a charm for luck and guidance," he explained, "or so the sailors told me. I fancied it guided me to your window, that night I found ye. But maybe that was a pipe-dream. Probably it has no power."

"Probably it has!" she exclaimed. "You told me it guided you to Captain Fournier and his fusiliers when first you escaped from the navy, and without Fournier's help you might never have come home."

He acknowledged the truth of that.

From time to time, Keane lessoned Rose in the use of firearms. "In case you ever need to defend yourself," he explained. She became proficient in the loading and firing of pistols, and when she shot at paper targets hung from a tree, her aim was true.

Occasionally Keane would pick the tiny, bright wildflowers that hid in the grasses and fashion floral crowns for Rose to wear. Other times he would rest his head in her lap while she combed the long ebony strands of his hair with her fingers, and chaffed him about his whiskers.

"Who lives behind that furze bush?' she teased. "You look completely different now. Even I did not recognise you, and I have known your features for most of my life. I have not truly seen your face for seven years. I wonder what you look like now. Maybe by chance you're actually handsome under there!"

"Assuredly!" he riposted.

If their joy was all-pervading, so was so was their unrequitable passion. This, they never discussed, and indeed they affected not to notice, but at times they pressed their hands together, trembling, or lay silently among the ferns in each others' embrace. The eagle eyes of the steward glittered from a high window beneath the eaves, as he kept virtuous watch on them.

Sometimes the young man would go running up the mountainside to the steep places where cascades draped themselves like quicksilver ribbons from the rocks. There he would plunge into the snow-melt and let icy threads course down his body, gasping at the shock of it.

The steward and the housekeeper did not fail to note the plight of their young guests. The woman felt sorry for them, and even MacTavish was almost moved to pity—almost, but not quite, because he believed that folk brought their own punishments down upon themselves, and people deserved their suffering. "Whit's fur ye'll no go past ye,"was one of his favourite sayings, meaning "you will get what you deserve." He felt piously satisfied that he himself was immune from sins of the flesh.

The two lovers kept company throughout every day, only parting at nights. Keane had brought a spyglass with him in his backpack, on his return to Ireland. This he gave to Rose, so that she might watch for danger when he was not at her side.

After the evening meal they would sit by the fire in the enormous main room. He told stories of his adventures at sea—the battles, the storms, the weird lights and strange visions. She recounted folktales she had learned from Mary and her mother, and tales of her own making in addition. Often, the housekeeper and the steward would steal in to listen discreetly from the corner, but as time passed their aloofness waned, and they openly joined the fireside gathering.

Eventually MacTavish and Priddy began to contribute stories, particularly about the ghosts of Heatherhill.

"You'll hear them mair often than you see them," said the Scotsman with relish. "There's the banshee, wha kin at times be heard shrieking thro' th' corridors, 'n' ye kin hear th' voices of former servants in th' scullery. Ye micht hear a phantom horse and carriage pullin' up ootside this once great hoose. Then there's th' slamming of doors, and th' sudden blowing-out of candles whin there's na draught. 'N' if you hear the voice o' a bairn screaming, laughing 'n' singing in th' deid o' nicht, that's wee Harriet, wha fell tae her death while playing oan th' stairs in 1861."

"And in the chapel," put in Priddy, "ye can sometimes 'ear the sound o' a pipe organ playin', or the chantin' o' voices insoide the walls. Though the place is empty! There ain't a day at 'eather'ill that Oi doesn't feel that there's summat or someone there with me. In some parts of the 'ouse Oi've seen abjects moved in front of moi oies!"

Not to be outdone MacTavish said, "I meself hae seen th' Red Lady carrying a dagger up th' back stairs."

"Oi seen 'er walkin' through walls," said Priddy, raising the stakes.

"'n' I've seen th' ghost o' a Spanish minstrel wha wis shipwrecked aff th' Irish coast," countered the steward.

"No yaw ain't," said Priddy. "'ow would a shipwrecked ghost get up this 'ere mountain?"

"Hmph," said the steward stiffly. "I beg tae differ."

Priddy eyed him with an air of mild annoyance.

"At any rate, that's how come fowk seldom come 'ere," said MacTavish. "They're afeard o' th' ghosts."

The four human inhabitants of Heatherhill House sat for a while without speaking, listening to the crackling chorus of the fire and the fluting of the wind in the eaves.

"And whenever travellers do pass through the village down below," said Priddy presently, "not that many ever do pass this way, moind—the village folk do tell 'em aboot our 'auntin's."

"The village of Drumnaveen?" queried Rose.

"Aye thats roight, Drumnaveen at the foot of the mountain. The people there allus tells their most 'orrifyin' ghost stories to passin' travellers. 'Tis tradition."

"And they got another tradition too," said the Scot.

"What might that be?" asked Keane.

"They git a special breid they bake thare, at the inn. A specialty o' th' local area, it is. They ca' it bitterblack."

"That's a curious name for bread. Why's that?"

"Because 'tis bitter. And black."

A companionable silence intervened.

"And they bakes a laif fur travellers, sometimes," added the steward.

"Not for us, they didn't," said Keane.

"Thats fur ye didn't stoap there fur th' nicht. An' forbye, ye wis hidden under some hay 'n' they didn't see you. But even if they did see you," said MacTavish, "they micht nae hae gi'en ye th' bitterblack."

"Why not?"

"Because it depends an their opinion o' ye," said Priddy, "whether they give you tha' 'ere rye loaf or not."

Rose and Keane remained mystified as to the nature of this strange rural tradition, but there was that about

MacTavish's report which felt disquieting, and they refrained from requesting elaboration.

Instead Keane said, "Mr MacTavish, pray tell us about Heatherhill's owner."

"Ah, you mean Monsieur le Chevalier de Mandeville," said MacTavish. "But I thought ye wur acquainted wi' th' master. 'twas he wha sent th' letter bidding us shelter twa fugitives, wax-sealed wi' his ain crest."

"We don't know him," said Keane.

MacTavish gave him a vinegary look. "Well I'll ask nae questions," he said at length. "Hearken 'n' I'll tell ye of his ways."

The house, he explained, was in the possession of a noble French family by the name of de Mandeville. Percy, the Chevalier de Mandeville, now abiding in in London, was a powerful man aged in his sixties, who was held high in the esteem of King George III.

Percy had a sister called Genevieve. Before the revolution, when the family was still living in Paris, she had—against her father's will—married beneath her station. In high dudgeon her father, Louis, cut her off without a penny. Genevieve and her husband, who was far from wealthy, were cast out and forced to live penuriously in a small rural village in France. Genevieve's brother Percy, however, felt sorry for her and made it a habit to send her money, discreetly, from time to time.

Genevieve bore a son, who they christened Jules. He grew up with scant knowledge of his relatives. Their family name was Fournier, a peasant name, so that when the revolution erupted, they remained relatively safe from persecution. None of their neighbours were aware of their aristocratic connection, so none could betray them. As for the de Mandevilles in Paris, however— that was another story. They were marked for the guillotine.

Seigneur Louis was seized and executed, and had it not been for the courage and wit of Percy's nephew Jules, the rest of the de Mandeville family would have suffered the same fate.

It was Jules Fournier who, risking the revelation of his own identity, saved his cousins from the guillotine and smuggled them out of France; Seigneur Percy—now the Chevalier de Mandeville—and his wife Marguerite, and their son Henri and daughter Louise.

The de Mandevilles forfeited their French property to the revolutionary government, but they were already the owners of a house in London, and another in Ireland. Long ago they were wont to use Heatherhill as a hunting lodge but now it stood empty, watched over by the steward and the housekeeper.

"Now Fournier's secret becomes clear," Keane murmured to Rose. "He has aristo blood in his veins, so he does. Such a secret could be lethal if it came to the ears of the Directory."

On Friday evenings, MacTavish played the fiddle. Priddy looked on in mute delight as Rose taught Keane how to perform the stately dance known as the minuet. Afterwards,

Rose played pretty folk-tunes on the harp—though its strings often went out of tune due to lack of regular maintenance—while Keane whirled Priddy around the floor in vigorous jigs and reels, accompanied by MacTavish clapping his hands. The steward refused to exert himself as far as to tap his toes, but fortunately he did not view dancing as sinful. "I dinna foot it myse', but I don't begrudge healthy exercise in others."

Rose and Keane reveled in their time together in their mountain sanctuary. It was a period of immense joy, but like blossom in springtime, it was not to last forever.

CHAPTER 27

A Reward for Information

During those summer months of the year 1801, while Rose and Keane sojourned on the Fairy Mountain, Sir Robert Westbourne's friend from court, the Baron of Maughinray, was residing at Charter Hall.

For some, the possession of unrestrained power while in the company of unquestioning sycophants, amplifies their worst tendencies. Over time, Lord Leighton's cruelty and arrogance had intensified. It was the usual practice in the Royal Navy for first-time deserters to be given the lash, if caught. If it happened again, they were shot. Leighton—who enjoyed involving himself in the affairs of his great friend at court, the First Lord of the Admiralty—advocated the dragging of recaptured prisoners behind a galloping horse, prior to execution. "As an example to the rest," he proclaimed.

Since his ignominious capture in the Austrian Netherlands he had grown a voluminous, bushy beard, possibly to disguise the unsightly merging of his sagging jowls with his neck. His paunch had also expanded in size, and due to gout, he now walked with a limp.

Years earlier, Leighton's interest in the out-of-the-way village of Allanwell had been sparked by the boastful words of that charismatic gambler Francis Delacey, who had been telling everyone at court about the beauty of his nieces.

Leighton took an interest in visiting the Westbournes because it suited him to be in Allanwell at that time. One of his preferred pursuits was seducing maidens—intimidating them with his wealth and power, bedazzling them with his blandishments and promises, until he cornered them and they could not escape. Afterwards, their shame, combined with his influence and status, kept them quiet.

He had his eye on young Elizabeth Delacey.

Many were the invitations Sir Robert extended to the Delacey family—on the insistence of his noble guest—to dine at Charter Hall. Appalled at the baron's blatantly salacious conduct towards his daughters, John Delacey strove to find excuses as to why they could not attend.

Many were the occasions upon which Leighton "chanced" to encounter Lizzie and her sisters when they were out walking. He would pressingly offer them rides in his custom-built phaeton, which was upholstered in fine leather and silk according to his own taste. The girls took to running for cover if they spied him approaching.

To display his riches and privilege, the baron ensured that his raiment was in the latest mode. He paraded himself in a long, high-collared coat with wide lapels, an embroidered waistcoat, and breeches made of fine wool or silk fabric, secured with gold buckles. His only fashion error was in wearing periwigs, which were quickly going out of style. Conceivably this was to disguise the state of his scalp. Over his wig he wore a top hat, and he often carried a riding crop in order to appear stylish and sporting.

Leighton took to aiding the Westbourne family in the search for Edwin's vanished bride. He and Sir Robert offered a substantial reward for information leading to her discovery— forty-seven golden guineas, equivalent to fifty pounds. In addition, he sent out spies to glean information.

A reward of fifty pounds was an attractive proposition. The people of Allanwell could earn between £3 and £20 per year, depending on their circumstances. It was a meager income, and most of them struggled to make ends meet. Their pride and resentment, however, prevented them from informing on one of their own. Some knew more than others, but all determined to keep silent.

All, that is, save one.

Lured by the chance of getting his hands on a financial reward greater than he had ever dared hope for, one Allanwell villager put about some inquiries. He even left the village for a week or two, which was unusual for him, undertaking a journey northwards in the direction of Ballyganna. He claimed he was looking for work, though everyone knew there was no work to be had up that way. Having ferreted out as much information as possible about the night the bride disappeared, he triumphantly began to draw a conclusion.

CHAPTER 28

Henri de Mandeville

It was late one night early in July when the hounds of Heatherhill suddenly awoke and rushed out to the front gates with a clamour of deep and resonant barking. Above the soughing of the wind, the clatter of hoofbeats could be heard, faint at first, rising in intensity. Springing from her bed Rose hastened to the window, where she put her spyglass to her eye and peered through.

A lone horseman was riding up the Green Lane.

The dogs ceased their rumpus as soon as the rider approached the gates. They wagged their tails and uttered soft whines and grunts, as if they recognised him.

Rose saw Keane, half-dressed, hastening from the gamekeeper's cottage at the back of the house, but MacTavish in a mournful banyan and nightcap like some pale scarecrow, lantern held high, was a few strides ahead of him. The steward unlocked the gates and ushered in the stranger.

That night there was to be scant sleep for anyone.

The newcomer turned out to be a friend—Henri, the son of the Chevalier de Mandeville, the owner of Heatherhill.

Instead of laying his head on a pillow after his ride up the mountain, the Frenchman called for food and drink, and for the guttering fire to be revived in the main dining-room.

"Rouse yourself, Priddy! Bring us your best roast beef!" he cried. "And bread and ham! I am famished. MacTavish, I want our best pinot noir, and be quick! Do not let ze cellar ghost get in ze way!"

Rose dressed herself hastily and descended the stairs to meet the visitor. He lay sprawled on a shabby chaise longue, his gold-trimmed riding-boots resting on the wooden carvings, gesticulating extravagantly with be-ringed hands, already engaged in animated conversation with Keane. Beside him on the floor lay his black felt tricorne hat, embellished with gold braiding that glinted in the candlelight.

The Irishman was standing before the fire, his back to the mantelpiece. The two young men looked to be about the same age, but there the resemblance ended. While Keane was tall and lean, with hair and whiskers as black as a crow's wing, Henri de Mandeville was stocky, goateed, his hair as fair as corn silk.

The Chevalier's son was clad in a long, navy-blue coat, trimmed with brass buttons, that reached down past his knees. Over his loose white linen shirt he wore a buttoned waistcoat, madder-red in colour. His loose-fitting knee-length breeches were made of leather, as was his ornate belt, upon which hung a gold-hilted sword in a scabbard, a cutlass and a couple of pistols in holsters. His fingers and earlobes glittered with heavy golden rings. His unkempt hair, covered with a decorative sash, was tied back into a loose club, and from his chin sprouted a pointed beard. The rest of his jaw was dusted with several days' worth of scruffy stubble.

The newcomer sprang to his feet and bowed to Rose as she entered the chamber, seizing her hand and kissing the back of it most gallantly. She shrank back, unsure of how to meet such lively looks and ebullience, but behind the Frenchman's back Keane caught her eye and smiled in reassurance.

Heartily the Frenchman greeted her, loudly proclaiming that he was pleased to meet any friend of his cousin and asserting his love for Jules, "In spite of Fournier being on the side of ze cursed Revolutionarys. 'Ow ironic, we Mandevilles find ourselves indebted to one of les sans-culottes!"

Priddy arrived bearing a tray of dishes, which she placed on the table, and MacTavish followed after her clutching two dusty wine-bottles. While the two servants busied themselves with setting out the supper, de Mandeville threw himself back onto the chaise longue.

"So, mon vieux, you braved the cellars eh?" he said to MacTavish with a laugh. "Did anything make you jump, eh?" Aside to Keane he added, "My taste is not really for ze wine. I prefer ale. But it is oh, so amusing to send our Scotsman down to ze cellars, for zere dwells the only ghost 'e fears in the entire house!" He roared with laughter, slapping his knee, then, "Oh, bring it to me 'ere, Priddy, I am too saddle-sore to rest my backside on your dining chairs of stone."

The housekeeper offered de Mandeville a heel of bread and a gobbet of beef, which he seized, one in each hand. He proceeded to eat and talk at the same time, explaining the purpose of his visit, while occasionally spitting crumbs or gravy, upon which the lurking wolfhounds pounced.

"I make ze journey 'ere just to meet you both, Mam'selle and Monsieur of Irlande. Nobody mentioned what an attractive couple you are, or I might 'ave bothered sooner. I see ze message from my cousin Fournier to my father, and I ask myself, 'oo are these people my cousin is to zem giving so much respect? And what do zey know about Marie Antoinette's jewels? I 'eard my cousin got his 'ands on zem."

They assured him they had no knowledge of any royal jewels. "I never heard him speak on the subject," said Keane, observing the ebullient Frenchman with quiet amusement.

"Hmm. A pity." De Mandeville brooded for a moment, but his regret was brief.

"From where have you travelled, Monsieur?" Keane asked. "From London? And did you come alone?"

"I rode from a joli little harbour called Allanwell, where my ship anchored two weeks ago."

"That is my home!" exclaimed Rose.

"I did not see much of it," said de Mandeville, "for we started out for 'eather'ill as soon as our boots touched land. My time is precious. I cannot stay 'ere long, as I 'ave business to attend to. And as for riding 'ere alone, par la mortbleu! I am not fool enough to travel without company on these roads, Monsieur et Mam'selle, especially decked in all this gold." De Mandeville jangled the rings on his hands. "I 'ave 'alf a dozen men down in Drumnaveen, awaiting my return. There in ze inn they will lie this night. Mouncy—my first mate—will make certain the innkeeper does not serve zem so much as a crumb of zat holy-fire bread. Mam'selle et Monsieur, 'ave zese two reprobates, my father's servants, been telling you ze ghost stories?"

"Why yes indeed Monsieur," said Rose, who could not help enjoying the company of this vivacious gentleman with his uncouth ways, "we've whiled away many an evening hearkening to them."

De Mandeville laughed again. "Ze 'eather'ill ghost tales—blood-curdling, eh? But upon my honour, ze ghost tales of pirates are equally as formidable."

"Pirates!" cried Rose. "Have you been so unfortunate as to encounter pirates on your travels, Monsieur?"

Laughing uproariously, de Mandeville replied, "Encounter zem? Why, certainly Mam'selle. In fact I encounter one every day in ze looking-glass."

Rose was astonished. "Surely sir, you don't mean. . . "

"Mon dieu, I do mean! I am myself a pirate! Monsieur O'Connell, I 'ear tell you were a nautical man yourself."

"Aye, thanks to His Majesty's Impress Service," said Keane.

"Ah, but you would much prefer a pirate's life to ze Royal

Navy. More riches, more freedom. A pirate is not bound by any legal or moral code! I act without any state support and attack who I please, but chiefly I prey upon ze ships of ze Spanish, Portuguese and Batavian. I leave ze French and British alone."

"But" said Rose, "I thought pirates were—"

"Untrustworthy? But of course! You are absolutely right Mam'selle. I am as untrustworthy as a fox in an 'en 'ouse."

Keane laughed and clapped de Mandeville on the shoulder. They fell to telling tales of the sea. By the time the sun rose the next morning, the two young men were on excellent terms.

It rained all the next day. Throughout the morning the Frenchman lay spreadeagled and snoring on the chaise longue in front of the fire. In the afternoon, bleary-eyed, he sat at the dining table playing chess with Keane and drinking sherry, while Rose settled herself nearby, helping Priddy to mend linen shirts. De Mandeville made use of this time to interrogate the Irishman gently but insistently, about Fournier's association, if any, with the royal jewels of the late French queen, Marie Antionette.

"Pray cast your thoughts back into the past," he said. "Per'aps my cousin let slip some word, some clue you 'ave forgotten."

Keane shrugged. "I've no recollection of it. In any case, how could a Chef de Brigade get hold of such valuables?

Surely they are locked in the government treasury with the jewels and paintin's the Directory seized from all the noble families!"

"You must understand, mon frere," explained de Mandeville, "the government of Le Republique insists that ze royal jewels are merely frivolous, and should be got rid of. According to zem, 'A democracy zat is sure of itself and confident in ze future has a duty to rid itself of zese objects of luxury, devoid of usefulness and moral worth.'"

He swigged some sherry from a chased goblet and leaned across the table towards Keane, to emphasize his words.

"But ze truth behind ze government's anger is different. Ze officials of Le Republique, zey live in constant fear of a monarchist restoration. Zey are concerned zat, if ze jewels remain in ze French treasury, anybody whose family 'as ever worn zem might suddenly lay claim to zem, and by extension, to the political power zey represent."

"Sure, no doubt they have a point," Keane commented, moving a knight on the chessboard.

"Mais oui! So ze government decide to auction ze important jewels. French jewelers, of course, were outraged, especially when ze stinking government decide to break apart many magnificent pieces of jewelry to sell as fragments and loose gems. Ze jewelers, zey start making look-alikes. And my cousin, you understand, 'e 'as many friends in 'igh places. He knows ze clever artificers who can make ze fakes to substitute for ze real jewels." de Mandeville snorted into his goblet. "If any man were so bold as to steal ze royal jewels and replace them with fakes, ze government, if they find out, zey will be too embarrassed to admit."

Keane could provide no information, for he knew nothing about such a scheme. Towards evening de Mandeville complained of weariness and announced that he would spend the night in a proper featherbed. Priddy ascended to the main bedchamber, where she slid a warming pan between the sheets for him, and kindled a fire.

After supper the Frenchman bade goodnight to the guests. He and the steward, both carrying candlesticks, set off up the stairs with the dogs at their heels. "Lead ze way my little Scotsman, " said de Mandeville, despite being shorter in stature than MacTavish.

Halfway up the stair he stopped suddenly and whirled about, his eyes darting from side to side.

"Wha' ails ye?" grumbled the steward.

"It occurs to me," said the Frenchman, "Zat somesing walks be'ind."

MacTavish peered over his shoulder at the empty steps descending, the naked curve of the balustrade. "Nothing here," he said, and continued to mount the stairs, with de Mandeville close at his heels.

"In this 'ouse the maister loikes to have someone walk before 'im, at nights," said Priddy when they were out of earshot. "'e says that once he saw a spectre with an axe on the landin', right beneath that ill-painted reproduction of Caravaggio's 'Judith Be'eading Holofernes' that 'angs on the wall."

"Well," said Rose, "that is a gruesome painting, to be fair."

An appalling scream tore through the fabric of the evening—the utterance of mortal terror, followed by a curse in French.

Keane leaped to his feet and made towards the staircase, for the sound had drilled down from the floor above.

"Wait! Wait sir!" cried Priddy, running after him and restraining him by the arm. He spun around to stare at her in astonishment. "All is well, I assure you. MacTavish is with the master."

A moment later they heard the voice of the Frenchman echoing down the stair, his words unintelligible, but his tone calmer.

Priddy released Keane's arm with an apology, and the young man returned to Rose's side.

"Perhaps he saw a ghost," he whispered in her ear, and her eyes sparkled with merriment.

After a while MacTavish returned alone, gliding down the stair somewhat complacently, with his candle held high.

"What happened on the landin'?" Keane asked.

"Oh dearie me," said Mc Tavish with an air of innocence, "the lights went out. Both candles together. It must ha' been a draught." As he shuffled away in his shroud-like banyan he said over his shoulder, "right beneath the fake Caravaggio."

"Did you detect a glimmer of satisfaction in his eye, my love?" Rose whispered to Keane.

"That MacTavish, he's some sleeveen right enough," said Keane, the corners of his fine-drawn mouth twitching with mirth.

"The master will leave his candle burning all night," foretold Priddy, "and have three of the dogs sleeping in his bedchamber, near the door."

Keane and Rose clasped each other close, and laughed into each other's hair.

"Goodnight my love," said she.

"Sleep soundly," he returned.

"Your friend's cousin is rather likeable, in spite of his pranks and boorishness," she subjoined as they parted. "Albeit once has no choice but to recall, only a brutal man could be a pirate."

"Aye, he's fine company, though 'tis clear he's not entirely to be trusted," said Keane. Gently, he kissed her. "Codladh sámh!"

CHAPTER 29

The Traitor in Allanwell

On a late afternoon in Allanwell, the sun's dying rays sent long, rubicund fingers across the sea and land. Amber-rose light winked from the window-panes of Charter Hall, that great house on Whitethorn Hill, and rinsed the high stone walls that surrounded the estate. Within the house four people sat conversing in the drawing room—Edwin Westbourne, his mother, his younger brother Albert, and Lord Leighton.

"The country is in chaos," grumbled Lady Westbourne, whose piled-up mass of powdered hair dripped with pearls. She rested her heavy head against the high back of her arm-chair. "It's just too dangerous, with all these rebels. There's nothing but rioting, looting, and destruction of property. Everywhere you look, our brave British soldiers are trying against great odds to maintain order, to suppress unrest and to enforce loyalty to the crown."

"Not to mention the sectarian violence," said Albert. He stared grumpily at the fire. Its light glinted off the pistols he wore at his belt.

Edwin remained silent.

"Our British soldiers and yeomanry know how to teach those Irish mobs and rioters a lesson," said Leighton, unbuttoning his waistcoat, which had become so tight after supper that the buttons threatened to burst off. "They deal out plenty of floggings, torture and killings to pacify them, but the fools refuse to learn what's good for them."

"There are more guards and watchmen on the estates around here than refined company, since our friends have departed," complained Lady Westbourne.

"And Father says it's getting harder to find workers, because so many of the labourers and their families are leaving the country," declared Albert.

Said his mother, "It's high time we followed the example of our friends. Your father has taken far too long over there in London, refurbishing the townhouse."

"While the place was being titivated we could have stayed with Georgiana," said Albert in injured tones, "Or Henrietta, or Alexandrina. They have nice homes over there in Albion."

"No dear, it's best not to impose on in-laws," said his mother. "Look what happened to—" she broke off. "I do detest gossip," she murmured, lowering her eyes and peeping out from beneath her lids at Lord Leighton.

A villager of Allanwell, his heart filled with desire for a purse of forty-seven golden guineas, presented himself one evening, after dusk, at the tall, metal gates of Charter Hall.

Two heavily-armed watchman did not wait to hear him speak. They seized him roughly and examined his person for hidden weapons, but found none. A third man, who was restraining two large dogs on chains, regarded the scruffy caller with suspicion. They were on the point of turning him away when the villager said, "Wait, in the name of heaven! I mean no harm. Sure, the lordships will welcome me so they will, for I bring the news they've been seekin'."

Six burly watchmen and the dog keeper escorted him through the grounds to the house, where one of them rapped loudly on a side door. It was opened by a young guard whose job it was to patrol the building's interior.

"Send word to their lordships that yer man here claims to have information."

The young guard sped away.

Leaving behind the dogs, the visitor was presently ushered in to the library, suffering many a scornful look from the watchmen and assorted footmen who jostled him. There, he stood looking around, marveling at the floor-to-ceiling mahogany bookshelves that lined the walls. Some were filled with leather-bound volumes, but others were bare. Wooden travelling-trunks stood open here and there, and more books could be seen closely packed inside them. He gaped, wondering what it must be like to sit in the deep buttoned leather armchairs arranged by the fireplace, and craning his neck to gawp at the plasterwork rosettes and garlands on the ceiling.

Two sturdy footmen poised themselves discreetly in a corner, regarding the villager with evident dislike.

"Well, come on fellow, what have you to tell us?" Leighton demanded without ceremony as he and Edwin Westbourne entered the book-lined chamber. He noticed the cadre of armed men and rounded on them. "You! Return to your stations!" he barked. "Are you fools enough to leave the boundaries unpatrolled?"

The patrolmen bowed and departed.

"What's your name?" asked Edwin. The man, cap in hand, told him.

"I know how the lady ye seek went from here," he said. "A man took her, hidden in a cartload of hay."

"Who drove the cart?" Leighton's voice was rusted iron.

"I cannot say! I do not know!" The informer quailed. Suddenly he was plagued with misgivings. He feared that if he revealed the driver was Flynn McGinty, then McGinty might somehow get the reward.

"Where did they go?" Edwin wanted to know.

"North."

"That is no help, you fool!" Leighton slammed his fist hard on the oak writing-table, making the candlesticks jump.

"Ah, sir, but after ye posted the reward I followed their trail. I tracked them along the road, village by village, axin' questions along the way. Folk tell a harmless buachaill like me what they see—things they do not tell yer men. I know where she went."

"Doubtless you are lying."

"I know more, lordship, for I have the knowledge o' who carried off the lady. 'Twas not the cart driver. I'll tell, if ye pay me now."

"You scoundrel! You will get your money only if, and when, we find her!"

"Is it not worth something to yer honour at this minute?"

"Confound you! Very well then, here's five silver shillings in advance." The coins changed hands. "Come on, tell us and we'll pay extra."

"Will yer pay the extra in gold?"

"Aye then, gold, devil take you."

"'Tis Heatherhill in the mountains," said the informant.

The two gentlemen exchanged glances.

"Who guards her?" Leighton demanded.

"Only an old man, an old woman and the feller who took the bride, himself."

"What fellow?"

"I did not see yer man, but I found out who it was."

"And?" said Edwin quickly.

"His name is Keane O'Connell."

Edwin turned pale when he heard the name, and Leighton flinched. The older man thrust his face close to that of the informant. "What does he look like, this O'Connell?"

Taken aback and quite alarmed, the villager stammered, "He—er—he's tall. Young. Wit' black hair. They say he's good-lookin', but I myself don't see it."

"Any other distinguishing features?" growled Leighton.

"Er—sure. His eyes, they are grey. Silver-grey, like seal fur."

Leighton cursed volubly and began muttering to himself.

"Have you any more to tell?" Edwin said sternly to the informant.

"No sir, but you have all the information you need to find the lady, so by rights I deserve my reward, if it please your lordship."

Edwin fished out another silver shilling from his waistcoat pocket and tossed it to him.

"Yer promised gold!"

"You had better hope we find her where you say, fellow," Leighton growled. "If we do, we'll pay you in gold sovereigns. If not, it will be you who pays. Now, begone!"

The first footman smartly escorted the man from the house, narrowly watching him in case he purloined the silverware.

"'Sdeath, Westbourne!" cried Leighton when the villager had fled down the hill and been swallowed by the darkness. "I know that name, O'Connell. If it is the same fellow who insulted my person in France, then he is my avowed enemy and I swear vengeance on him!"

"What is your meaning?"

"I have strong reason to hate a man by that name. Such a one was among those French barbarians who captured me and dared to humiliate me as I was on my way to Salzburg. An Irishman he was, a deserter and a traitor to boot, wearing the uniform of the Royal Navy. I heard someone address him as O'Connell."

"How can you be sure it is the same fellow?"

"He matches the description. On my return to England I sought to discover his identity. I asked my friend John Markham, First Lord of the Admiralty—you know him?—to look up the muster rolls of every ship, and find out which had a crewman by the name of O'Connell. There were several by that name, but Markham said there was only one it could be—a pressed Irish fellow from Allanwell who deserted from H.M.S. Victory to the Austrian Netherlands, and was shot dead by the French. That is, he was listed as having been killed, but now it appears he survived. And joined the puking frog-eaters! 'Fore gad! There will be retribution!'"

Edwin threw himself moodily into one of the leather armchairs. "I know that name too," he said morosely.

"Whats the matter with you, sir? You're continually brooding these days. Are you ailing? Have you lost your spirit? Rejoice! We have the news we want, if this clod-hopper is to be believed. Your little bit is discovered at last."

"I pray you, do not speak of my bride in that fashion."

Leighton gestured exasperatedly. "All right, if you insist. In any case, let us depart for Heatherhill forthwith! We'll seize your wife and force her to return to her lawful spouse. No doubt she's been ruined by now, but you should have what's yours, and I must get hold of that traitor O'Connell."

"My wife is loyal and faithful to her word," Edwin said stiffly. "She is still a maiden that I'll guarantee. Recall, I told you of that broken ring she wore for seven years? She keeps her word, and she will keep her wedding vows. She promised to abide by her mother's dying wish."

"All the better, then!" said Leighton. "I have heard of that house, Heatherhill. It's in the uplands, and owned by that accursed French family, the de Mandevilles. We'll ride there immediately, with a hand-picked band of our best men."

CHAPTER 30

The Departure of de Mandeville

Far off in the mountains at Heatherhill, Henri de Mandeville regaled his guests with tales of piracy on the high seas, omitting some of the more horrifying stories when the lady was present. Despite Rose's distaste for his violent way of life she found herself drawn in by his rousing tales of adventure, and wanting to know more.

He described his ship, the *Royal Revenge,* "A 120 ton two-masted brig, with both masts fully square-rigged. Crewed by 110 men, she's ninety feet long and four-and-twenty feet across ze beam."

The brig was a fast and maneuverable vessel, he said, highly suitable for chasing down merchant ships. De Mandeville had had her extensively modified to gain speed; her hull was streamlined, and she possessed extra sail area.

"My beauty, she carries fourteen cannon," he declared proudly, "mounted on 'er main deck and able to fire from either side. Swivel guns and small cannon are stationed along ze railings. She 'as also a large arsenal of pistols, cutlasses, blunderbusses, grenades, and other arms for ze crew.

"We are 'eavily armed and more zan a match for merchant-men, but of course," he added, "we would never be such fools as to fight a naval vessel in a pitched battle, unless we were desperate! We avoid engagement with ze military ships."

"How do you hide from British and French naval patrols?" Rose wanted to know. "Yes, and the Spanish Navy too, and the rest. They all keep a vigilant look-out for pirates!

"Ah, Mam'selle,"—de Mandeville's lively eyes twinkled—"we 'ave many clever techniques! We 'ave informants in many port towns. Zey tell us ze location of naval ships, so we can steer clear of patrolled areas. We avoid ze main shipping routes, except when we attack some rich merchant-man in the lanes. After we seize their cargo, we make for isolated areas—thinly populated or remote islands are our preferred 'ideouts. Or sometimes, a little coastal 'aven, such as Allanwell. Ze little bay there is quite secluded, isn't it? And that little 'eadland, Sharpnose 'ook, it can conceal a ship from the prying eyes of coastal traders, and even landlubbers! Such a clever little 'iding place, so close to ze village and with ze Allanwell 'arbour-master in my pay—it is ideal for my purposes."

The shades of bitter memories flitted across Keane O'Connell's countenance. "Your words call to mind the tactics of the Conqueror's press-gang."

"Allanwell is the closest 'arbour to this god-forsaken 'ouse on this god-forsaken mountain," said de Mandeville. "My proud beauty is anchored zere now, waiting for me. She will remain for about a fortnight, while we prepare.

"Naturally, my crew needs time to rest before we go out raiding. Zey must be alert during ze attack. While Revenge lies at anchor zey play games, tell stories, drink rum. Never fear, I do not unleash zem on your unsuspecting villagers. We save ze wenching for our port of call after our next raid— Agadir in Morocco."

"You have grand plans indeed, sir," said Rose. "Morocco— it is far away, a long voyage."

"Ah oui, but ze bother is worth all!"said de Mandeville. "Many merchantmen, zey catch ze Canary Current to sail down past Morocco, laden with cargoes of bullion from ze silver mines of ze Americas. Fat prizes indeed, no?"

The Canary Current, he told them, was an important sea route connecting Europe with the Americas, Africa, and the East Indies, and it passed through the Canary Islands, which served as strategic stopover points for ships heading to and from the New World to resupply, refit, and repair.

"When we reach ze Canary Route, we keep a lookout for ze potential prizes. We 'ave many cunning ways to trick zem, my friends, but in ze end, even with all our techniques, luck and secrecy, zey are our best allies. If a naval force caught us looting a ship, or stumbled upon our 'ideout, our freedom must depend on our cleverness to escape by whatever means necessary—even abandoning ship, 'eaven forbid!" de Mandeville crossed himself and rolled his eyes skywards.

"But please monsieur," said Rose, who had developed a kind of macabre fascination with the topic of piracy, "how in heaven's name do you conceal your ship from hostile eyes when you are sailing on the high seas, with the sun shining brightly in the sky and nowhere to hide?"

"My dear Mam'selle, we are skilled at ze camouflage and deception," said the Frenchman, who clearly enjoyed expounding upon his favourite subject, "I simply disguise ma belle as a merchant vessel to avoid suspicion. She can change quickly 'er appearance, and fly false colors until we are ready to attack our target." He laughed. "It is all part of ze sport!"

"But ships' names are painted on their figureheads, and across the stern!" Rose cried. "How is it possible to change that?"

"Revenge 'as a reversible figure'ead," explained de Mandeville, his eyes lively with mischief. "Our beautiful wooden mermaid is installed backwards, so 'er name is not visible from other ships. We show merely a carved eagle. When it is time to attack, ze figure'ead we spin around quickly. As for ze name on ze stern—we use a false transom zat perfectly fits around the existing stern name. Zis backboard, it 'as ze new fake name, "Fancy", and can be slipped onto the transom and temporarily fastened, then removed when no longer needed."

"So clever! And when you attack, do you drop your disguise and raise a skull-and-crossbones flag, sir?" Rose asked with morbid incredulity.

"Of course Mam'selle! It works well to terrify our targets. We 'oist it when pursuing a ship, but we now 'ave what is even better than ze Jolly Roger," he went on. "We ave ze black sails." He paused for effect, then continued, "*Royal Revenge*, she 'oists ze black sails to signal she is a pirate vessel. Black as ze pits of 'ell! When zey see our sails, ze target ships know their enemy is not bound by the usual rules of engagement and will take what 'e wants by force. Such canvas intimidates zem into surrendering without a fight."

Next day, de Mandeville swung himself up on his horse and departed for Drumnaveen. He and his men would soon be on their way to Allanwell Bay where their brig, *Royal Revenge*, waited at anchor in the secluded inlet behind Sharpnose.

CHAPTER 31

At Foley's Inn

The pirate posse arrived in Allanwell at dusk on Tuesday 7th July. As inconspicuously as possible in the gloaming, they guided their horses straight to the stables of the harbour-master, who was in de Mandeville's pay. It was easy for pirates and smugglers to bribe officials, port authorities, and even naval officers to gain information or safe passage.

Soon thereafter, the captain and his crew rowed out in a longboat to the brig *Royal Revenge*.

Unbeknownst to de Mandeville, he had narrowly missed encountering another band of riders. They departed from Allanwell early the following morning. Had he been aware of them, and their purpose, he might have stayed to bar their way.

Others noted their departure, and the direction in which they were heading. Flynn McGinty was among them. It chanced that he was ready to start for Slieve Sidhe that very day, bearing news for his friends at Heatherhill. He had already saddled Clover when, with a jolt of alarm, he spied the riders cantering down Whitethorn Hill and turning along the road to the north, out of the village. Driven by an instinctive sense of urgency he bade goodbye to his mother and sister, and set off in the wake of the horsemen. Riding his slow draught horse, he could not hope to keep pace with the mettlesome steeds of those who galloped ahead of him, but if he were not too late, there might be something he could do to help those at Heatherhill, who might be in peril.

Leighton and his mercenaries were twelve in number, clad in black coats with shiny steel buttons, and bristling with weapons—swords, pistols, muskets, daggers, blunderbusses. Their mounts were young, fit and strong. Easily, the company cantered northwards along the rutted roads to the uplands and by the evening of 10th July they arrived at the village of Drumnaveen.

There they halted and sought refreshment at Foley's Inn. A spindly young lad and a hostler led their horses through the courtyard to the stables.

"Landlord," shouted Huntley, the mercenary captain, "give us your best meat and ale, for we have come a long way and we are hungry!" He followed his employer into the low-ceilinged hostelry, with the other rough-looking fellows crowding in at his back. "And be quick about it, for we ride up the mountain this night."

"Ach, good sir," said Foley, bustling about fetching benches for his customers to sit on at his long table, "meat and drink ye shall have, but I take the liberty to advise ye against venturin' along dat road at night. Da road winds tightly up the mountainside. 'Tis a steep and treacherous pat' indeed and yer horses will need more dan lantern light to keep their footin'. Pray stay here till mornin' and we will ensure yer grand comfort."

"All right, all right!" said Leighton impatiently, having overheard the innkeeper's words. "We'll settle into this rat-hole and await the daylight hours."

Foley pressed home his point. "Sure, no living soul could be findin' safe passage up dat road at night, sir, or in foul wedder."

"That's first-rate, " said Leighton, "because if anyone goes up to Heatherhill ahead of us to announce our forthcoming visit, we'll burn down this hovel." He looked around to ensure that any local men who were present at the inn had hearkened to his words, and indeed they showed clear evidence of having done so.

Leighton and his men arranged themselves around the table, while Foley disappeared into the kitchen. A thin-faced young girl timidly placed foaming tankard on the boards, and presently the innkeeper's son came in from the stables.

"Who's living up at the big house?" Leighton demanded of the boy.

Foley's lad looked uncomfortable. He stood on one leg, rubbing one foot behind the other. "A fine lady, sir, and Mr

MacTavish, and Mrs Priddy. And Gamekeeper Driscoll."

"Gamekeeper Driscoll, eh? What does he look like?"

"Donal Beg!" squawked a woman's voice. A shiny, red face appeared around the frame of a doorway. "What are you at? Stop pesterin' the gentleman and give me a hand wit' the kitchen fire."

"Go away, woman," the baron said irritably. "Leave the lad to me."

"If it please your lordship,' said the woman, "I need my son's help to stoke de fire, if I'm to be cookin' supper for you and your officers."

Leighton pulled a penny out of his pocket and tossed it to the boy.

"Don't listen to your mother. What do women know, eh? Tell me about this gamekeeper."

The boy, having deftly captured the winking metal disc, blinked owlishly at Leighton. Then he turned his head and took in his mother's expression.

He returned his attention to Leighton and pocketed the coin. "He's a fat old chunk of lard, sir, with a t'atch of hair like a straw stable-broom."

"Confound you, you corny-faced little liar. Get you gone before I box your ears!" The baron dismissed the lad with a wave of his hand, and the child scuttled away.

Leighton murmured to his captain, "No doubt 'Driscoll the Gamekeeper' is in fact the deserter Keane Connor."

"No doubt at all, sir."

Foley reappeared. "Don't mind de lad I pray ye, good sir," he said. "No doubt he's flummoxed by seein' such brave gentlemen as yez, who dares to go visitin' de big house."

Leighton grunted.

Huntley said, "What is your meaning, fellow?"

"De ghosts yer know, sir," said Foley. He noted that the other mercenaries, with nothing else to do but quaff ale, were now leaning slightly towards him. "Heatherhill is de most haunted house in Ireland. Ach sir, I cannot barely describe de blood-curdling sounds dat come out o' dat place, and de terrible sights I seen wit' me own eyes."

He proceeded to recount the macabre history of the Red Lady and her bloody dagger. The room fell quiet as he spoke, his words being tempered only by the sudden soft explosion of a log on the fire, and the clatter of dishes in the kitchen.

Before the innkeeper finished speaking Leighton interrupted. "Be off with you, bog-trotter. You and your superstitions! I've never heard such a load of tosh!"

"Begging your pardon, lordship. I myself did not mean to offend," said Foley with a bow, before heading for the kitchen once again.

There, he spoke with his wife. "An bhfuil tú chun aráin a bhácáil le bheith agat leis an anraith tráthnóna inniu, a ghrá?" the innkeeper wanted to know. ("Going to bake bread to have with the soup this evening, my love?")

"Níl sé seo san oíche seo," was his wife's reply. "Tá stoirm ag teacht." ("Not this evening. Storm's a-coming.") "Tomorrow I'll bake."

She raised her voice. "Donal Beg! Fetch a sack o' flour from the cellar!"

Overnight, thunder awoke and growled in the west. By morning, storm clouds bruised the sky and the wind's voice was rising clamourously.

As Leighton and his men sat at the inn's table consuming their breakfast, the heavens opened and rain cascaded down in a deluge, hanging from the clouds like a million crystal strings.

The innkeeper's wife shuttered the small windows against the weather, and lit a lamp. Its flame blossomed like a yellow crocus against the gloom. Outside, the wind rose to a gale, forged in the crucible of the storm, spinning its currents through the ether like steel threads.

"Don't suppose yez'll be goin' anywhere in dis wedder, sir," said the innkeeper to the baron, who merely grunted in reply.

Foley persevered. "Beggin' yer pardon sir, I myself take de liberty of advisin' against travellin' de Green Lane in de rain, so I do."

"Oh, a little water don't discourage us," said Leighton.

"Sir, beg pardon, I've lived here all me life and I go by dat road once a week. I seen horses and riders washed straight off dat road in a downpour. Dey're after fallin' to their doom down the cliff face, so they are, to be sure."

Ignoring Foley with blatant contempt, the baron turned to speak to his captain. "We'll wait for the damned rain to ease," he said exasperatedly. "Driscoll the Gamekeeper can wait another hour or two for Judgement Day."

"Aye, m'lord."

Displaying remarkable equanimity, the innkeeper made himself scarce.

The voice of the wind beyond the walls was the howling of wolves. Raindrops battered at the shuttered windows and in the heart of the storm lightning unveiled itself, a cobweb of bright silver tracing the livid face of the sky.

That morning Foley's wife, who appeared oblivious of the weather's screechings, started making rye bread. The dough, markedly dark in colour, was set by the hearth to prove all day. It pervaded every room of the inn with a sharp smell.

Late in the afternoon the storm blew away to the east. Rays of the westering sun poured through rents in the clouds, and laved the landscape, as warm and golden as mulled cider.

"I can't stand another night in this hovel," Leighton said to Huntley. "There's enough daylight to see us up the mountainside. I plan to sleep in a good featherbed this night. To horse!"

The innkeeper's wife had baked several loaves. Just before her customers set out, she served them the bread, warm from the oven, giving off tendrils of steam and deliciously slathered with butter and salt.

CHAPTER 32

The Despoiling of Heatherhill

Late that afternoon, after the rain petered out, the westering sun gleamed rose-gold in a sky slashed with frayed clouds. It seemed, however, that this was merely a temporary lull in the atmospheric violence, for curiously, a rampart-like wall of purple-black clouds was slowly rolling down from the north, stretching from horizon to horizon and blotting out the skies behind it.

It took Leighton's cavalcade longer than they expected to navigate the Green Lane. The recent deluge had gouged thin, twisted channels in the steep and unpaved road. Their horses had to pick their way among loose stones and across rivulets still trickling down the mountainside. By the time they arrived at the gates of Heatherhill estate and reined in their mounts, the fortress of cloud had rolled close—almost overhead—and the mountain wind was rising once more.

Rose, carrying her spyglass in a leather case that hung on a strap from her shoulder, ascended the ladder and clambered through the attic trapdoor to the roof of Heatherhill House. There, standing like a slender sapling among the stonework crenelations and gargoyles and grotesques, her hair and gown blowing in the wind, she put the brass instrument to her eye and looked northwards. The grounds seemed laid out like a map. Mists submerged the distant uplands. She was observing the approach of the long cloud-bank when the dogs began to bark. A faint drumming of hooves intensified, and she ran across the roof-terrace to the south side, peering in the direction of the gates.

On spying the band of horsemen she slid the spyglass into its case, hitched up her skirts and darted down through the trapdoor. It was with all haste that she descended the ladder and staircase, but by the time she rushed into the front hall, gasping for breath, Keane was already there, and so was MacTavish.

"They've discovered us!" she cried.

"We know," said Keane, before she had finished the sentence. Their eyes met in a loving glance; his look transmitted strength and certainty, hers signalled steadfastness and stoicism. "Be comforted, darlin'. We've all prepared for this day." He returned his attention to his work. He and the steward were strapping scabbards and holsters to their belts, arming themselves with as many weapons as they could carry. The frantic dogs barked and bayed. They hurled themselves at the front door—a massive portal of thick oaken planks, bound and studded with iron, fastened with a couple of heavy locks.

"Every door and winder is locked and barred," said MacTavish with grim virtuousness.

The posse had drawn up at the gates. Over their heads, the boughs of the ancient yew trees lashed back and forth in the gale. The horses, agitated by the cries of the dogs, pranced skittishly. Captain Huntley stood up in his stirrups and bellowed through the wrought iron lilies, "Open the gates. The law demands you yield to us the deserter, O'Connell, and the stolen bride of Westbourne."

"Law?" scoffed MacTavish in an undertone as he stood in the hall loading an ancient fowling-piece. "They've as muckle tae dae wi' the law as my great-aunt's laundry pinnie. An' if they were the sheriffs in truth, that'd mak' them a' the mair deserving o' a skelpin'. I've niver had muckle o' a likin' for thae blackguards."

Priddy materialised in the hall.

"Rose, ye must go with Nest into the chapel," said Keane. "Take shelter there and lock yourselves in. 'Tis the strongest chamber in this house. Take these." He handed four loaded pistols to her and the housekeeper.

"But you and MacTavish—" Rose protested.

"We will be guardin' the chapel doors."

"No! You must come to safety with us!"

"If we do not, those men will break down the doors."

"But if you fall—"

"If we fall, and if they find a way to ye, that is what the guns are for."

Before Rose could utter another word of protest, Keane swung around to face the front door. He called out in resonant, authoritative tones that carried far, "Go away. There's no deserter here. This is private property."

The dogs fell silent, and for a moment, nothing could be heard save for the agonised wailing of the wind, rising and falling.

Then Captain Huntley took aim with his pistol and shot the lock off the gates. He kicked them open with his boot, and the riders charged in.

Simultaneously, Priddy caught Rose by the elbow and dragged her out of the hall. She was surprisingly strong for such a small woman.

With their attention fixed on the front door, Keane O'Connell and MacTavish, each aiming a musket, walked slowly backwards across the parquetry in the wake of the two women.

Once inside the gates, Leighton's riders sprang from their saddles. Some ran up to the massive portal, while others hared off around the back towards the gamekeeper's cottage.

Deep in the house's core, Priddy pushed Rose unceremoniously into the chapel, dashed in after her and turned the key in the lock. The Irishman and the Scotsman positioned themselves outside those doors, feet braced and weapons at the ready.

Rose found herself in a dim chamber with Nest Priddy at her side. The chapel was windowless, and there had been no time to light candles, but she knew the place well enough to locate her position within it. The consecrated space was divided into two areas: the nave, with its simple wooden pews that offered seating for no more than twenty persons, and the chancel, with its altar. A pulpit stood to one side of the nave and a few icons decorated the walls. The air smelled stagnant, faintly tinged with a sickly odour of incense. Fumbling in the darkness, the housekeeper pulled her charge into the front row of pews, then fell to her knees and began to pray.

Rose listened, with every nerve, to the noises daggering in from beyond the walls.

Explosions and splintering crashes erupted through the cavities and arteries of the house as Leighton's men shot the locks off the front door. The great portal crashed inwards, and the invaders' boots trampled the doorstep as they burst into the hall.

The outraged dogs lunged at them, but the men kicked them away and slashed at them with swords. One sank his teeth into Huntley's calf, whereupon the man pointed his pistol at the fearless defender and shot him dead on the spot. Thunder roared, a sable lion unleashing its power as the onrushing cloud bank finally enveloped the house, blotting out the setting sun. In a heartbeat, all was drowned in an eerie, submarine dimness.

"O'Connell!" shouted a harsh voice. "O'Connell! Where are you? Stand forth!"

Rose sat curled up on the unyielding oaken pew, her arms clasped tightly around her knees, her pulse pounding in the cage of her ribs. Her were fixed on Keane, and she longed to run to his side, but instead suppressed all movement and sound, becoming as still as an icon. Outside the chapel, antique floorboards creaked under the burden of heavy footwear. The intruders were moving around on both the lower and upper floors, broadcasting a rumble of laughter and coarse shouts. It was only a matter of time before they chanced upon the chapel doors.

From her hiding-spot she heard a loud bang, as some heavy object crashed to the floor. Men's voices uttered curses of surprise and alarm. There was no more laughter now, only edgy murmurs.

An unnatural cold seeped into her bones, as if her veins were transmuting to conduits of ice. There came a resounding double-detonation, as if a door had been kicked open by an invisible foot, and the shock of it made her gasp. Yowls—unearthly—pierced the gloom. Next, the bright shattering of glass, and more cacophony of destruction.

In the murk of the chapel, terror choked her throat. For a suffocating moment a weird silence imprisoned the house, but the cold remained, an icy claw with a grip of iron. A peculiar feeling of horror fixed on her. All ominous noises had ceased, but somehow she guessed that appalling sensation had fixed also on every other living thing in that house.

She glanced across at Nest Priddy, whose face, in the gloom, was a barely discernible pale blob. The housekeeper seemed at once terrified and serene in equal measure.

For Rose, the grip of fear intensified.

The silence was shattered by the discharge of firearms. Men began yelling, as if in rising panic and confusion.

Amidst the chaos, there arose a low, guttural growl, like nothing Rose had ever heard before. It seemed to come from everywhere at once, filling the entire house, the chapel, the hollow of her own skull.

This was overlaid by the screaming and hysterical howling of men struck by abject terror and despair, and the urgent rapping of their boots on wood and stone as they fled, or tried to flee. It was all she could do to restrain herself from calling out to the two who guarded the doors, "What is happening out there?" Footsteps were rapidly approaching the chapel. She drew a deep breath and prayed, but another sound caused her to freeze again.

It was a high-pitched, piercing, long-drawn screech, like a thousand voices crying out in agony.

Gradually the screech died away, followed by more echoes and running footsteps, as if men were scrambling to escape the house. She heard the front door slam back hard against the wall, and more demented shrieks, growing fainter. . .

Presently, quietness settled on the house like a soft shower of featherdown.

Rose crouched in the chapel beside Priddy, who had ceased praying. Feeling with her fingers in the darkness, the housekeeper found the small tinderbox that depended from her chatelaine belt. She used it to light a candle. The tiny, butterfly glow of the flame caressed their faces. It seemed bright and cheerful, as if offering hope.

Nonetheless it seemed an eternity until they heard the voice of Keane through the locked doors.

"'Tis safe to come out, now. They've gone. I'm here with MacTavish."

Priddy turned her key in the lock and and the two women emerged, dazed.

Keane embraced his sweetheart. "Are ye both well?"

"We are. And you?"

"Not a scratch." Keeping his arm about Rose's shoulders he addressed the housekeeper. "Mistress Priddy, pray take Mistress Rose to the kitchen and prepare possets for all of us. MacTavish and I shall inspect the house and perimeters, and make any temporary repairs necessary. For the moment, I believe we are secure."

"Aye, for th' moment," said MacTavish portentously, his gimlet eyes gleaming from beneath his beetling brows.

That night, nobody slept.

Rose and Priddy examined the three dogs who had survived their encounter—though not unscathed—with the invaders. They applied ointments, splinted limbs and bound up bleeding ears before burying faithful Rufus in the garden, marking his grave with a great stone.

Keane O'Connell and MacTavish searched the house, barred the broken gates and hammered timbers across the splintered front door. When they returned to the kitchen, Priddy handed each of them a hot drink.

Hounds and human beings lounged wearily by the kitchen fire. Presently Keane said, "Plainly 'tis no longer wise for us to remain here."

"Agreed," said Rose. "We must depart at daybreak."

"Aye, ye'll get no argument from me," said MacTavish. "Until then, we keep watch,"

"I am sorry for bringin' this on ye," Keane said to the servants.

Priddy had fetched a loaf of bread and a round of cheese from the larder and she was busy slicing them at the table. As usual she kept her own counsel, merely nodding acknowledgment to Keane.

"A's weel 'at ends weel," said MacTavish with unexpected calmness, and apparently also with relish.

Rose glanced at him inquiringly. "Mr MacTavish," she said, "what exactly happened here this night?"

"The ithers 'at bide in this hoose took matters intae their ain hands," the steward replied with satisfaction.

The Irishman shot him a skeptical, slightly amused look. "'Tis hard to know what occurred," he said to Rose.

Aware of the reason for Keane's hesitation she said, "Tell me. No, pray do not try to spare my feelings. I am no shrinking violet. I would rather know the truth, even if it is unpalatable."

"As you wish, a chuisle. The trut' is, we ourselves discharged no firearm last night. Men died, but it was not at our hands. We found two corpses when we did our rounds, and one poor fellow close to deat'. He passed away soon after we found him, despite our attempts to revive him. We laid them in the old dairy. Foley can carry them down to the churchyard on his next visit.

"One we discovered was lyin' lifeless at the foot of a staircase. Another died of gunshot wounds—killed by a ball from his comrade's musket I suppose—and the last seems to have fallen from a balcony. He survived the fall but I have never seen anyone in such as state as he—convulsin', ravin' like a madman, his eyes startin' from his head, his face twisted in terror, howlin' that he was being tormented by t'ings that were unseen by our eyes."

MacTavish put in, "It wis a mercy fan he suddenly stoppit a' that an' fell stane deid."

"The 'ouse is in a disgraceful mess," said Nest Priddy. "Trails o' blood all ower the floors, an' the wainscotin' all riddled wi' bullet 'oles 'cause of them shootin' at each other."

"At each other!" exclaimed Rose.

"Aye." MacTavish nodded.

"Some grand confusion has caused a ruckus among those fellows," said Keane.

"At the end," said the steward, "they ran screamin' an' jabberin' fae the hoose, some nae even stoppin' tae mount their nags in their haste tae pit this place ahind them."

Keane said, "A voice that I know well was shoutin' commands at them, callin' curses upon their heads, namin' them cowards. It was the voice of that English slaoiste Leighton. I wonder whether he himself dared enter this house."

"Leighton! That friend of the Westbournes!" cried Rose.

"The very one. His croak is known to me, for I heard it plenty when we had him captive in the Austrian Netherlands. I'd bet me last penny he was the ringleader of this venture."

"Somehow he has seen through your disguise and found out that you are here."

A cloud passed across Keane's visage. "There is only one way that could've happened," he said. "There's a turncoat in Allanwell."

They waited out the rest of the night. MacTavish was dozing in the dining room, his head on his arms, which in turn rested on the table. Priddy sat in a rocking chair with her eyes closed, but she might have been awake.

Rose drew closer to her sweet-heart. "During the break-in, did you see anything you're not telling me about?" she whispered.

"Aye, mo grá, but I believe 'twas but a trick of the mind. No need to upset you wit' a mere delusion."

"What was it? Please tell me!"

Searchingly, he looked into her apple-blossom face.

"Alright then, if ye're truly wantin' to know. . . As I stood with MacTavish before the chapel doors I t'ought I glimpsed some tall creature in a billowin' coat fly past with impossible speed. A frightful face, the eyes starin'. An upraised hand graspin' the shadow of a blade, and all bathed in a weird light, a dim reddish glow, like blast furnaces seen from afar in the night. The villains soon took to their heels. I stood at the wreckage of the front door, watchin' them as they bolted for the gates. And I thought I saw, trackin' behind them, the raw shape o' that thing, movin' like a wolf after its prey. It hounded them as far as the gates, then melted into the dark."

CHAPTER 33

The Leaving of Heatherhill

Come morning, the weather had turned fine and sunny. One of the thoroughbred horses that belonged to the attackers was found wandering loose in the grounds. Keane and MacTavish led her into the stables, where they removed her saddle and gave her feed and water.

"Yer a bonny lass that ye are," said MacTavish to the mare, caressing her long nose.

Rose, in the meantime, packed a small bag with essential items. Now that their sanctuary had been violated, she and her sweetheart were at risk. There was no knowing whether Leighton's men might return with reinforcements at any time. If they captured Rose, they would return her to the Westbournes. If they caught Keane, they would most likely execute him, with or without a trial. The fugitives had nowhere else to go, but Heatherhill was one place they could not stay. They must take to the open road and trust in fortune.

"I have an uncle," said Rose, clutching at straws. "If we could find him, he would give us shelter. Perhaps my father knows his whereabouts. . ." He voice trailed away. She did not invest much faith in Frank Delacey. The last she had heard of him, he was running a gambling scheme in Portugal.

In the middle of the morning, with a rattle of hooves and a cry of greeting, Flynn McGinty came trotting up to the gates on horseback. Recognising him, MacTavish bade the dogs be quiet and stand aside, and opened the gates.

Flynn swung his leg over Clover's broad back and slid down to the ground, as Rose and Keane emerged to greet him.

"What news from Allanwell?" they both wanted to know.

"Our friends and families are safe and well," Flynn said, grinning widely, "and I'm delighted to see that you are the same. When I spied Leighton and his bully boys takin' the road nort' out of Allanwell, I had strong misgivin's."

Keane O'Connell led Clover into the stables. Veils of daylight, swarming with motes, filtered into the thatched building through small windows. They pinned tiny silver stars on each polished rim of the tack and equipment hanging on the walls. The air was lush with the scent of hay and manure. Keane steered Clover into one of the stalls, where she stood arching of her neck over the wooden partition to sniff the face of the thoroughbred mare in the next compartment.

Flynn, Rose and MacTavish gathered around.

"Listen," said Flynn, with a note of triumph in his voice, "for I have important news and I cannot wait to tell you all."

"We're listenin'!" said Keane.

"'Tis secure for Rose to return home to Allanwell!" McGinty took delight in their looks of surprise and doubt, adding exuberantly, "Tis true! The Westbournes have packed up and gone to 'fidious Albion. Master Edwin has rejoined the dragoons and sailed overseas. Mistress Rose, it is truly safe for you to return to your people!"

"Thank you Mr McGinty," said Rose, "but perhaps not, for Lord Leighton came here last night seeking us out. His mission was disastrous, but it probably failed to dampen his greed for retribution against Keane, and his penchant to gain fame by restoring Edwin Westbourne's wife to him. If we return to Allanwell, he will remain a threat to us."

"I t'ink not," said Flynn with a knowing look. "I lay last night at Foley's Inn in Drumnaveen. And a strange night it was, to be sure. I do not have the knowledge o' what you did to them ruffians who rode up here ahead of me, but 'twas serious."

"What's your meanin'?" Keane asked.

"Around sunset yesterday, after the sky went dark, I came to the inn. Me heart was sick when Foley told me that Leighton's band of rascals had ridden up the mountainside that very afternoon.

"Foley said 'twas too dark to follow them up the Green Lane. There was not'in' for it but to stay put for the night. The young lad was helpin' me rub down Clover in the stables when we heard a clamour and commotion comin' down the road in the blackness. We rushed outside with lanterns, just as a band of riders, about seven or eight of them, came gallopin' and slippin' down the slope, hatless, their coattails flyin' as if the very divil was at their backs.

"They went careerin' t'rough the village without stoppin', scatterin' everyone and everyt'in' in their path, and made off sout'wards. I spotted a couple o' riderless horses among them, keepin' pace. As for the men themselves—I've never seen such bewitched and haggard faces. Some were barely stickin' to their saddles, their limbs were twitchin' so.

"Indeed, when I rode up here this mornin' I happened to look over the cliff edge and saw a terrible sight down below—a gentleman in black clothes lyin' dead and broken on the rocks. Sure, at least one of 'em lost his grip and toppled to his doom. Twelve men went up the mountain, so they said at the inn, but only eight returned. And of those eight, the only one unscathed was their leader, that Leighton gobdaw. I spied him as he charged past at the head of his pack, his great pumpkin face swollen purple, like as if choked with fury. By all the saints, what did you do to them?"

"We did not'in'," said Keane.

"There was naught we needed tae dae," interjected MacTavish somewhat smugly. "The hoose has always took guid care o' its freends."

"Ah, the ghosts," said Flynn, casting an apprehensive look around.

"Maybe," said Rose uncertainly.

"At any rate," concluded Flynn, "none of those fellers looked as if they'd be comin' after yez again soon. Leighton's raid failed, and wit'out the support of the Westbournes, he has no reason or right to t'reaten your freedom, Miss Rose."

"Thank the very heavens! I may see my family again!" exclaimed Rose rapturously. "We can return to my father's house. He will be pleased to welcome you, my love," she said to Keane. "But oh!" her face changed as a thought struck her. "You will not be safe in Allanwell! Leighton still seeks you!"

"I'll wear my disguise," said Keane, "and keep goin' by the name of Driscoll. Besides, he's not sure who I am. He only has suspicions. And where else can we go?"

"I would rejoice to see my loved ones again," she said, "but only if you are safe."

"I'll have the whole village on my side," he replied, though a darkness briefly crossed his brow, and Rose recollected he had spoken of a traitor in Allanwell.

She took his hand and pressed it lovingly, then turned to address Flynn. "Our belongings are already packed and we could set out with you this very day, only, you and Clover must rest before you begin another long journey."

"We are rested enough to set out now wit'out delay," said Flynn, eying Heatherhill House with a dubious air.

There was much rejoicing at the prospect of a homecoming. After Keane had tended to Clover, all persons repaired indoors to take refreshment and learn more about events at Allanwell.

For this is what had happened, on the very evening the traitor had divulged secrets and offered his services to Edwin Westbourne—

In the library of Charter Hall, Master Westbourne had been reclining in a buttoned leather armchair while Lord Leighton was exerting his powers of persuasion.

"I have heard of that house, Heatherhill," said the baron. "It's in the uplands, and owned by that French family, the de Mandevilles. We'll ride there with a hand-picked band of our best men."

Edwin glanced up at his interlocutor. "No, we will not," he said quietly.

"What? What in thunder are you talking about?" the baron expostulated.

"I will not do it," said Edwin. "Do you think I want to be viewed as a man who had to force his wife to return to him? I would make myself a laughing-stock."

Leighton blustered. "Your family is preparing to go to England. After we seize her you can take her to your house in London. High society need never know what's happened."

"O'Connell is back from the dead," said Edwin with a bitter smile, "and she is with him. But she can never be truly with him. Perhaps that is punishment enough for her—a lifetime of cruel denial. There is nothing more I need do."

The baron remonstrated with the younger man for half an hour, but he would not change his mind.

"I will have no part of it."

"Then I shall go without you," Leighton declared at last.

"It's de Mandeville's house, you say. I believe he is a court favourite. Do you think he would welcome trespassers?"

"I will not ask permission from any French Jack-a-sauce, to hunt for a traitor on British territory. I care not whether the garlic-eating fop's servants roll out a welcome mat or set the hounds on me. They will find I am a force to be reckoned with. I want to find out where O'Connell is, and bring him to justice, and that I will do!"

"Do as you please," said Edwin." I will not be here to discover the consequences."

"What do you mean?"

"I am weary," the younger man said abruptly. "I wish to seek my bed. Good night."

And with no further ado, he walked out of the room.

It was true that Edwin was a changed man since his wedding night. His anger having burned away, he had fallen into a dark mood, becoming listless and lethargic. None of his old pursuits seemed to interest him.

That same evening, instead of repairing to his bedchamber he went to see his mother. She sat at the dressing-table in her boudoir, with her lady's maid standing at her shoulder, combing out her long tresses.

Edwin sank to the floor at his mother's feet and rested his head on her knee.

Absently, she stroked his hair. "What is it, dear?"

"I am come to tell you, mother, "he said, "I am leaving."

"But we are all leaving, my dear." She frowned. "We are

going to live where people behave in a civilised fashion. Heaven knows, I never wanted to come back here but your father would insist. You know what he's like."

"No. I am not going with you to London."

Lady Westbourne sat up sharply, turned aside from the looking-glass and batted away the hands of her maid. "Go!" she snapped, and the woman hastily departed. "My darling boy, what can you mean?"

"I intend to re-enlist in my old regiment."

"But why?" consternation crumpled Lady Westbourne's visage. "You have everything you need! Your son, your loving mother, your sisters, your nieces and nephews, your wealth and prospects—you'll find mistresses aplenty—" under her breath she added, "you've never had any trouble with that—"

"I seek adventure. I miss the excitement of the cavalry charge and the duty of defending His Majesty's dominions. Besides, the Rathskillens urgently need officers."

His mother stared down at him, tears starting in her eyes.

"Do you expect me to believe that, my boy? I know you too well. You've no heart for life, any more, do you! Since that"— she fumbled for an epithet that would not offend him—"that young lady did what she did."

"And methinks her whereabouts is now discovered, Mama. It seems she bides with the man whose ring she wore on her finger for seven years, he who was thought to be dead, but who is somehow resurrected."

"What?"

"It comes to me now," Edwin continued, "that she has rejected me utterly. She is willing to exile herself from her home and family to avoid living as my wife. I cannot be bothered to bring back such an ungrateful wench."

"But you must not throw your life away by returning to active service! You might be killed!"

"On the contrary. It gives me strength, the notion of making my mark upon the rolls of the Rathskillens, there to etch a name not soon forgotten."

Lady Westbourne stood up and began to pace back and forth agitatedly, her silk skirts rustling with every step. Presently she said, "I see it now. This Irish peasant whose ring she wore—he went to sea with the navy did he not? And now he's returned as some nautical hero, while you have resigned your commission and may no longer wear your yellow sash and plumed helmet. You wish to impress her with your courage. No doubt she is one of those girls who is easily swayed by the sight of a man in uniform."

"Mother!" Edwin rose to his feet. "It does you no credit to speak of Rose that way. While she's an ungrateful chit, she was my choice of wife."

"I am sorry my boy," she said, suddenly contrite in the face of her son's displeasure. "Forgive your mother's weakness. But I beg you to reconsider."

"I have made my decision," he said tightly. "It is done."

The servants packed the last of the family's belongings into travelling-trunks and the Westbournes left Allanwell again, this—in all likelihood—being the final time. They had endured enough of the atrocious conditions, the attacks, the hatred, the need for security wherever they went. To London they voyaged, leaving a caretaker at the house, and allowing the land of the estate to lie fallow, or under-stocked, with armed patrols riding the borders regularly to repel trespassers.

Edwin Westbourne did not accompany his family to their town house. On his return to England he rejoined the Royal Rathskillen Dragoon Guards and was posted with his regiment to Spain.

As soon as Edwin and his family had departed, and without their knowledge, Leighton had arranged the raid on Heatherhill.

At noon on the day after Leighton's failed incursion, Rose, Keane and Flynn took their leave of the two servants of Heatherhill, not without some emotion.

"Keane and I each carry a cross of St Brigid," said Rose, "and we would give them to you as a parting gift, dear Priddy and MacTavish."

"Keep them," bluntly said the steward. "We are weel-protected here, as ye've no doubt seen fur yerselves."

"Aye, keep them," echoed Nest Priddy, nodding.

"Fare weel, and lang may yer lum reek" MacTavish intoned in mysterious farewell, before explaining that this was a traditional Scottish way of wishing someone a long and healthy life, and it meant, "may your chimney smoke for a long time".

Nest Priddy said, "Duw genowgh. Dursona!" to Rose's surprise, because she had not guessed that the housekeeper spoke Cornish, nor did she know what it meant, though it sounded benign.

They named the abandoned mare "Bonny". The Scotsman excavated, from the darkest depths of the stable, one of Lady de Mandeville's side-saddles.

"I'll bring Bonny back to ye, MacTavish," Keane promised, "When I return the saddle."

"My sister Ilvenna has an ointment that will blur the brand on Bonny's flank," Flynn said with a wink, "and a dye to alter her markin's. A young thoroughbred mare is the least reparation them divils ought to pay to ye, for the damage they did to the house here."

"What use would a fine nag like that be, here on the mountainside?" MacTavish said disparagingly. "Tak' her and keep her!"

"What use would a fine nag like that be at an Allanwell cottage, indeed?" rejoined Keane. "There'd be plenty of folk who'd start suspiciously sniffin' about, if they saw such a sight."

"Ach well, mebbe," muttered MacTavish.

Keane placed the side-saddle on the mare's back and tightened the girths. He helped Rose to mount, and she sat with her skirts draped over the horse's right side. She was wearing her own clothes again, leaving behind her borrowed raiment. It belonged to the de Mandevilles, and besides, had she been dressed as a lady, the trio of travellers would have attracted attention.

Flynn tied two sacks either side of Clover's saddle, including two large bags of provisions packed by Priddy. He hoisted a knapsack on his own back.

Led by the two young men on foot, the two horses walked through the gates of Heatherhill. As they started down the Green Lane Rose turned her head and waved to the two figures standing on the threshold. For an instant she thought she caught a flash of cinnabar at one of the upstairs windows, but probably it was only a reflection, a trick of the light.

Thus, after a week of travel, stopping at wayside inns at nightfall, these three returned to Allanwell on 19th July—Rose Westbourne, "Conor Driscoll" and Flynn McGinty.

CHAPTER 34

The Return

It was late in the afternoon when they reached the outskirts of the village. Breezes, carrying whispers of the sea, coursed across the hillsides. The air smelled fresh, carrying hints of earth and the faint fragrance of blooming flowers.

The July weather was balancing itself between a delicate semblance of warmth and the familiar embrace of a soft chill. The sun, no longer a timid guest, cast a golden veil over the sprawling fields and the lacework of stone walls that crisscrossed the countryside. The landscape, bathed in the unique summer light, took on an enchanted quality.

Flynn went ahead to make sure the coast was clear. He found no sign of mercenary patrols or soldiers, so he returned to his friends and they made their way along the leafy lanes to the Delacey cottage.

There ensued a family reunion of the greatest astonishment and happiness. Everyone seemed to be talking at once, refreshments were shared around, and news was exchanged. Rose could scarcely allow herself to believe she was surrounded by all those she loved best. Her joy was so immense it seemed impossible to contain, though there was a puzzling flaw. Her sister Lizzie appeared cowed, and quieter than usual. She only roused from this state once, when Flynn entered the room, but her radiant smile was short-lived.

Lizzie refused to admit that there was anything wrong, nonetheless.

After a bite and a sup and handshakes all around, Flynn departed, taking the two horses back to his home where his mother and sister waited.

"At last you are returned to us, dear Rosie!" exclaimed John Delacey, embracing his daughter. "And you, sir," — he addressed Keane with warm respect and no regard for distinctions of class —"You are welcome to stay with us, Mr O'Connell, though I can offer only the stable loft for your sleeping quarters, I'm afraid. We've no spare beds."

"I'm t'inkin' I must seek refuge somewhere else sir," said Keane, "though I'm thankful for your generous offer. Leighton's still on the hunt for me. He's a spiteful man, and were I to stay wit' you and your kin, he'd surely notice our connection and take it as proof that beneath the whiskers of Connor Driscoll is the face of O'Connell."

"I have no knowledge of Leighton's whereabouts," said John Delacey, "but he's no longer here in this village. Soon after he and his mercenaries returned in such disarray, he departed in haste. Some say he went to England. No-one knows when he will return, if ever. There is not much reason for him to stay in a quiet backwater like Allanwell. He owns no property here. Charter Hall stands vacant. I've heard it is available to rent. The house is shuttered and dark, only inhabited by some caretakers."

"He's not here, but his spies remain, maybe," said Keane. "I'm takin' no chances. We know there is at least one turncoat in this village, who informed against us and led Leighton to Heatherhill."

There ensued much discussion on who that traitor might be, but no conclusions were drawn.

"Any news of Uncle Frank?" asked Rose.

"The last we heard," said her father, "he was still in Portugal, running some kind of betting operation. Sometimes he is good enough to send us a little money. At games of chance he is a first-rate player, and I hope there is no cheating, but. . . ah, to be honest, I know him too well. And to be wholly honest, I despair of him." His shoulders slumped.

Katherine changed the subject, with the eager air of someone imparting exciting news.

"Rose, during the last fortnight, quantities of seafarers have been coming and going in the village. They're the crew of a merchant ship called Fancy, that is lying in the harbour. You should see them! Some are men the like of whom no-one has ever seen before, so we are sending ourselves distracted trying not to stare at them when they are not looking. Their skin is the colour of polished ebony, and they are called blackamoors. The Murphy children walk right up and stand gawking at them, but of course they've never been taught proper manners. The ship's officers have been buying up foodstuffs and chandlery, paying with gold coins. They've been magnificently good for business around here."

Said Margaret, "Good for business, but bad for moral standards. They are, all of them, the most disreputable bunch I have ever seen."

"Maybe so, but at least they are partial to cleanliness," said Katherine. "A great number— some blackamoor, some not— seem to have a perfect infatuation with washing their clothes. No sooner had they arrived when they hauled bundles of shirts and vests, and breeches down to the riverbank. There they could be seen, those great hulking brutes, all scratched with tattoos and scars, doing women's work, up their their elbows in soapsuds."

"Not all of them are great and hulking," Lizzie pointed out. "There are some scrawny ones."

Katherine ignored her. "And Maureen Kelly, I mean O'Hara as is her married name, says the captain of this ship hired Mrs Rafferty to wash his clothes and bedding for him in her big tub, with proper hot water and all. Paid her with a silver crown, too! I ain't seen one of those coins for donkey's years."

"Haven't," Margaret corrected absentmindedly.

"You can understand why they want to wash their clothes as soon as they get to land," said Lizzie. "They must be very scratchy and uncomfortable. Fresh water is in short supply on ships, and you can't do your laundry in seawater. Probably they have fleas, too, from the rats on board."

"The funniest thing," Katherine ploughed on, her eyes

shining, "was seeing their smallclothes strung up to dry in the ship's rigging! And it's a mystery, because they're not just purchasing goods from the village. A couple of big six-horse wagons came in from Galway, offloading crates of heaven-knows-what onto the longboats that the sailors row out to the ship. They were so cumbersome, they had to lift them on board with a winch. I cannot imagine why the Fancy doesn't just sail round to the port of Galway, it would be much easier to load goods straight from the pier!"

"No doubt you were hoping your English sailor Mr Watson might be among the crew," said Margaret.

"Watson?" said Keane. "I met a sailor by that name aboard the Victory. He was the captain maintop."

"James Watson?" asked Katherine, agog.

"Why, that's the very name. A Londoner, and a decent fellow."

"It's the man himself!" exclaimed Katherine.

"Oh, don't be foolish," reprimanded Margaret. "How many James Watsons do you think there are in this world? There's probably a million. It won't have been him."

"But it might have been," said her sister.

When Henri de Mandeville learned that the erstwhile guests of Heatherhill were back in Allanwell, he sent his cabin boy to the home of the Delaceys with a message. The freckled lad recited it with his hands clasped behind his back and a blank stare directed earnestly upwards, as he strained to recall it verbatim.

"Cap'n says 'e sends 'is good wishes to Mister Driscoll and 'is good lady. 'e is sorry but—um—'e is too busy wiv preparations for 'is—um—forthcomin' voyage to speak wiv 'em."

"Thank you, my boy," said John Delacey, giving the lad a silver threepence, which he eagerly pocketed before skipping back to the harbour.

That night, Keane slept at the McGinty cottage, in the loft over the stable.

Beyond his bedchamber lay the lavender fields, a striking sight, now in full blossom, their vibrant, purple-feathered rows contrasting with the soft pearliness of the skies. Clouds of sweet scent soothed everyone in the vicinity to a deep and gentle slumber.

In her family home, Rose, snuggled into the bedclothes beside Lizzie. Sleep evaded her. Images of her sweetheart formed before her eyes, and being away from his side felt like a wound. She was aware, too, that Lizzie was lying awake, contemplating the ceiling.

"Its almost midnight, Lizzie," she said eventually. "What ails you?"

"I could ask you the same question. Go to sleep."

"I cannot sleep. I want to know what ails you."

After much coaxing, Rose managed to persuade her sister to divulge the truth. During Lord Leighton's sojourns at Allanwell, he had been trying to persuade Lizzie to become his mistress, but she consistently spurned him. Her rebuffals only made him the more determined.

"But Rosie," confessed Lizzie brokenly, "if blandishments were all I had to contend with, I would never give in to that monster. You must tell no-one what I am about to say, for I confide in you alone. That evil creature has threatened Flynn McGinty's freedom if I do not consent to a tryst, but so far I have managed to keep putting it off. He suggests that Flynn might be arrested for illegal activities such as cheating the revenuers, and thrown into jail or transported to the colonies. He swears to leave Flynn alone, or even to see that he gets an official pardon, if I give in. I feel sure Flynn would be clever enough to outwit him, but I am so glad that detestable man has gone away to England."

Rose felt too shocked to speak.

Presently she gathered her wits, drew a deep breath and said, "Oh Lizzie. My dear one. You have had to suffer this torment all alone. I do not know what to do! I will think on this, and hope to find a solution."

"Rosie, how can that detestable man know that I care for Flynn? I thought I'd kept my feelings secret. Don't tell me everyone in the village knows!"

"No, no," Rose assured her. "It is probably just because of our family's close association with the McGintys."

"How would he know about that? He's too stuck-up to notice what's going on in the village."

"No doubt the traitor told him!"

"What traitor?"

"Someone living in Allanwell is in the pocket of Lord Leighton."

"There is? That is scandalous! Let's hope Ilvenna puts a curse on him, whoever he is."

Much relieved at having shared her secret, Lizzie drifted off to sleep and Rose soon fell into her own slumber.

CHAPTER 35

Postage Fully Paid

In the morning a post rider arrived in the village. This being a relatively uncommon occurrence, it attracted some attention from the populace. The rider asked for Mr Conor Driscoll of Allanwell, and was directed to the home of the McGintys.

His horse began to pick its way along the rutted lane towards the cottage.

Keane O'Connell had just come into the kitchen from the yard, where he had been washing at the pump. Shirtless, he threw back his dripping mane of hair and reached for a linen towel to dry himself. His finely-thewed body glistened with pearly droplets. Ilvenna, who had been busy stirring a bowl on the table, was unable to refrain from covertly scrutinising him. Suddenly she frowned, paused her activity and took a second, more blatant look.

"What's that on your arm?" she said, using her wooden spoon to indicate the tattoo on his right shoulder.

He turned his head to peer at it. "T'ank the gods, I t'ought you'd seen a spider. 'Tis a compass rose, a tattoo of good luck and guidance."

"Hmph," said Ilvenna. "Good luck is it?" She dropped the spoon in the bowl, spattering batter across the table-top, and leaned over to examine the mark more closely. "Surprisingly there is some power in this t'ing,' she said at length, while Keane, diverted by her interest, toweled his hair with one hand. "But it needs more. There's wisdom in havin' such a charm engraved on yer person, for whereas a cross or a a ring or some other such artifact can be lost or stolen, 'tis hard to lose an engravin' in yer skin, so it is."

"Unless someone carves it off you," said Keane.

"And then it would be losin' its power," said Ilvenna matter-of-factly. "Now, I can boost the magic in this tattoo, if yer'll allow me."

"Mistress Ilvenna, I am grateful!"

She could tell by the twinkle in his eyes that he was merely indulging her, but ignoring the implied slight, she fetched a small vial of blessed water and a wand of rowan wood and performed what she called a spell.

Keane seated himself and calmly gazed out the open door while she worked. As the last words of the arcane chant left her lips, he started, as if stung.

"Ah!" She exclaimed in triumph, "ye felt somet'ing did ye?"

"I did indeed," he admitted. "'Twas like a dart piercin' me shoulder, but only for an instant. It wasn't your revenge was it?"

328

"It should have been, for no doubt ye deserve it. But it was the magic," she said demurely, as she went to put away the vial and wand.

"Are you helpin' me wit' the bakin' or what?" her mother called out peevishly.

Keane had just donned his shirt when the post rider arrived at the door, dismounted and stood on the threshold.

"Mr Conor Driscoll of Allanwell?"

"The same." In two strides, Keane was standing before the newcomer. Ma and Ilvenna peered from the shadows of the kitchen.

The messenger said, "This letter was delivered to Ireland by the Spanish Royal Company of the Philippines, whose ship is docked at Castletownbere, County Cork. Thence has it been carried overland." He gave an envelope into the hands of Keane.

The packet had "postage fully paid" scrawled on the back, with an official ink-stamp, so Keane was able to send the messenger away with just a couple of copper coins. This was fortunate, because without payment somewhere along the line, the man would not have handed it over.

Keane seated himself at the kitchen table and examined the envelope for any indication of who had sent it, but could find none. He slit it open with a small knife.

At his back Ilvenna and Ma hovered, appearing to bake potato bread, acutely interested in the contents of the letter but keeping a respectful, silent distance.

The young man extracted a card from the envelope. A strange passage was written thereon: "Farewell you sweet and turtle dove. On you alone, I fixed my love. And if you never can be mine, I never can no comfort find!" Some amateur hand had drawn, with coloured pencils, a picture of a dove with wings unfurled and a letter in its beak, surrounded by a flowery wreath, and some pink hearts.

"A Valentine's Day card?" Keane murmured. A moment later the significance of this puzzling missive came to him. He jumped to his feet and, seizing his knapsack, started rifling through the contents.

Ma and Ilvenna exchanged bemused glances.

Soon enough, Keane extracted from his bag a small bottle of liquid. He sat down again at the table and, after setting aside the card, carefully slid his knife-blade through the adhered seams on the envelope until he had unfolded it flat. He unscrewed the lid of the bottle.

"Ilvenna, Ma, do you have a small brush I could borrow?"

Mystified, Ilvenna handed him a goat-hair paintbrush, whereupon he dipped the bristles sparingly into the liquid and brushed the inside of the envelope.

By this time both women had abandoned all pretence of baking and were closely observing the proceedings. Lines of faint handwriting materialised on the paper, and they watched, spellbound, as Keane perused it without speaking. After he had read it twice through, he crumpled it in his fist and threw it into the hearth-fire, which briefly flared. Then he planted his elbows on the table and sat brooding, head in his hands.

"Oh, sweet Jesus, man," Ilvenna burst out after a few long moments had passed. "Can't you tell us anything?"

"I have been called to Tenerife," Keane replied. "And I am bound to answer the call."

The two McGinty women found themselves not much the wiser for this revelation, but before they could inquire further Keane said, "I must go to Rose." Grabbing his cap and coat, he rushed out the door.

Ilvenna stood in the doorway, hands on hips, watching the young man run swiftly down towards the willow-lined stream in the blowing golden strands of morning sunlight.

"I have a lonely feeling about this," she said to Ma.

"Tá," said Ma. "Agus na comharthaí trioblóid dom." (Yes. And the signs trouble me.)

"Me darlin'! Pray come outside!" Keane called as soon as he arrived at the Delacey cottage.

The front door opened and Katherine's head appeared. "Is it something to do with that letter this morning from the Spanish conquistador?"

Elbowing her sister aside, Rose stepped out onto the doorstep. "For heaven's sake Kitty," she said crossly. "Other people's letters are none of your business, and I don't know how you even found out such a thing, for I never knew of it."

"I just heard one of the Murphy children shouting about it," said Katherine, "that's all."

She withdrew, leaving Rose to take Keane's arm and walk with him among the summer flowers in the garden, so that their conversation could be private.

They sauntered with their arms so closely entwined that their bodies brushed together with every step. Rose sensed her beloved's nearness like a tingling flame down one side. It was a sweetness almost unbearable. She knew he felt it too, but by mutual consent, they both feigned ignorance.

"I've received a letter from my friend Fournier," said Keane, regarding her with tender intensity. "Do ye recall the gentleman I told ye about—he who was responsible for my return to Ireland, and our shelter at Heatherhill?"

An stab of premonition struck through Rose like a levin bolt. She forced herself to remain outwardly calm. "I remember," she replied. "We are indebted to him for his kindness."

"Indeed we are," said Keane. He hesitated, as if unsure how to impart the contents of the letter.

Rose reached up and pushed aside a lock of the midnight hair that had fallen across his face. She took the opportunity to say, "I fear the message brings ill tidings. I pray that we may postpone discussion of it for a short while, for I would like to ask your advice."

"Ask away."

"I am not at liberty to say this, and by doing so I am breaking a promise to Lizzie, but she is living in constant fear of Lord Leighton's return."

Rose told Keane what her sister had told her, whereupon ire could be seen to rise in him like a tiger from slumber. He swallowed his curses, though his eyes burned with cold fire.

"She is safe now, but if that divil ever returns to Allanwell," he said, "she must be hidden and smuggled away."

"Where to?"

"Your uncle Francis?"

"He's in Portugal, but no-one knows where."

"Perhaps to England, then. Maybe the Chevalier de Mandeville would offer her shelter."

"She could not go alone. I would accompany her!"

"I will ask Fournier to write to the Chevalier. And ye must take my purse, for the fare. All my fortune is within it, though 'tis meagre enough."

"We may argue that point later! Now pray tell me, what is in Fournier's message?"

"He writes that he's stationed on the Spanish island of Tenerife, and has urgent need of me. 'Come to me in my hour of need,' he wrote. He would never have been after sendin' such a message unless he was in a dire spot, because of the risk. I promised to lend him a hand if ever he was in a terrible bind. Now he's callin' on me, but I'm not knowin' for what reason."

Rose's mind raced. She felt dizzy. What if Keane should be torn from her side once more? If he ventured far across the seas, would she ever see him again? After their short period of happiness together, was there to be another agonising separation, with no guarantee they would ever be reunited? At the same time she was painfully aware of his dilemma, for he, too, was torn—between keeping his word to his friend and staying with his sweetheart.

She forced herself to speak calmly. "You are bound by your word of honour to go to this gentleman who helped you."

"But no! I am bound to stay wit' you and protect you!"

"Protect me from what? I am secure here, now. Master Westbourne has renounced me, his family is no longer in this country—even Leighton has gone. I am safe at home with my family!"

"Darlin'. I cannot leave you."

Denying her own heart's most ardent wishes for the sake of her sweetheart, Rose continued, "Besides, my love, if you stay here in Allanwell, you will always be in danger. My mind will only be at peace if you leave this place, because it will put a good distance between you and Leighton, should he ever return and look for you. That monster has a vendetta against you. Your disguise and false name will not hide your identity for long. Everyone fears you will be accused of deserting to the enemy, if you ever fall into British hands, and the punishment is death."

Keane shook his head, but she sensed indecision.

"Do it for my sake!" she pushed on. "Besides, by a stroke of luck de Mandeville's ship is still in the harbour. He told us he would be sailing the Canary Route, recall? Tenerife is one of the Canary Islands, if I rightly recall the great atlas globe in the library at Charter Hall. You could speak to him about taking passage."

The two lovers debated the point fiercely for three quarters of an hour. In the end, Keane accepted Rose's reasoning, though reluctantly.

"Very well. I will go, but only because I am certain you are safe here. I will return as soon as I am able. Flynn and Ryan will help your father watch over you."

When Keane informed his brother, however, that he intended to sail for Tenerife, Ryan insisted on accompanying him.

"I will not let you go alone," he said with determination. "We will not be separated again! You need your brother beside you. Besides why should you be enjoyin' all the excitement and adventure?"

Nothing Keane could say would dissuade him, so with due haste the O'Connell brothers made their way down to the harbour in search of de Mandeville.

Rose informed her family that Keane was going away over the sea on a mission to help a friend, but she would not divulge the details. "The less everyone knows, the better," she said. "For Keane has a powerful enemy, and there is a traitor in Allanwell."

Only to Lizzie did she reveal her beloved's destination.

"He's been summoned to the island of Tenerife. He's going to ask the captain of the Fancy to take him, and to bring him home afterwards. For the captain is a friend of ours, and the

Fancy is in truth a pirate ship in disguise, but you must tell no-one."

"Oh Rosie! A pirate?" Lizzie cried in consternation.

"Please! Promise you won't tell!"

"Very well then, my lips are sealed, but I don't like it!"

"Neither do I. Truth to tell, I am beset by a terrible fear that I may never see my darling again. This forthcoming separation goes hard with me. Every beat of my heart measures my yearning for our reunion, and he has not even departed yet."

"Of course, dearest!" Lizzie cried compassionately.

"Until he returns," said Rose, "I will have no way to know whether he lives, or if I have lost him forever. The agony of not knowing his fate—and thus mine—will be like coals of fire smouldering in my very bones every minute of every day."

She wept. Lizzie embraced her sister comfortingly. Presently she said, "I have been considering, and I have an idea. Perhaps you will deem it whimsical, but hear me out. There may be a way to cut short your ignorance of Keane's fate, and thus your suffering, if only by few hours."

Rose raised a tear-stained face to gaze at her sister. "Tell me."

"This pirate brig is to bring him home, correct? And pirate ships carry black sails, you told me. And that impudent rogue of a captain is your friend, yes?"

Rose nodded.

"Why then say this to the captain: He must give you a signal when they come sailing back into Allanwell Bay. If

Keane is aboard, they must hoist white sails, to show that he is alive and well. And if—heaven forbid—your love has gone to heaven, let Fancy return with black sails aloft. By this means, we will know the truth as soon as we sight the ship from afar."

Rose considered this notion for a moment.

"You're right, it is a whimsical proposition, but somehow it comforts me. I can but put the request to de Mandeville. The notion might appeal to the man's rakish sense of gallantry. If he refuses, well, c'est la vie. But I must try."

CHAPTER 36

The Royal Revenge

The captain of the *Royal Revenge* was easy to find, for he stood on the pebble-strewn beach with his first mate, one hand on his hip and the other gesticulating, loudly arguing with the port-master about some complicated financial arrangements. Near the water's edge, rocked by restless wavelets, a silver branch of driftwood floated. Meanwhile, in the shallows, a group of seamen loaded crates and barrels from a wagon into a longboat, using a block and tackle. The horses waited patiently between the shafts at the waterline, the jetty being too narrow for a horse-drawn cart to turn around.

De Mandeville greeted Keane warmly, looked measuringly at Ryan, and readily granted their request to take them aboard.

"Tenerife is an important port of call for ships 'eading to and from ze New World," he said. "By good fortune it is served by our 'unting grounds, ze Canary Current. My proud beauty will carry you there! Aye, and bring you back 'ome, too, some time! Probably one day we will return to Allanwell 'arbour. I 'ave spies 'ere 'oo tell me when ze coast is clear.

"Welcome aboard, my friends. One day more and you would 'ave been too late. We weigh anchor this very evening and sail with ze tide. We 'ave today completed checking and preparing our weapons, and we 'ave stocked up on ammunition and supplies. So my cousin is in Tenerife, eh? I did not know this. Could it be 'e is on ze trail of some treasure, yes? If 'e 'appens to reveal any words about ze jewels of the queen you will relay this to me, yes?"

Without waiting for a reply, de Mandeville began shouting furious imprecations at his crewmen loading the longboat, who had accidentally let let slip a heavy barrel into the waves.

The O'Connells took the opportunity to depart for home.

That day Keane and Ryan prepared to embark.

Late in the afternoon, they went down to the seashore and walked out along the ricketty wooden jetty, accompanied by the entire Delacey family, Mary, and all three McGintys. A straggling group of onlookers assembled nearby in desultory fashion. It included Father Joseph, Michael O'Sullivan and his comrade Kevin O'Flaherty, the Raffertys, and the Murphys, complete with a gaggle of inquisitive children. What the villagers expected to behold was anyone's guess, but the departure of a ship of any size greater than that of a fishing-boat was ever an entertaining spectacle for them.

The sun was westering. Towering over the harbour, the cliffs of Madigan's Leap, loomed, a bulwark against the sea. A ruddy glow rinsed their walls, tinting them with hues of flame. Sunlight, like liquid gold, laved the cloudbanks ranged along the horizon.

Small fishing boats danced on the water, their wooden frames weathered and salt-streaked. Fishing nets were spread out to dry along the shore, like huge cobwebs. Among them, a group of fishermen sat with their needles, repairing tears in the mesh.

Beside the jetty a longboat bobbed up and down, tied to a bollard as it waited to ferry the last of the passengers and crew to the brig. One burly crewman from the Fancy was seated in the stern while another loitered on the jetty. The tang of stranded seaweed drifted on the breeze.

Ryan lingered in the company of the McGinty family, saying his last farewells.

"Give this charm bag to your brother," said Ilvenna, handing him a tiny leather pouch. "Terrifyin' is its power, for I crafted it with me own hands, whilst chantin' words of power. It can mend him if he's sick or hurt. Its influence is equal to that of the dragonfly amulet, my gift to you."

"That gift I always treasure, my Áine of the daybreak hair." Ryan put his hand to his collarbone, against which nestled the token he had carried with him through all his journeys and adventures, and Ilvenna smiled.

"What's inside the pouch?" he asked.

"Salt, iron, and rowan berries, herbs with healing properties and a mighty rune of the ancient Druids, written on a scrap of parchment."

Ryan thanked her gravely and stowed the gift in an inner pocket of his waistcoat. Ma and Flynn had by then drifted away towards the beach, and Ryan stood alone with Ilvenna.

"What gift shall I bring back for you?" softly he asked her.

"You yourself, of course. And a lookin'-glass," she added as an afterthought. "A good one, as clear as a pond on a windless mornin'."

She half-expected him to tease her with clichéd banter about a woman's vanity, as so many might have done. But he did not, and by this, his esteem for her became doubly evident.

"You'll have your wish," he answered. Then, impulsively, he leaned down and kissed her cheek. "I'll come back for you, Ilvenna McGinty," he said with conviction.

Uncharacteristically she blushed; nonetheless it was not the self-conscious reaction of a shy maiden, but a quickening of recognition, for it came to her that he understood her as so few did, as perhaps no one else did, or could.

A little apart from the rest, Rose stood clasped in Keane's arms. The susurrus of the waves overlaid their voices, so that none could overhear their conversation. Her gaze brimmed with anguish. His eyes were wells of torment.

"Every moment that you are away will stretch into an eternity for me," she said, fighting back tears.

"Don't look so sorrowful, my love," he said softly, smoothing a stray wisp of hair from her brow. "I promise you that we shall meet again on this earth."

"Then, let us re-affirm the pledge of the two half-rings," she whispered.

And thus they did.

Boots clattered on the jetty's planks. De Mandeville, with his first mate following at his shoulder, strode up to the couple. The former gestured impatiently. "Come, come! It is time to go! Ze tide does not wait for us."

"One moment, I beseech you!" said Rose. "Monsieur de Mandeville, I have a favour to ask of you."

"Ask away, Mam'selle," he said. "If it is in my power to grant zis favour, I will. But be quick about it!"

"Promise me you will bring Keane O'Connell back. If not alive, then find his body and bring his mortal remains back to me, for I would fain share my final resting place with my love."

"I will do what I can!"

Rose continued, "Let there be a signal. When your ship returns to Allanwell if my love lives, leave your white sails aloft on the Fancy's masts. If it is his body you bring back, order your crew to hoist the black. I will keep watch from the cliffs. I desire to know his fate—and mine—as soon as possible, as soon as your ship comes within sight—even before she enters the bay."

"A request most strange!" said de Mandeville in some astonishment. "But novel enough," he added with a shrug, "and passionate enough. It catches my imagination. It shall be done! But what if I do not know if 'e lives or not?"

"If you do not have that knowledge, or if he has perished on some foreign shore, then hoist a flag. Choose a flag that is distinct and easily recognizable, so that I may quickly understand your communication."

"Per'aps a black flag," mused de Mandeville, rubbing his goateed chin. "But non, we use that as a signal of plague or pestilence. I will use a red flag. Agreed?"

"Agreed!"

"Now O'Connell brothers, come away, or my proud beauty will leave you be'ind!"

The four men moved to the jetty's edge, and de Mandeville commenced clambering into the longboat. Keane could hardly take his eyes from his sweetheart. Unbridled tears were streaming down her face. He turned his head to regard the moored boat, then looked back at Rose.

Abruptly he broke away from the group by the bollard and ran back to her. She held out her arms for one last embrace, and they clasped one another so tightly, it was as if they would fuse and become one.

"Make haste!" Ryan called out to his brother. De Mandeville was seated in the boat now, and Mouncy was stepping in beside him. Keane murmured a word to Rose, kissed her, and tore himself away.

Ryan boarded and settled himself in the boat, finding his balance. Keane made to enter the little vessel in his turn but, once again, he looked back at Rose standing on the jetty bathed in tears, and as before, he paused in an agony of indecision. Next moment he spun around and ran back to her a second time. Again, they wrapped their arms about each other, as if their lives depended on it, and pressed their faces together, buried in each other's hair. And a second time he pulled away from her.

Holding her by the shoulders, he gave her a look that could make iron bleed. Then he ran back to the boat. The pirate who remained on the jetty was unwinding the hawser from the bollard, while down in the longboat the burly crewman and the first mate gripped the oars, ready to row away.

At the last moment, just as he was about to step down, Keane turned third time and ran back to the slender figure weeping on the jetty. A third time he enfolded her in his embrace, and her tears would drown the ocean.

"You're too late," yelled the captain. "We're leaving without you!"

The pirate on the jetty tossed the untied rope into the longboat and lightly jumped in after it, with practised skill, so as not to disturb its equilibrium.

He pushed off from the jetty, and the oarsmen began to row. The vessel pulled away, see-sawing over the licking tongues of the waves, the oars rhythmically lifting and falling like the preposterous wings of some strange waterbird.

They had put only a few yards between themselves and the jetty, however, when they heard a splash, followed by screams from the onlookers. Keane had launched himself into the icy water and was swimming towards them. The captain cried out, "We will not let you aboard, for you would capsize us all!"

Nevertheless Keane kept swimming, cleaving the waves with powerful strokes.

And as fast as the boat travelled, so the swimmer travelled, so that by the time the vessel reached the ship he was there beside it, wet and shining as a young seal, droplets flying from his hair like strings of crystals.

Treading in the glacial water he waited uncomplaining, while the captain climbed the rope ladder the crew had thrown out over the side, for de Mandeville submitted his precedence to no man, if he could help it, and tried to spurn the swimmer with his foot, and even insisted on his first mate following him. Finally, Keane took his turn on the ladder, and thus he came aboard the ship with the rest.

High above the bay, the ruins atop the Madigan's Leap caught the last ruby gleams of sunset.

Rose lingered on the little pier while the Fancy's crew made preparations for the ship's departure. They weighed anchor, accompanied by a chorus of rough male voices raised in a sea-chant as they trudged around the capstan. The wind blew cold and the young woman was shivering. Her family waited with her, concerned for her well-being, pleading, "Come away! Come away!"

But she would not.

At length, the brig's mainsail billowed like a cloud, and the jib unfurled like a dove's wing. Then followed the topsail on the main-mast and the foresail on the foremast.

As the sails caught the wind and bellied forth, and the vessel began to move away, Rose spied Keane climbing into the rigging. He climbed high, until he stood upon the main topgallant yard, leaning out from the braces, holding on to the ropes with one hand and waving to her with the other, as if floating among the billowing sails. There he stayed, and there she stayed on the jetty, waving back to him, until distance and sea mists intervened.

The canvas petals of the "merchant ship Fancy" glimmered with a rosy light, blossoming in an offshore breeze as she sailed away into the last rays of the sunset.

Positioned on the quarterdeck with his first mate, Captain de Mandeville watched the land recede.

"Are we going to show black sails if we bring back the Irishman's corpse, cap'n?" asked the first mate.

De Mandeville laughed. "Do not be absurd. We won't raise ze black sails whether 'e's alive or dead or anything in between. It eez a fanciful notion, non? Why give our bird black wings coming into port? People might mistake us for pirates!"

"Just so, cap'n, but these days 'tis not only pirates who use black sails," said Mouncy. "I've 'eard tell that some merchantmen use 'em in the tropics to stop the glare."

"Pshaw!" de Mandeville exclaimed contemptuously, spitting on the deck. "We save the black canvas for raids! We won't bother pandering to the whims of some Irish coquette, no matter how pretty."

From their airy vantage point on the cliff-top, the black silhouettes of the antique stone fort seemed steeped in some secret knowledge as they watched the ship depart. The wind whined among the crumbling walls and tilted gravestones, where, so it was said, the ghost of Bridget O'Day wandered and wept with her child in her arms.

Under cloud-racked skies the crowd dissipated from the jetty and the beach, but Rose and Ilvenna stayed behind. Arm in arm they watched the ship until it dwindled out of sight, and darkness swept across the landscape. Stars pricked out overhead, one by one. The lacy foam stitched along the edges of the waves shone with a faint luminescence.

When Rose returned home, she found Mary holding a purse and a rush-woven St Brigid's cross.

"Master O'Connell left these here today," said the servant. "He said they belong to ye and Lizzie. He said the cross in particular is for Lizzie. Those charms are powerful ain't they, especially if Ilvenna makes 'em. Did you know she's workin' on a mighty one to lead her to a crock o' gold at the end of a rainbow?"

"Sweet Jesus, he's left all his money with us!" cried Rose brokenly, "and his good luck too!"

"No he ain't," said Mary, "because Ilvenna made healin' charms, one for each o' dem two boys. They'll be fine."

But Rose was inconsolable. At nights she went to sleep with the golden half-ring on her thumb pressed to her lips, praying for the safe and swift return of Keane and Ryan.

Clouds piled up over Allanwell, and rain came streaming down in shimmering, crystal curtains. As it cleared, the clouds began to tease themselves apart. Spindly beams of sunlight shot earthwards and fractured. An arc of magical colours, silent, majestic, emerged from the fine mist and soared across the sky.

Alone in the morning, Ilvenna climbed a grassy hillside. Her hair fell around her like an autumnal briar, and she carried a looking-glass in her hand. Standing in that high place with her back to the rainbow she held up the mirror and gazed at the reflection. She spoke—the words were a kind of verse, though lacking in rhyme and meter. The curved streamers of radiant colour filled the frame of the cheap hand-glass, but they were blurred, slightly distorted and mottled by its imperfections.

After a long while, the rainbow faded. With a sigh, Ilvenna lowered the mirror, picked up her damp skirts and made her way down the hill.

THE END

This story continues in -

Madigan's Leap Book 3: Words of Power

If you enjoyed this book, please write a short (or long) review on Amazon.
Reviews signal to potential readers that others are interested in the book, and like it.
Writing and posting book reviews on Amazon is a small, but powerful thing you can do to support authors from whose work you have derived some value.

~ Cyberchicks in Love ~

"Science Fiction with a Good Dose of Humor"

"Cyberchicks in Love" is an eccentric combination of humor and sci-fi-fantasy. The story, revolving around a group of young women infatuated with a movie star, offers a delightful spoof of various genres - from fanfiction to chick lit and science fiction.
~ The Reader's Gazette

www.professorsbookshelf.com

For more about the Professor's Bookshelf series, visit
www.professorsbookshelf.com/

www.ingramcontent.com/pod-product-compliance
Lightning Source LLC
Chambersburg PA
CBHW011406010726
47495CB00009B/2802